Best Shorts

Favorite
Short Stories
for
Sharing

Best Shorts

Favorite
Short Stories
for
Sharing

SELECTED BY

Avi

with Carolyn Shute

HOUGHTON MIFFLIN COMPANY
Boston 2006

The editors wish to extend particular thanks to the authors and publishers who have generously allowed us to include their stories in this collection. May you reap the reward of many readers! Grateful acknowledgment is also made to Erica Zappy, Terri Schmitz, Lauren Raece, Andrea Pinkney, Judy O'Malley, and Eden Edwards for their contributions to this volume's creation.

■ ■ ■

Introduction copyright © 2006 by Avi
Afterword copyright © 2006 by Katherine Paterson
Illustrations copyright © 2006 by Chris Raschka

A list of credits appears on page 341.

www.houghtonmifflinbooks.com

The text of this book is set in Columbus MT.
Book design by Sheila Smallwood
Printed in the United States of America
Library of Congress Cataloging-in-Publication Data
Best shorts : favorite short stories for sharing / selected by Avi ; assisted by Carolyn Shute ; afterword by Katherine Paterson ; [illustrations by Chris Raschka].
p. cm.
ISBN-13: 978-0-618-47603-9 (hardcover)
ISBN-10: 0-618-47603-2 (hardcover)
1. Children's stories. [1. Short stories.] I. Avi, 1937- II. Shute, Carolyn. III. Paterson, Katherine. IV. Raschka, Christopher, ill.
PZ5.B4313 2006
[Fic]—dc22   2006011535

Manufactured in the United States of America
MP 10 9 8 7 6 5 4 3 2 1

Contents

Introduction

Welcome to *Best Shorts: Favorite Short Stories for Sharing,* a collection of short stories that have been gathered together for your reading and listening pleasure. We offer no overriding message, theme, or subject, just good short stories, stories that are particularly good to share.

But first, what exactly is a short story? A spoken or written story that is brief. Written short stories can be as short as one paragraph. They may be as long as sixty pages. You are probably most accustomed to reading longer stories—chapter books or novels. While a novel takes strength from its *many* details, a short story takes strength from a *few* revealing details. A novel may present a whole life. A short story can compress a whole life into a few moments. If a great novel is a mighty river, a short story is a sparkling brook. In a novel we reveal life by bonfire; a short story allows us to look at life with a candle.

All cultures have short stories that entertain, explain, and sometimes teach—and these traditions continue, right up to the present, carried on by gifted storytellers and those who collect and adapt stories into print. It's probably fair to suggest that written short stories derive from *told* tales. And, historically, while intended for older folks, short stories are often taken over by young people. *Aesop's Tales* and *The Arabian Nights* have clear oral roots. Other examples include *The City Mouse and the Country Mouse,* which comes from a first-century (BC) tale by the Roman writer Horace; the fascinating medieval collection of stories called the *Gesta Romanorum,* which Shakespeare used for ideas; and the familiar *Tales of Mother Goose.*

When, then, did writers first compose short stories? Perhaps the first real short story in children's literature may be found in James Janeway's *A Token for Children: Being an Exact Account of the Conversion, Holy and Exemplary Lives and Joyful Deaths of Several Young Children* (1672). Happily, the short story for children moved beyond mere moralizing. In 1819 Washington Irving published "Rip Van Winkle" and thereby marked the traditional beginning of the American short story. That story is included here, not just to celebrate that fact, but because it remains a wonderfully engaging tale.

The stories in this collection are old and new, written both by people whose names you may know well and by those whom you may never have heard of before. When Frank Stockton published "The Lady or the Tiger?" in 1882, it was a literary sensation, partly because it has no ending. Readers have to supply their own. By contrast, the last line in Francisco Jiménez's story "The Circuit" has a shocking finality.

"The Woman in the Snow" deals with real history—that of the pre–civil rights era in the South—even though Patricia McKissack tells it as a ghost story. In "The Caller," Robert D. San Souci brings an otherwise traditional ghost story right up to date with the haunting taking place via a cell phone.

My own story, "Scout's Honor," based on something that really happened to me, was far more fun when I composed it as a story. And there's more fun here—a clever woman outsmarts the Devil in Natalie Babbitt's very brief, funny story "Nuts"; a group of bandits give up their wicked ways under the influence of a librarian in "The Librarian and the Robbers," by Margaret Mahy.

Are the stories in this collection the very best? They are surely *some* of the best that have been published over a long period of time—from "Rip Van Winkle," published almost two hundred years ago, to one of the most recent stories, "The Baby in the Night Deposit Box," published in 2003. Still, the universe of short stories has many stars, and it would be silly to suggest that there are no brilliant lights other than the ones we have assembled here. Indeed, we hope these stories inspire you to search out more for yourself and share them with others, because above all, *Best Shorts* is meant to be shared. Shared by families. Shared by teachers with students. Shared by kids like you with your friends. These stories can certainly be read alone, but if read aloud, my guess is that they will provoke much thought, moments of laughter and sadness, and perhaps even talks longer than the stories themselves. Short these stories may be, but their impact can be long.

Reach in and help yourself!

Avi
2006

Rogue Wave

by Theodore Taylor

A killer wave, known to mariners as a "rogue wave," was approaching a desolate area of Baja California below Ensenada. It had been born off the east coast of Australia during a violent storm; it had traveled almost 7,000 miles at a speed of 20.83 miles an hour. Driven by an unusual pattern of easterly winds, it was a little over 800 feet in length and measured about 48 feet from the bottom of its trough to its crest. On its passage across the Pacific, it had already killed thirteen people, mostly fishermen in small boats, but also an entire French family of five aboard a 48-foot schooner . . .

Melissa "Scoot" Atkins went below into the *Old Sea Dog*'s tiny galley, moving down the three steps of the companionway, closing the two solid entry doors behind her, always a good idea in offshore sailing. The three horizontal hatch boards that were on top of the doors were also firmly in place, securing the thirty-foot Baba type against sudden invasion of seawater.

Rogues and sneakers have been around since the beginning of the oceans, and the earliest sea literature makes note of "giant" waves. The U.S. Navy manual Practical Methods for Observing and Forecasting Ocean Waves *says, "In any wave system, after a long enough time, an exceptional high one will occur. These monstrous out-sized waves are improbable but still possible and the exact time of occurrence can never be predicted." Naval hydrography studies indicate that waves 15 to 25 feet high qualify for "sneaker" or "sleeper" status; the freak rogue is up to 100 feet or over. As waters slowly warm they seem to be occurring more frequently. In 1995 the* Queen Elizabeth 2 *(the* QE2*), the great British passenger liner, encountered a 95-foot rogue south of Newfoundland. More than 900 feet long, the* QE2 *rode over it, but her captain said it looked like they were sailing into the White Cliffs of Dover.*

Sullivan Atkins, Scoot's oldest brother, was steering the cutter-rigged boat on a northerly course about fifteen miles off desolate Cabo Colnett, south of Ensenada. Under a brilliant sun, the glittering blue Pacific rose and fell in long, slick swells, a cold light breeze holding steady.

Below deck Scoot was listening to Big Sandy & His Fly-Rite Boys doing "Swingin' West," and singing along with them while slicing leftover steak from last night's meal. They'd grilled it on a small charcoal ring that was mounted outboard on the starboard side at the stern, trailing sparks into the water. The *Sea Dog* had every blessed thing, including a barbecue pit, she marveled.

Scoot was learning how to be a deep-water sailor. She was fourteen years old and pretty, with dark hair. Though small in size, not even five feet, she was strong. She'd started off with eight-foot Sabots. On this trip, her first aboard the *Sea Dog,* she'd manned the wheel for most of the three days they'd been under way. She'd stood four-hour watches at night. Sully was a good teacher.

It was one of those perfect days to be out, Sully thought: the three Dacron sails belayed and whispering, white bow waves singing pleasant songs as the fiberglass hull, tilting to starboard, sliced through the ocean. It was a day filled with goodness, peace, and beauty. They'd come south as far as Cabo Colnett, turning back north only an hour ago. They'd sailed from Catalina Island's Avalon Harbor, the *Sea Dog's* home port, out in the channel off Los Angeles. Sully had borrowed the boat from a family friend, Beau Tucker, a stockbroker with enough money to outfit it and maintain it properly. Built by Ta-Shing, of Taiwan, she was heavy and sturdy, with a teakwood deck and handsome teakwood interior, and the latest in navigation equipment. Sully had sailed her at least a dozen times. He'd been around boats, motor and sail, for many of his nineteen years. He thought the *Old Sea Dog* was the best, in her category, that he'd ever piloted.

As he was about to complete a northeast tack, Sully's attention was drawn to a squadron of seagulls diving on small fish about a hundred yards off the port bow, and he did not see the giant wave that had crept up silently behind the *Sea Dog.* But a split second before it lifted the boat like a carpenter's chip, he sensed something behind him and glanced backward, toward the towering wall of shining water.

It was already too late to shout a warning to Scoot so she could escape from the cabin; too late to do anything except hang on to the wheel with both hands; too late even to pray. He did manage a yell as the *Sea Dog* became vertical. She rose up the surface of the wall stern first and then pitch-poled violently, end over end, the bow submerging and the boat going upside down, taking Sully and Scoot with it, the forty-foot mast, sails intact, now pointing toward the bottom.

Scoot was hurled upward, legs and arms flying, her head striking the after galley bulkhead and then the companionway steps and the interior deck, which was now the ceiling. She instantly blacked out.

Everything loose in the cabin was scattered around what had been the overhead. Water was pouring in and was soon lapping at Scoot's chin. It was coming from a four-inch porthole that had not been dogged securely and a few other smaller points of entry.

* * * *

Sully's feet were caught under forestay sailcloth, plastered around his face, but then he managed to shove clear and swim upward, breaking water. He looked at the mound of upside-down hull, bottom to the sky, unable to believe that the fine, sturdy *Sea Dog* had been flipped like a cork, perhaps trapping Scoot inside. Treading water, trying to collect his thoughts, he yelled, "Scoot," but there was no answer. Heart pounding, unable to see over the mound of the hull, he circled it, thinking she might have been thrown clear. But there was no sign of her.

He swam back to the point of cabin entry, took several deep breaths, and dove. He felt along the hatch boards and then opened his eyes briefly to see that the doors were still closed. She *was* still inside. Maneuvering his body, he pulled on the handles. The doors were jammed, and he returned to the surface for air.

He knew by the way the boat had already settled that there was water inside her. Under usual circumstances, the hull being upright, there would be four feet, nine inches of hull below the waterline. There would be about the same to the cabin overhead, enabling a six-foot-person to walk about down there.

Panting, blowing, Sully figured there was at least a three-foot air pocket holding the *Sea Dog* on the surface, and if Scoot hadn't been knocked unconscious and drowned, she could live for quite a while in the dark chamber. How long, he didn't know.

* * * *

In the blackness, water continued to lap at Scoot's chin. She had settled against what had been the deck of the galley alcove, her body in an upright position on debris. Everything not tied down or in a locker was now between the overhead ribs. Wooden hatch covers from the bilges were floating in the water and the naked bilges were exposed. Just aft of her body, and now above it, was the small diesel engine as well as the batteries. Under the water were cans of oil, one of them leaking. Battery acid might leak, too. Few sailors could imagine the nightmare that existed inside the *Sea Dog.* Scoot's pretty face was splashed with engine oil.

Over the next five or six minutes, Sully dove repeatedly, using his feet as a fulcrum, and using all the strength that he had in his arms, legs, and back, in an effort to open the doors. The pressure of the water defeated him. Then he thought about trying to pry the doors open with the wooden handle of the scrub brush. Too late for that, he immediately discovered. It had drifted away, along with Scoot's nylon jacket, her canvas boat shoes—anything that could float.

Finally he climbed on top of the keel, catching his breath, resting a moment, trying desperately to think of a way to enter the hull. Boats of the Baba class, built for deep-water sailing, quite capable of reaching Honolulu and beyond, were almost sea-tight unless the sailors made a mistake or unless the sea became angry. The side ports were supposed to be dogged securely in open ocean. Aside from the cabin doors, there was no entry into that cabin without tools. He couldn't very well claw a hole through the inch of tough fiberglass.

He thought about the hatch on the foredeck, but it could only be opened from inside the cabin. Then there was the skylight on the top of the seventeen-foot cabin, used for ventilation as well as a sun source; that butterfly window, hinged in the middle, could be opened only from the inside. Even with scuba gear, he couldn't open that skylight unless he had tools.

He fought back tears of frustration. There was no way to reach Scoot. And he knew what would happen down there. The water would slowly and inevitably rise until the air pocket was only six inches; her head would be trapped between the surface of the water and the dirty bilge. The water would torture her, then it would drown her. Seawater has no heart, no brain. The Sea Dog would then drop to the ocean floor, thousands of feet down, entombing her forever.

Maybe the best hope for poor Scoot was that she was already dead, but he had to determine whether she was still alive. He began pounding on the hull with the bottom of his fist, waiting for a return knock. At the same time, he shouted her name over and over. Nothing but silence from inside there. He wished he'd hung on to the silly scrub brush. The wooden handle would make more noise than the flesh of his fist.

Almost half an hour passed, and he finally broke down and

sobbed. His right fist was bloody from the constant pounding. Why hadn't *he* gone below to make the stupid sandwiches? Scoot would have been at the wheel when the wave grasped the *Sea Dog*. His young sister, with all her life to live, would be alive now.

They'd had a good brother-sister relationship. He'd teased her a lot about being pint-sized and she'd teased back, holding her nose when he brought one girl or another home for display. She'd always been spunky. He'd taken her sailing locally, in the channel, but she'd wanted an offshore cruise for her fourteenth birthday. Now she'd had one, unfortunately.

Their father had nicknamed her Scoot because, as a baby, she'd crawled so fast. It was still a fitting name for her as a teenager. With a wiry body, she was fast in tennis and swimming and already the school's champion in the hundred-yard dash.

Eyes closed, teeth clenched, he kept pounding away with the bloody fist. Finally he went back into the ocean to try once more to open the doors. He sucked air, taking a half-dozen deep breaths, and then dove again. Bracing his feet against the companionway frames, he felt every muscle straining, but the doors remained jammed. He was also now aware that if they did open, more water would rush in and he might not have time to find Scoot in the blackness and pull her out. But he was willing to take the gamble.

Scoot awakened as water seeped into her mouth and nose. For a moment she could not understand where she was, how she got there, what had happened . . . Vaguely, she remembered the boat slanting steeply downward, as if it were suddenly diving, and she remembered feeling her body going up.

That's all she remembered, and all she knew at the moment was that she had a fierce headache and was in chill water in total darkness. It took a little longer to realize she was trapped in the *Sea Dog*'s cabin, by the galley alcove. She began to feel around herself and to touch floating things. The air was thick with an oil smell. Then she ran her hand over the nearest solid thing—a bulkhead. *That's strange,* she thought—her feet were touching a pot. She lifted her right arm and felt above her—the galley range. The galley range above her? *The boat was upside down.* She felt for the companionway steps and found the entry doors and pushed on them; that was the way she'd come in. The doors didn't move.

Sully crawled up on the wide hull again, clinging to a faint hope that a boat or ship would soon come by; but the sun was already in descent, and with night coming on, chances of rescue lessened with each long minute. It was maddening to have her a few feet away and be helpless to do anything. Meanwhile the hull swayed gently, in eerie silence.

Scoot said tentatively, "Sully?" Maybe he'd been drowned. Maybe she was alone and would die here in the foul water.

She repeated his name, but much more loudly. No answer. She was coming out of shock now and fear icier than the water was replacing her confusion. To die completely alone? It went that way for a few desperate moments, and then she said to herself, *Scoot, you've got to get out of here! There has to be some way to get out . . .*

Sully clung to the keel with one hand, his body flat against the smooth surface of the hull. There was ample room on either side of the keel before the dead-rise, the upward slope of the hull. The *Sea Dog* had a beam of ten feet. Unless a wind and waves came up, he was safe enough in his wet perch.

Scoot again wondered if her brother had survived and if he was still around the boat or on it. With her right foot she began to probe around the space beneath her. The pot had drifted away, but her toes felt what seemed to be flatware. That made sense. The drawer with the knives and forks and spoons had popped out, spilling its contents. She took a deep breath and ducked under to pick out a knife. Coming up, she held the knife blade, reaching skyward with the handle . . .

Eyes closed, brain mushy, exhausted, Sully heard a faint tapping and raised up on his elbows to make sure he wasn't dreaming. No, there was a tapping from below. He crawled back toward what he thought was the source area, the galley area, and put an ear to the hull. *She was tapping!* He pounded the fiberglass, yelling, "Scoot, Scooot, Scooot . . ."

* * * *

Scoot heard the pounding and called out, "Sully, I'm here, I'm here!" Her voice seemed to thunder in the air pocket.

Sully yelled, "Can you hear me?"

Scoot could only hear the pounding.
"Help me out of here . . ."

Ear still to the hull, Sully shouted again, "Scoot, can you hear me?" No answer. He pounded again and repeated, "Scoot, can you hear me?" No answer. The hull was too thick and the slop of the sea, the moan of the afternoon breeze, didn't help.

Though she couldn't hear his voice, the mere fact that he was up there told her she'd escape. Sully had gotten her out of jams before. There was no one on earth that she'd rather have as a rescue man than her oldest brother. She absolutely knew she'd survive.

Though it might be fruitless, Sully yelled down to the galley alcove, "Listen to me, Scoot. You'll have to get out by yourself. I can't help you. I can't break in. Listen to me, I know you're in water, and the best way out is through the skylight. You've got to dive down and open it. You're small enough to go through it . . ." She could go through either section of the butterfly window. "Tap twice if you heard me!"

She did not respond, and he repeated what he'd just said, word for word.

No response. No taps from below.

* * * *

Scoot couldn't understand why he didn't just swim down and open the doors to the cabin, release her. That's all he needed to do, and she'd be free.

Sully looked up at the sky. "Please, God, help me, help us." It was almost unbearable to know she was alive and he was unable to do anything for her. Then he made the decision to keep repeating: "Listen to me, Scoot. You'll have to get out by yourself. I can't break in. Listen to me, the best way out is through the skylight. You've got to dive down and open it. You're small enough to go through it . . ."

He decided to keep saying it the rest of the day and into the night or for as long as it took to penetrate the hull with words. *Skylight! Skylight!* Over and over.

He'd heard of mental telepathy but had not thought much about it before. Now it was the only way to reach her.

Scoot finally thought that maybe Sully was hurt, maybe helpless up on that bottom, so that was why he couldn't open the doors and let her out. That had to be the reason—Sully up there with broken legs. *So I'll have to get out on my own,* she thought.

Over the last two days, when she wasn't on the wheel she had been exploring the *Sea Dog,* and she thought she knew all the exits. Besides the companionway doors, which she knew she couldn't open, there was the hatch on the foredeck for access to the sails; then there was the skylight, almost in the middle of the long cabin. Sully had opened it, she remembered, to air out the boat before they sailed. As she clung to a light fixture by the alcove, in water up to her shoulders, something kept telling her she should first try the butterfly windows of the skylight. The unheard message was compelling—*Try the skylight.*

Sully's voice was almost like a recording, a mantra, saying the same thing again and again, directed down to the position of the galley.

Scoot remembered that an emergency flashlight was bracketed on the bulkhead above the starboard settee, and she assumed it was waterproof. From what Sully had said, Beau Tucker took great care in selecting emergency equipment. It might help to actually see the dogs on the metal skylight frame. She knew she wouldn't have much time to spin them loose. Maybe thirty or forty seconds before she'd have to surface for breath. Trying to think of the exact position of the upside-down flashlight, she again tapped on the hull to let her brother know she was very much alive.

He pounded back.

Sully looked at his watch. Almost four-thirty. About three hours to sundown. Of course, it didn't make much difference to Scoot. She was already in dank night. But it might make a difference if she got out after nightfall. He didn't know what kind of shape she was in. Injured, she might surface and drift away.

The mantra kept on.

Scoot dove twice for the boxy flashlight, found it, and turned it on, suddenly splitting the darkness and immediately feeling hopeful. But it was odd to see the *Sea Dog*'s unusual overhead, the open hatchways into the bilge and the debris floating on the shining water, all streaked with lubricants; odd to see the toilet upside down. She held the light underwater and it continued to operate.

Every so often, Sully lifted his face to survey the horizon, looking for traffic. He knew they were still within sixteen or seventeen miles of the coast, though the drift was west. There was usually small-boat activity within twenty miles of the shore— fishermen or pleasure boats.

Scoot worked herself forward a few feet, guessing where the skylight might be, and then went down to find the butterfly windows, the flashlight beam cutting through the murk. It took a few seconds to locate them and put a hand on one brass dog. She tried to turn it, but it was too tight for her muscles and she rose up to breathe again.

Not knowing what was happening below or whether Scoot was trying to escape, Sully was getting more anxious by the moment. He didn't know whether or not the crazy telepathy was working. He wished she would tap again to let him know she was still alive. It had been more than twenty minutes since she'd last tapped.

Scoot had seen a toolbox under the companionway steps and went back to try to find it. She guessed there'd be wrenches inside it, unless they'd spilled out. Using the flashlight again, she found the metal box and opened it. Back to the surface to breathe again, and then back to the toolbox to extract a wrench. With each move she was becoming more and more confident.

A big sailboat, beating south, came into Sully's view; but it was more than two miles away and the occupants—unless he was very lucky—would not be able to spot the *Sea Dog*'s mound and the man standing on it, waving frantically.

Four times Scoot needed to dive, once for each dog; and working underwater was at least five times as difficult as trying to turn them in usual circumstances. She'd aim the light and rest it to illuminate the windows. Finally, all the dogs were loose and she rose once again. This time, after filling her lungs to bursting, she went down and pushed on the starboard window. It cracked a little, but the outside sea pressure resisted and she had to surface again.

Sully sat down, almost giving up hope. How long the air pocket would hold up was anybody's guess. The boat had settled at least six inches in the last two hours. It might not last into the night.

＊ ＊ ＊ ＊

On her sixth dive Scoot found a way to brace her feet against the ceiling ribs. She pushed with all her strength, and this time the window opened. Almost out of breath, she quickly pushed her body through and the *Old Sea Dog* released her. Treading water beside the hull, she sucked in fresh air and finally called out, "Sully . . ."

He looked her way, saw the grin of triumph on the oil-stained imp face, and dived in to help her aboard the derelict.

Shivering, holding each other for warmth all night, they rode and rocked, knowing that the boat was sinking lower each hour.

Just after dawn, the *Red Rooster,* a long-range sports fishing boat out of San Diego bound south to fish for wahoo and tuna off the Revilla Gigedo Islands, came within a hundred yards of the upside-down sailboat and stopped to pick up its two chattering survivors.

The *Red Rooster*'s captain, Mark Stevens, asked, "What happened?"

"Rogue wave," said Sully. That's what he planned to say to Beau Tucker as well.

Stevens winced and nodded that he understood.

The *Old Sea Dog* stayed on the surface for a little while longer, having delivered her survivors to safety; then her air pocket breathed its last and she slipped beneath the water, headed for the bottom.

The Caller

by Robert D. San Souci

It was hot at Aunt Margaret's funeral. Being in church had been tiring, but this was worse. Lindsay Walters had to stand in the hot sun, sweating in the ugly, black, too-heavy dress her parents had made her wear, while the minister prayed on and on. The bunches of flowers draped across the coffin had wilted. Lindsay almost giggled as she thought of Aunt Margaret in her coffin turning golden brown like a big biscuit in a toaster oven.

Lindsay was angry because she *should* be at Missy's, helping her best friend get ready for a party. Except for her mother and father and two brothers, there were only a few dried-up men and ladies from the old folks' home. And *they* got to sit on folding chairs, Lindsay thought, while we have to *stand*.

A cell phone rang. Lindsay knew from the stupid "Yankee

Doodle Went to Town" tune that it was her father's. He went red in the face. At least *she* knew enough to turn hers off so it wouldn't ring in church or at the cemetery. Her father pulled his phone out of its carrying case and shut off the signal but glanced at the caller's phone number. He made a face and checked his watch. Then he put the phone back in its case and looked across at the minister. Happily, Lindsay saw that the reverend was just about done.

As soon as the final prayers were said, and the minister was patting her mother's hand, Lindsay ducked behind a tree, took out her own cell phone, and dialed Missy's number. It was busy. Probably her friend was making plans with Noelle or Candice for the party. She made a face at the phone, turned, and bumped into her father, who was talking into his phone. He shooed her back to her mother while he kept talking. *Like my calls aren't that important,* Lindsay thought sourly.

Her mother introduced her to some boring old ladies. She had to nod and look sad as they yakked about her aunt, while her mother and brothers talked to the minister. When her father returned, Lindsay asked, "Can we go now?"

"I just have to make one more call," her father said. He moved off to where they couldn't overhear him.

When the last old lady and the minister had gone, Lindsay begged her mother, "Please, please, *please* make Daddy get off the phone so we can go!"

"Stop whining," her mother said. But she waved impatiently

at Lindsay's father. "Show some respect," she ordered Lindsay's brothers, who were trying to trip each other in one of their weird games. Darren fell on his seat a few feet from Aunt Margaret's coffin. She would be buried when they had left. David laughed. Their mother ordered all of them to the car, then marched over to where Mr. Walters was still talking on the phone. The kids could see she wanted to get going. She made their father end his call. Now both of them were angry. Mr. Walters shoved his phone into his coat pocket, not into its holster. "All right, let's get this show on the road," he said. But he had to go after Darren and David, who had climbed out of the car and were now playing tag.

Some people from the funeral had stopped by the house. Lindsay and her brothers had to sit around and smile while their sad-faced parents and guests drank coffee and tea and talked about how nice Aunt Margaret had been.

"As long as you didn't make her angry," said Mr. Walters with a sharp laugh. "I remember as a kid that she could be a holy terror if she thought someone had been rude or was lying or cruel." Lindsay knew what he was talking about. Her aunt had a real temper. Lindsay thought of the woman in heaven, terrorizing the angels for not being holy enough. She'd tune up the heavenly choir, all right, or feathers would fly. It was all the girl could do to keep from laughing aloud at the picture in her mind.

But the guests finally left. Lindsay ran to her room to change so that her father could drive her to Missy's party. When she was ready, she opened her red velvet jewel case and took out Aunt Margaret's ring, set with real diamonds in white gold. She had always loved it, and Aunt Margaret had promised it to her just before she died. Her mother had wanted to keep it until Lindsay was older, but Lindsay had thrown one of her best tantrums and said that the old woman had wanted her to wear it always. (She had made up that part, but it seemed to work on her mother, who told her only to wear the ring at special times. Well, showing off to Missy and Noelle and Candice and the others was special!)

Her cell phone, beside the jewel box, rang.

There was some strange crackling, then a lot of whispering, sounding like a crowd. Finally a voice so tired and dry and old that it was hard to tell if it was a man or a woman said, "Lindsay, darling, this is Aunt Margaret."

"Right! Nice try, Missy, guys—see you in a few minutes." Lindsay hung up and put her phone into her party bag. Slipping the ring in her jeans pocket so her parents wouldn't see, she rushed down the steps two at a time.

"Where's Dad? He's supposed to drive me to Missy's."

"He's out in the car looking for his cell phone," her mother said. "It fell out of his pocket."

Sighing at the hopelessness of all grownups, Lindsay helped her father search the car; but the phone was gone. He was in a bad mood. She was glad she was spending the night at Missy's after the party.

Aunt Margaret's ring helped make up for arriving late. All the girls at Missy's were jealous of the real diamonds on Lindsay's finger. She forgot about their phone joke.

"I hated to go to that smelly old folks' home," Lindsay told them. "I just pretended I wanted to go, because I wanted this ring. But Aunt Margaret thought I was nice, so she left me her ring when she died last week."

Her cell phone rang. She grabbed her purse from beside the couch and answered it.

Lots of static, more whispers, then the same dried-up voice saying, "Lindsay, this is Aunt Margaret. I must talk to you."

Clearly it wasn't her friends trying to trick her. That meant it had to be Darren and David. She covered the mouthpiece and whispered, "It's my creepy brothers pretending to be my aunt's ghost." The others rolled their eyes, knowing what jerks younger brothers could be.

"Is it *really* you, Aunt Margaret?" asked Lindsay, trying to sound little-girl scared, playing along with the game.

"Yes. I just wanted to hear your sweet voice again."

How corny could they get? Lindsay wondered.

"You were always my favorite. You loved me best."

Lindsay held up the ring and wiggled her fingers as she talked. "Well, it was really your ring I loved." The other girls put their hands over their mouths and giggled. "I hated going to that place where you stayed. And I hated it when you kissed me, because your breath always smelled like sour milk or tuna fish. And all that stuff you told me about when you were young was as boring as my jerks of brothers talking about football scores. So thanks for the ring and goodbye, *Aunt Margaret!*" Lindsay disconnected the call.

She pushed *69 to see where her brothers were calling from. The readout was her father's cell phone number.

"They're using my dad's phone that he was looking for. They're never supposed to touch it. They must have found it in the car. I'm going to see that they get *so busted* for this when I get home."

When the party ended and the other girls left after dinner, Missy's parents said they were going to visit neighbors. They left the number where they could be reached, even though Missy reminded them that she and Lindsay often stayed home alone. As soon as they were gone, the girls went upstairs to Missy's room to call their friends and talk about boys and clothes and MTV. Lying at opposite ends of Missy's bed, they chatted into their cell phones.

Lindsay was just about to dial her boyfriend of the week when her phone rang.

"Lindsay, I am very disappointed in you." The same voice.

"Get lost!"

"I don't think you deserve my ring. I'm coming to get it back."

"Get real!" She broke the connection. The readout showed her father's cell phone. She punched the number, but the line just rang and rang. She hung up and dialed her home. Her mother answered.

"Mom," she said, "Darren and David found Dad's phone. They've been using it to call and bug me. They just did it again."

"That's not possible," said her mother. "They've been watching a game for the past hour. And your father is sure he dropped his phone at the cemetery this afternoon. He's going to check there tomorrow morning." Now her mother sounded worried. "Do you think it's a real crank caller?"

"The readout shows Dad's cell phone number," Lindsay explained. "But—"

There was a burst of static. The phone went dead. Missy looked up as her phone went dead, too. The lights in the house flickered, dimmed, then went out. "Blackout," said Missy. All the other houses in the neighborhood were dark.

"I don't think that would shut off our phones," said Lindsay.

"Well, it did," said Missy. "Anyhow, I was bored with what Noelle was telling me. And this is cool. We can tell ghost stories."

"I don't want to," said Lindsay, wishing she were home and not spending the night in a lightless house. The cut-off conversation with her mother had worried her more than she liked to admit. But Missy's folks would be home soon, she decided.

"Chicken!" her friend teased.

There was a knocking downstairs at the front door. It had an odd, echoing sound to it. *Thunk. Thunk. Thunk.*

Missy got up to answer it.

"Don't!" cried Lindsay. She couldn't say why she was frightened, but in truth she was suddenly feeling scared.

"You are *so* stupid," said Missy. "My folks forgot their keys or something. Probably the doorbell doesn't work like the phones don't."

"Please, don't go!"

"Stay here if you're so scared," said Missy, shaking her head. "What a wuss!" She left. A moment later Lindsay heard her running down the stairs two at a time.

Lindsay closed the bedroom door and locked it. She heard the front door open and slam a moment later. She thought she heard a soft sound, like something heavy being dropped. Then quiet. She listened harder, hoping to hear the sound of familiar voices. But there was only silence.

Her cell phone rang.

She snatched it up, hoping it was her mother calling back.

"Lindsay, I've come for my ring, you unhappy child. I'm at the foot of the stairs right now. Let's play that game I played when you were a little girl. The one your father told me not to play, because it frightened you so? But you loved it—you loved being scared. Don't you like being scared anymore?"

"Missy? Are you playing a trick on me? This isn't funny."

But Missy's phone was still on the bed where she had left it.

"One step, two—I'm coming for you," said the voice on the phone.

Thump, thump on the stairs.

"Three steps, four—better lock the door."

Two more *thumps.*

But Lindsay had already locked the door. Part of her wanted to shut off the phone, but she didn't dare.

"Five steps, six—say your prayers quick."

If the phone were working, Lindsay thought, she could call for help. She hung up and dialed her home phone number. It was answered on the third ring.

"Seven steps, eight—not long to wait," said her mother's voice.

She hung up and dialed 911.

"Nine steps, ten—we're near the end," said a man's voice.

She hung up and threw the phone onto the bed beside Missy's.

"Eleven, twelve, and one step more—too late for you, I'm at the door!" It was Aunt Margaret's angry voice, the one she'd used when Darren and David's football broke a window in her house before she moved to the old folks' home.

Someone rattled the door handle, found it locked, and knocked loudly.

THUMP! THUMP! THUMP!

"Go away! Leave me alone! I didn't mean what I said!" Lindsay started to cry.

"Gotcha!" cried Missy through the door. "You're crying! This is better than telling ghost stories! Wait till Noelle and Candice hear I made you cry. You and that stupid ring you think is so cool."

Angry at how she'd been tricked, Lindsay wiped away her tears and yanked open the door. "I never want to talk to you again!" she yelled.

But it wasn't Missy holding Lindsay's father's phone in a muddy hand as the lights came on.

Scout's Honor

by Avi

Back in 1946, when I was nine, I worried that I wasn't tough enough. That's why I became a Boy Scout. Scouting, I thought, would make a man of me. It didn't take long to reach Tenderfoot rank. You got that for joining. To move up to Second Class, however, you had to meet three requirements. Scout Spirit and Scout Participation had been cinchy. The third requirement, Scout Craft, meant I had to go on an overnight hike in the *country*. In other words, I had to leave Brooklyn on my own for the first time in my life.

Since I grew up in Brooklyn in the 1940s, the only grass I knew was in Ebbets Field, where the Dodgers played. Otherwise, my world was made of slate pavements, streets of asphalt (or cobblestone), and skies full of tall buildings. The only thing "country" was a puny pin oak tree at our curb, which was noticed mostly just by dogs.

I asked Scoutmaster Brenkman where I could find some country. Now, whenever I saw Mr. Brenkman, who was a church pastor, he was dressed either in church black or Scout khaki. When he wore black, he'd warn us against hellfire. When he wore khaki, he'd teach us how to build fires.

"Country," Scoutmaster Brenkman said in answer to my question, "is anywhere that has lots of trees and is not in the city. Many boys camp in the Palisades."

"Where's that?"

"Just north of the city. It's a park in Jersey."

"Isn't that a zillion miles from here?"

"Take the subway to the George Washington Bridge, then hike across."

I thought for a moment, then asked, "How do I prove I went?"

Mr. Brenkman looked deeply shocked. "You wouldn't *lie,* would you? What about Scout's honor?"

"Yes, sir," I replied meekly.

My two best friends were Philip Hossfender, whom we nicknamed Horse, and Richard Macht, called Max because we were not great spellers. They were also Scouts, Tenderfoots like me.

Horse was a skinny little kid about half my size whose way

of arguing was to ball up his fist and say, "Are you saying . . . ?" in a threatening tone.

Max was on the pudgy side, but he could talk his way out of a locked room. More important, he always seemed to have pocket money, which gave his talk real power.

I wasn't sure why, but being best friends meant we were rivals, too. One of the reasons for my wanting to be tougher was a feeling that Horse was a lot tougher than I was, and that Max was a little tougher.

"I'm going camping in the Palisades next weekend," I casually informed them.

"How come?" Max challenged.

"Scout Craft," I replied.

"Oh, *that*," Horse said with a shrug.

"Look," I said, "I don't know about you, but I don't intend to be a Tenderfoot all my life. Anyway, doing stuff in the city is for sissies. Scouting is real camping. Besides, I like roughing it."

"You saying I don't?" Horse snapped.

"I'm not saying nothing," I said.

They considered my idea. Finally, Horse said, "Yeah, well, I was going to do that, but I didn't think you guys were ready for it."

"I've been ready for *years*," Max protested.

"Then we're going, right?" I said.

They looked around at me. "If you can do it, I can do it," Max said.

"Yeah," Horse said thoughtfully.

The way they agreed made me nervous. Now I really was going to have to be tough.

We informed our folks that we were going camping overnight (which was true) and that the Scoutmaster was going with us—which was a lie. We did remember what Mr. Brenkman said about honesty, but we were baseball fans, too, and since we were prepared to follow Scout law—being loyal, helpful, friendly, courteous, kind, obedient, cheerful, thrifty, brave, clean, *and* reverent—we figured a 900 batting average was not bad.

So Saturday morning we met at the High Street subway station. I got there first. Stuffed in my dad's army surplus knapsack was a blanket, a pillow, and a paper bag with three white-bread peanut butter and jelly sandwiches—that is, lunch, supper, and Sunday breakfast. My pockets were full of stick matches. I had an old flashlight, and since I lived by the Scout motto—Be Prepared—I had brought along an umbrella. Finally, being a serious reader, I had the latest Marvel Family comics.

Horse arrived next, his arms barely managing to hold on to a mattress that seemed twice his size. As for food, he had four cans of beans jammed into his pockets.

Max came last. He was lugging a new knapsack that contained a cast-iron frying pan, a packet of hot dogs, and a box of saltine crackers—plus two bottles. One bottle was mustard, the other, celery soda. He also had a bag of Tootsie Rolls and a shiny hatchet. "To build a lean-to," he explained.

Max's prize possession, however, was an official Scout compass. "It's really swell," he told us. "You can't ever get lost with it. Got it at the Scout store."

"I hate that place," Horse informed us. "It's all new. Nothing real."

"This compass is real," Max retorted. "Points north all the time. You can get cheaper ones, but they point all different directions."

"What's so great about the north?" Horse said.

"That's always the way to go," Max insisted.

"Says who?" I demanded.

"Mr. Brenkman, dummy," Horse cried. "Anyway, there's always an arrow on maps pointing the way north."

"Cowboys live out west," I reminded them. They didn't care.

On the subway platform, we realized we did not know which station we were heading for. To find out, we studied the system map, which looked like a noodle factory hit by a bomb. The place we wanted to go (north) was at the top of the map, so I had to hoist Horse onto my shoulders for a closer look. Since he refused to let go of his mattress—or the tin cans in his pockets—it wasn't easy. I asked him—in a kindly fashion—to put the mattress down.

No sooner did he find the station—168th Street—than our

train arrived. We rushed on, only to have Horse scream, "My mattress!" He had left it on the platform. Just before the doors shut, he and I leaped off. Max, however, remained on the train. Helplessly, we watched as his horror-stricken face slid away from us. "Wait at the next station!" I bellowed. "Don't move!"

The next train took forever to come. Then it took even longer to get to the next stop. There was Max. All around him— like fake snow in a glass ball—were crumbs. He'd been so nervous he had eaten all his crackers.

"Didn't that make you thirsty?"

"I drank my soda."

I noticed streaks down his cheeks. Horse noticed them, too. "You been crying?" he asked.

"Naw," Max said. "There was this water dripping from the tunnel roof. But, you said don't move, right? Well, I was just being obedient."

By the time we got on the next train—with all our possessions—we had been traveling for an hour. But we had managed to go only one stop.

During the ride, I got hungry. I pulled out one of my sandwiches. With the jelly soaked through the bread, it looked like a limp scab.

Horse, envious, complained *he* was getting hungry.

"Eat some of your canned beans," I suggested.

He got out one can without ripping his pocket too badly. Then his face took on a mournful look.

"What's the matter?" I asked.

"Forgot to bring a can opener."

Max said, "In the old days, people opened cans with their teeth."

"You saying my teeth aren't strong?"

"I'm just talking about history!"

"You saying I don't know history?"

Always kind, I plopped half my sandwich into Horse's hand. He squashed it into his mouth and was quiet for the next fifteen minutes. It proved something I'd always believed: The best way to stop arguments is to get people to eat peanut butter sandwiches. They can't talk.

Then we became so absorbed in our Marvel Family comics that we missed our station. We got to it only by coming back the other way. When we reached street level, the sky was dark.

"I knew it," Max announced. "It's going to rain."

"Don't worry," Horse said. "New Jersey is a whole other state. It probably won't be raining there."

"I brought an umbrella," I said smugly, though I wanted it to sound helpful.

As we marched down 168th Street, heading for the George Washington Bridge, we looked like European war refugees. Every few paces Horse cried, "Hold it!" and adjusted his arms around his mattress. Each time we paused, Max pulled out his compass, peered at it, then announced, "Heading north!"

I said, "The bridge goes from east to west."

"Maybe the bridge does," Max insisted with a show of his compass, "but guaranteed, *we* are going north."

About then, the heel of my left foot, encased in a heavy rubber boot over an earth-crushing Buster Brown shoe, started to get sore. Things weren't going as I had hoped. Cheerfully, I tried to ignore the pain.

The closer we drew to the bridge, the more immense it seemed. And the clouds had become so thick, you couldn't see the top or the far side.

Max eyed the bridge with deep suspicion. "I'm not so sure we should go," he said.

"Why?"

"Maybe it doesn't have another side."

We looked at him.

"No, seriously," Max explained, "they could have taken the Jersey side away, you know, for repairs."

"Cars are going across," I pointed out.

"They could be dropping off," he suggested.

"You would hear them splash," Horse argued.

"I'm going," I said. Trying to look brave, I started off on my own. My bravery didn't last long. The walkway was narrow. When I looked down, I saw only fog. I could feel the bridge tremble and sway. It wasn't long before I was convinced the bridge was about to collapse. Then a ray of hope struck me: Maybe the other guys had chickened out. If they had, I could quit because of *them.* I glanced back. My heart sank. They were coming.

After they caught up, Horse looked me in the eye and said, "If this bridge falls, I'm going to kill you."

A quarter of a mile farther across, I gazed around. We were completely fogged in.

"I think we're lost," I announced.

"What do we do?" Horse whispered. His voice was jagged with panic. That made me feel better.

"Don't worry," Max said. "I've got my compass." He pulled it out. "North is that way," he said, pointing in the direction we had been going.

Horse said, "You sure?"

"A Scout compass never lies," Max insisted.

"*We* lied," I reminded him.

"Yeah, but this is an *official* Scout compass," Max returned loyally.

"Come on," Max said and marched forward. Horse and I followed. In moments, we crossed a metal bar on the walkway. On one side a sign proclaimed NEW YORK; on the other it said NEW JERSEY.

"Holy smoke," Horse said with reverence as he straddled the bar. "Talk about being tough. We're in two states at the same time."

It began to rain. Max said, "Maybe it'll keep us clean."

"You saying I'm not clean?" Horse shot back.

Ever friendly, I put up my umbrella.

We went on—Max on one side, Horse on the other, me in

the middle—trying to avoid the growing puddles. After a while, Max said, "Would you move the umbrella? Rain is coming down my neck."

"We're supposed to be roughing it," I said.

"Being in the middle isn't roughing it," Horse reminded me.

I folded the umbrella up so we all could get soaked equally.

"Hey!" I cried. "Look!" Staring up ahead, I could make out tollbooths and the dim outlines of buildings.

"Last one off the bridge is a rotten egg!" Horse shouted and began to run. The next second, he tripped and took off like an F-36 fighter plane. Unfortunately, he landed like a Hellcat dive-bomber as his mattress unspooled before him and then slammed into a big puddle.

Max and I ran to help. Horse was damp. His mattress was soaked. When he tried to roll it up, water cascaded like Niagara Falls.

"Better leave it," Max said.

"It's what I sleep on at home," Horse said as he slung the soaking, dripping mass over his shoulder.

When we got off the bridge, we were in a small plaza. To the left was the roadway, full of roaring cars. In front of us, aside from the highway, there was nothing but buildings. Only to the right were there trees.

"North is that way," Max said, pointing toward the trees. We set off.

"How come you're limping?" Horse asked me. My foot *was* killing me. All I said, though, was "How come you keep rubbing your arm?"

"I'm keeping the blood moving."

We approached the grove of trees. "Wow," Horse exclaimed. "Country." But as we drew closer, what we found were discarded cans, bottles, and newspapers—plus an old mattress spring.

"Hey," Max cried, sounding relieved, "this is just like Brooklyn."

I said, "Let's find a decent place, make camp, and eat."

It was hard to find a campsite that didn't have junk. The growing dark didn't help. We had to settle for the place that had the least amount of garbage.

Max said, "If we build a lean-to, it'll keep us out of the rain." He and Horse went a short distance with the hatchet.

They saw a tree they wanted, and Max whacked at it. The hatchet bounced right out of his hand. There was not even a dent in the tree. Horse retrieved the hatchet and checked the blade. "Dull," he said.

"Think I'm going to carry something sharp and cut myself?" Max protested. They contented themselves with picking up branches.

I went in search of firewood, but everything was wet. When I finally gathered some twigs and tried to light them, the only thing that burned was my fingers.

Meanwhile, Horse and Max used their branches to build a lean-to directly over me. After many collapses—which didn't help my work—they finally got the branches to stand in a shaky sort of way.

"Uh-oh," Horse said. "We forgot to bring something for a cover."

Max eyed me. "Didn't you say you brought a blanket?"

"No way!" I cried.

"All in favor of using the blanket!"

Horse and Max both cried, "Aye."

Only after I built up a mound of partially burned matchsticks and lit *them* did I get the fire going. It proved that where there's smoke there doesn't have to be much fire. The guys meanwhile draped my blanket over their branch construction. It collapsed twice.

About an hour after our arrival, the three of us were gathered inside the tiny space. There was a small fire, but more light came from my flickering flashlight.

"No more rain," Horse said with pride.

"Just smoke," I said, rubbing my stinging eyes.

"We need a vent hole," Horse pointed out.

"I could cut it with the hatchet," Max said.

"It's my mother's favorite blanket."

"And you took it?" Max said.

I nodded.

"You *are* tough," Horse said.

Besides having too much smoke in our eyes and being wet, tired, and in pain, we were starving. I almost said something about giving up, but as far as I could see, the other guys were still tough.

Max put his frying pan atop my smoldering smoke. After dumping in the entire contents of his mustard bottle, he threw in the franks. Meanwhile, I bolted down my last sandwich.

"What am I going to eat?" Horse suddenly said.

"Your beans," I reminded him.

Max offered up his hatchet. "Here. Just chop off the top end of the can."

"Oh, right," Horse said. He selected a can, set it in front of him, levered himself onto his knees, then swung down—hard. There was an explosion. For a stunned moment, we just sat there, hands, face, and clothing dripping with beans.

Suddenly Max shouted, "Food fight! Food fight!" and began to paw the stuff off and fling it around.

Having a food fight in a cafeteria is one thing. Having one in the middle of a soaking wet lean-to with cold beans during a dark, wet New Jersey night is another. In seconds, the lean-to was down, the fire kicked over, and Max's frankfurters dumped on the ground.

"The food!" Max screamed, and began to snatch up the franks. Coated with mustard, dirt, grass, and leaves, they looked positively prehistoric. Still, we wiped the franks clean on our pants, then ate them—the franks, that is. Afterward, we picked beans off each other's clothes—the way monkeys help friends get rid of lice.

For dessert, Max shared some Tootsie Rolls. After Horse swallowed his sixteenth piece, he announced, "I don't feel so good."

The thought of his getting sick was too much. "Let's go home," I said, ashamed to look at the others. To my surprise—and relief—nobody objected.

Wet and cold, our way lit by my fast-fading flashlight, we gathered our belongings—most of them, anyway. As we made our way back over the bridge, gusts of windblown rain pummeled us until I felt like a used-up punching bag. By the time we got to the subway station, my legs were melting fast. The other guys looked bad too. Other riders moved away from us. One of them murmured, "Juvenile delinquents." To cheer us up, I got out my comic books, but they had congealed into a lump of red, white, and blue pulp.

With the subways running slow, it took hours to get home. When we emerged from the High Street station, it was close to midnight.

Before we split up to go to our own homes, we just stood there on a street corner, embarrassed, trying to figure out how to end the day gracefully. I was the one who said, "Okay, I admit it. I'm not as tough as you guys. I gave up first."

Max shook his head. "Naw. I wanted to quit, but I wasn't tough enough to do it." He looked to Horse.

Horse made a fist. "You saying I'm the one who's tough?" he demanded. "I hate roughing it!"

"Me, too," I said quickly.

"Same for me," Max said.

Horse said, "Only thing is, we just have to promise not to tell Mr. Brenkman."

Grinning with relief, we simultaneously clasped hands. "No matter what," Max reminded us.

To which I added, "Scout's honor."

The Dog of Pompeii

by Louis Untermeyer

Tito and his dog Bimbo lived (if you could call it living) under the city wall where it joined the inner gate. They really didn't live there; they just slept there. They lived anywhere. Pompeii was one of the gayest of the old Roman towns, but although Tito was never an unhappy boy, he was not exactly a merry one. The streets were always lively with shining chariots and bright red trappings; the open-air theaters rocked with laughing crowds; sham battles and athletic sports were free for the asking in the great stadium. Once a year the emperor visited the pleasure city, and the fireworks and other forms of entertainment lasted for days.

But Tito saw none of these things, for he was blind—had been blind from birth. He was known to everyone in the poorer quarters. But no one could say how old he was; no one remembered his parents; no one could tell where he came from. Bimbo was another mystery. As long as people could remember seeing Tito—several years at least—they had seen Bimbo. The dog never left his side. He was not only a watchdog, but mother and father to Tito.

Did I say Bimbo never left his master? (Perhaps I had better say "comrade," for if anyone was the master, it was Bimbo.) I was wrong. Bimbo did trust Tito alone exactly three times a day. It was a custom understood between boy and dog since the beginning of their friendship, and the way it worked was this:

Early in the morning, shortly after dawn, while Tito was still dreaming, Bimbo would disappear. When Tito awoke, Bimbo would be sitting quietly at his side, his ears cocked, his stump of a tail tapping the ground, and a fresh-baked loaf of bread—more like a large round roll—at his feet. Tito would stretch himself, Bimbo would yawn, and they would breakfast.

At noon, no matter where they happened to be, Bimbo would put his paw on Tito's knee, and the two of them would return to the inner gate. Tito would curl up in the corner (almost like a dog) and go to sleep, while Bimbo, looking quite important (almost like a boy), would disappear again. In a half-hour he would be back with their lunch. Sometimes it would be a piece of fruit or a scrap of meat; often it was nothing but a dry crust. But sometimes there would be one of those flat, rich cakes, sprinkled with raisins and sugar, that Tito liked so much.

At suppertime the same thing happened, although there was a little less of everything, for things were hard to snatch in the evening with the streets full of people.

But whether there was much or little, hot or cold, fresh or dry, food was always there. Tito never asked where it came from, and Bimbo never told him. There was plenty of rainwater in the hollows of soft stones; the old egg woman at the corner sometimes gave him a cupful of strong goat's milk; in the grape season the fat winemaker let him have drippings of the mild juice. So there was no danger of going hungry or thirsty. There was plenty of everything in Pompeii if you knew where to find it— and if you had a dog like Bimbo.

As I said before, Tito was not the merriest boy in Pompeii. He could not romp with the other youngsters or play hare-and-hounds and I-spy and follow-your-master and ball-against-the-building and jackstone and kings-and-robbers with them. But that did not make him sorry for himself. If he could not see the sights that delighted the lads of Pompeii, he could hear and smell things they never noticed. When he and Bimbo went out walking, he knew just where they were going and exactly what was happening.

As they passed a handsome villa, he'd sniff and say, "Ah, Glaucus Pansa is giving a grand dinner here tonight. They're going to have three kinds of bread and roast pigling and stuffed goose and a great stew—I think bear stew—and a fig pie." And

Bimbo would note that this would be a good place to visit to-morrow.

Or "Hmm," Tito would murmur, half through his lips, half through his nostrils. "The wife of Marcus Lucretius is expecting her mother. She's airing all the linens; she's going to use the best clothes, the ones she's been keeping in pine needles and camphor, and she's got an extra servant cleaning the kitchen. Come, Bimbo, let's get out of the dust!"

Or, as they neared the forum, "Mmm! What good things they have in the marketplace today! Dates from Africa and salt oysters from sea caves and cuttlefish and new honey and sweet onions and—ugh!—water buffalo steaks. Come, let's see what's what in the forum." And Bimbo, just as curious as his comrade, hurried on. Being a dog, he, too, trusted his ears and nose more than his eyes, and so the two of them entered the center of Pompeii.

The forum was the part of town to which everybody came at least once during the day. Everything happened there. There were no private houses; all was public—the chief temples, the gold and red bazaars, the silk shops, the town hall, the booths belonging to the weavers and the jewel merchants, the wealthy woolen market. Everything gleamed brightly here; the build-ings looked new. The earthquake of twelve years ago had brought down all the old structures; and since the citizens of Pompeii were ambitious to rival Naples and even Rome, they had seized the opportunity to rebuild the whole town. Hence there was scarcely a building that was older than Tito.

Tito had heard a great deal about the earthquake, although, since he was only about a year old at the time, he could hardly remember it. This particular quake had been a light one, as earthquakes go. The crude houses had been shaken down, and parts of the outworn wall had been wrecked, but there had been little loss of life. No one knew what caused these earthquakes. Records showed they had happened in the neighborhood since the beginning of time. Sailors said that it was to teach the lazy cityfolk a lesson and make them appreciate those who risked the dangers of the sea to bring them luxuries and to protect their town from invaders. The priests said that the gods took this way of showing their anger to those who refused to worship properly or failed to bring enough sacrifices to the altars. The tradesmen said that the foreign merchants had corrupted the ground and it was no longer safe to traffic in imported goods that came from strange places and carried a curse upon them. Everyone had a different explanation and everyone's explanation was louder and sillier than his neighbor's.

People were talking about it this afternoon as Tito and Bimbo came out of the side street into the public square. The forum was crowded. Tito's ears, as well as his nose, guided them to the place where the talk was loudest.

"I tell you," rumbled a voice that Tito recognized as that of the bath master, Rufus, "there won't be another earthquake in my lifetime or yours. There may be a tremble or two, but earthquakes, like lightning, never strike twice in the same place."

"Don't they?" asked a thin voice Tito had never heard before. It had a high, sharp ring to it, and Tito knew it as the accent of a stranger. "How about the two towns in Sicily that have been ruined three times within fifteen years by the eruptions of Mount Etna? And were they not warned? And does that column of smoke above Vesuvius mean nothing?"

"That?" Tito could hear the grunt with which one question answered another. "That's always there. We use it for our weather guide. When the smoke stands up straight, we know we'll have fair weather; when it flattens out, it's sure to be foggy; when it drifts to the east—"

"Very well, my confident friend," cut in the thin voice, which now sounded curiously flat. "We have a proverb: 'Those who will not listen to man must be taught by the gods.' I say no more. But I leave a last warning. Remember the holy ones. Look to your temples. And when the smoke tree above Vesuvius grows to the shape of an umbrella pine, look to your lives!"

Tito could hear the air whistle as the speaker drew his toga about him, and the quick shuffle of feet told him that the stranger had gone.

"Now what," said Attilio, the cameo cutter, "did he mean by that?"

"I wonder," grunted Rufus. "I wonder."

Tito wondered, too. And Bimbo, his head at a thoughtful

angle, looked as if he were doing a heavy bit of pondering. By nightfall the argument had been forgotten. If the smoke had increased, no one saw it in the dark. Besides, it was Caesar's birthday, and the town was in a holiday mood. Tito and Bimbo were among the merrymakers, dodging the charioteers, who shouted at them. But Tito never missed his footing. He was thankful for his keen ears and quick instinct—most thankful of all for Bimbo.

They visited the open-air theater; then went to the city walls, where the people of Pompeii watched a sham naval battle in which the city, attacked from the sea, was saved after thousands of flaming arrows had been burned. Though the thrill of flaring ships and lighted skies was lost to Tito, the shouts and cheers excited him as much as anyone.

The next morning there were two of the beloved raisin cakes for his breakfast. Bimbo was unusually active and thumped his bit of a tail until Tito was afraid he would wear it out. Tito couldn't imagine whether Bimbo was urging him to some sort of game or was trying to tell him something. After a while he ceased to notice Bimbo. He felt drowsy. Last night's late hours had tired him. Besides, there was a heavy mist in the air—no, a thick fog rather than a mist—a fog that got into his throat and made him cough. He walked as far as the marine gate to get a breath of the sea. But even the salt air seemed smoky.

Tito went to bed before dusk, but he did not sleep well . . .

He awoke early. Or rather, he was pulled awake, Bimbo doing the pulling. The dog had dragged Tito to his feet and was urging the boy along. Where, Tito did not know. His feet stumbled uncertainly; he was still half asleep. For a while he noticed nothing except the fact that it was hard to breathe. The air was hot and heavy, so heavy that he could taste it. The air, it seemed, had turned to powder, a warm powder that stung his nostrils and burned his sightless eyes.

Then he began to hear sounds, peculiar sounds. Like animals under the earth. Hissings and groanings and muffled cries. There was no doubt of it now. The noises came from underneath. He not only heard them—he could feel them. The earth twitched; the twitching changed to an uneven shrugging of the soil. Then, as Bimbo half pulled, half coaxed him along, the ground jerked away from his feet and he was thrown against a stone fountain.

The water—hot water!—splashing in his face revived him. He got to his feet, Bimbo steadying him, helping him on again. The noises grew louder; they came closer. The cries were even more animal-like than before, but now they came from human throats. A few people began to rush by; a family or two, then a group, then, it seemed, the whole city of people. Tito, bewildered though he was, could recognize Rufus's voice as he bellowed like a water buffalo gone mad.

It was then that the crashing began. First a sharp crackling, like a monstrous snapping of twigs; then an explosion that tore earth and sky. The heavens, though Tito could not see them, were shot through with continual flickerings of fire. Lightning above was answered by thunder beneath. A house fell. Then another. By a miracle the two companions had escaped the dangerous side streets and were in a more open space. It was the forum. They rested here awhile; how long, the boy did not know.

Tito had no idea of the time of day. He could feel it was black—an unnatural blackness. Something inside, perhaps the lack of breakfast and lunch, told him it was past noon. But it didn't matter. Nothing seemed to matter. He was getting drowsy, too drowsy to walk. But walk he must. He knew it. And Bimbo knew it; the sharp tugs told him so. Nor was it a moment too soon. The sacred ground of the forum was safe no longer. It began to rock, then to pitch, then to split. As they stumbled out of the square, the earth wriggled like a caught snake, and all the columns of the Temple of Jupiter came down. It was the end of the world, or so it seemed.

To walk was not enough now. They must run. Tito, too frightened to know what to do or where to go, had lost all sense of direction. He started to go back to the inner gate; but Bimbo, straining his back to the last inch, almost pulled his clothes from him. What did the dog want? Had he gone mad?

Then suddenly he understood. Bimbo was telling him the way out. The sea gate, of course. The sea gate—and then the sea, far from falling buildings, heaving ground. He turned, Bimbo guiding him across open pits and dangerous pools of bubbling mud, away from buildings that had caught fire and were dropping their burning beams.

New dangers threatened. All Pompeii seemed to be thronging toward the marine gate, and there was the chance of being trampled to death. But the chance had to be taken. It was growing harder and harder to breathe. What air there was choked him. It was all dust now, dust and pebbles as large as beans. They fell on his head, his hands—pumice stones from the black heart of Vesuvius! The mountain had turned itself inside out. Tito remembered what the stranger had said in the forum two days ago: "Those who will not listen to man must be taught by the gods." The people of Pompeii had refused to heed the warnings; they were being taught now, if it was not too late.

Suddenly it seemed too late for Tito. The red-hot ashes blistered his skin; the stinging vapors tore his throat. He could not go on. He staggered toward a small tree at the side of the road and fell. In a moment Bimbo was beside him. He coaxed, but there was no answer. He licked Tito's hands, his feet, his face. The boy did not stir. Then Bimbo did the thing he least wanted to do. He bit his comrade, bit him deep in the arm. With a cry of pain, Tito jumped to his feet, Bimbo after him. Tito was in despair, but Bimbo was determined. He drove the boy on, snapping at his heels, worrying his way through the crowd, barking, baring his teeth, heedless of kicks or falling stones.

Sick with hunger, half dead with fear and sulfur fumes, Tito plodded on, pursued by Bimbo. How long, he never knew. At last he staggered through the marine gate and felt soft sand under him. Then Tito fainted.

Someone was dashing sea water over him. Someone was carrying him toward the boat.

"Bimbo!" he called. And then louder, "Bimbo!" But Bimbo had disappeared.

Voices jarred against each other. "Hurry! Hurry!" "To the boats!" "Can't you see the child's frightened and starving?" "He keeps calling for someone!" "Poor child, he's out of his mind." "Here boy, take this!"

They tucked him in among them. The oarlocks creaked; the oars splashed, the boat rode over the toppling waves. Tito was safe. But he wept continually. "Bimbo!" he wailed. "Bimbo! Bimbo!"

He could not be comforted.

Eighteen hundred years passed. Scientists were restoring the ancient city; excavators were working their way through the stones and trash that had buried the entire town. Much had already been brought to light—statues, bronze instruments, bright mosaics, household articles, even delicate paintings that had been preserved by the ashes that had taken over two thousand lives. Columns were dug up, and the forum was beginning to emerge.

It was at a place where the ruins lay deepest that the director paused.

"Come here," he called to his assistant. "I think we've discovered the remains of a building in good shape. Here are four huge millstones that were most likely turned by slaves or mules, and here is a whole wall standing, with shelves inside it. Why, it must have been a bakery! And here's a curious thing—the skeleton of a dog!"

"Amazing!" gasped his assistant. "You'd think a dog would have had sense enough to run away at that time. What is that flat thing he's holding between his teeth? It can't be a stone."

"No, it must have come from this bakery. Do you know, it looks to me like some sort of cake, hardened with the years. And bless me, if those little black pebbles aren't raisins! A raisin cake almost two thousand years old! I wonder what made him want it at such a moment?"

"I wonder," murmured his assistant.

LAFFF

by Lensey Namioka

In movies, geniuses have frizzy white hair, right? They wear thick glasses and have names like Dr. Zweistein.

Peter Lu didn't have frizzy white hair. He had straight hair, as black as licorice. He didn't wear thick glasses, either, since his vision was normal.

Peter's family, like ours, had immigrated from China, but they had settled here first. When we moved into a house just two doors down from the Lus, they gave us some good advice on how to get along in America.

I went to the same school as Peter, and we walked to the school bus together every morning. Like many Chinese parents, mine made sure that I worked very hard in school.

In spite of all I could do, my grades were nothing compared

to Peter's. He was at the top in all his classes. We walked to the school bus without talking because I was a little scared of him. Besides, he was always deep in thought.

Peter didn't have any friends. Most of the kids thought he was a nerd because they saw his head always buried in books. I didn't think he even tried to join the rest of us or cared what the others thought of him.

Then on Halloween he surprised us all. As I went down the block trick-or-treating, dressed as a zucchini in my green sweats, I heard a strange, deep voice behind me say, "How do you do."

I yelped and turned around. Peter was wearing a long black Chinese gown with slits in the sides. On his head he had a little round cap, and down each side of his mouth drooped a thin long mustache.

"I am Dr. Lu Manchu, the mad scientist," he announced, putting his hands in his sleeves and bowing.

He smiled when he saw me staring at his costume. It was a scary smile, somehow.

Some of the other kids came up, and when they saw Peter, they were impressed. "Hey, neat!" said one boy.

I hadn't expected Peter to put on a costume and go trick-or-treating like a normal kid. So maybe he did want to join the others after all—at least some of the time. After that night he wasn't a nerd anymore. He was Dr. Lu Manchu. Even some of the teachers began to call him that.

When we became too old for trick-or-treating, Peter was

still Dr. Lu Manchu. The rumor was that he was working on a fantastic machine in his parents' garage. But nobody had any idea what it was.

One evening, as I was coming home from a baby-sitting job, I cut across the Lus' backyard. Passing their garage, I saw through a little window that the light was on. My curiosity got the better of me, and I peeked in.

I saw a booth that looked like a shower stall. A stool stood in the middle of the stall, and hanging over the stool was something that looked like a great big showerhead.

Suddenly a deep voice behind me said, "Good evening, Angela." Peter bowed and smiled his scary smile. He didn't have his costume on and he didn't have the long, droopy mustache. But he was Dr. Lu Manchu.

"What are you doing?" I squeaked.

Still in his strange, deep voice, Peter said, "What are *you* doing? After all, this is my garage."

"I was just cutting across your yard to get home. Your parents never complained before."

"I thought you were spying on me," said Peter. "I thought you wanted to know about my machine." He hissed when he said the word *machine*.

Honestly, he was beginning to frighten me. "What machine?" I demanded. "You mean this shower-stall thing?"

He drew himself up and narrowed his eyes, making them into thin slits. "This is my time machine!"

I goggled at him. "You mean . . . you mean . . . this machine can send you forward and backward in time?"

"Well, actually, I can only send things forward in time," admitted Peter, speaking in his normal voice again. "That's why I'm calling the machine LAFFF. It stands for Lu's Artifact For Fast Forward."

Of course Peter always won first prize at the annual statewide science fair. But that's a long way from making a time machine. Minus his mustache and long Chinese gown, he was just Peter Lu.

"I don't believe it!" I said. "I bet LAFFF is only good for a laugh."

"Okay, Angela. I'll show you!" hissed Peter.

He sat down on the stool and twisted a dial. I heard some bleeps, cheeps, and gurgles. Peter disappeared.

He must have done it with mirrors. I looked around the garage. I peeked under the tool bench. There was no sign of him.

"Okay, I give up," I told him. "It's a good trick, Peter. You can come out now."

Bleep, cheep, and *gurgle* went the machine, and there was Peter, sitting on the stool. He held a red rose in his hand. "What do you think of that?"

I blinked. "So you produced a flower. Maybe you had it under the stool."

"Roses bloom in June, right?" he demanded.

That was true. And this was December.

"I sent myself forward in time to June when the flowers were blooming," said Peter. "And I picked the rose from our yard. Convinced, Angela?"

It was too hard to swallow. "You said you couldn't send things back in time," I objected. "So how did you bring the rose back?"

But even as I spoke I saw that his hands were empty. The rose was gone.

"That's one of the problems with the machine," said Peter. "When I send myself forward, I can't seem to stay there for long. I snap back to my own time after only a minute. Anything I bring with me snaps back to its own time, too. So my rose has gone back to this June."

I was finally convinced, and I began to see possibilities. "Wow, just think: If I don't want to do the dishes, I can send myself forward to the time when the dishes are already done."

"That won't do you much good," said Peter. "You'd soon pop back to the time when the dishes were still dirty."

Too bad. "There must be something your machine is good for," I said. Then I had another idea. "Hey, you can bring me back a piece of fudge from the future, and I can eat it twice: Once now, and again in the future."

"Yes, but the fudge wouldn't stay in your stomach," said Peter. "It would go back to the future."

"That's even better!" I said. "I can enjoy eating the fudge over and over again without getting fat!"

It was late, and I had to go home before my parents started

to worry. Before I left, Peter said, "Look, Angela, there's still a lot of work to do on LAFFF. Please don't tell anybody about the machine until I've got it right."

A few days later I asked him how he was doing.

"I can stay in the future time a bit longer now," he said. "Once I got it up to four minutes."

"Is that enough time to bring me back some fudge from the future?" I asked.

"We don't keep many sweets around the house," he said. "But I'll see what I can do."

A few minutes later, he came back with a spring roll for me. "My mother was frying these in the kitchen, and I snatched one while she wasn't looking."

I bit into the hot, crunchy spring roll, but before I finished chewing, it disappeared. The taste of soy sauce, green onions, and bean sprouts stayed a little longer in my mouth, though.

It was fun to play around with LAFFF, but it wasn't really useful. I didn't know what a great help it would turn out to be.

Every year our school held a writing contest, and the winning story for each grade got printed in our school magazine. I wanted desperately to win. I worked awfully hard in school, but my parents still thought I could do better.

Winning the writing contest would show my parents that I was really good in something. I love writing stories, and I have lots of ideas. But when I actually write them down, my stories never turn out as good as I thought. I just can't seem to find the right words, because English isn't my first language.

I got an honorable mention last year, but it wasn't the same as winning and showing my parents my name, Angela Tang, printed in the school magazine.

The deadline for the contest was getting close, and I had a pile of stories written, but none of them looked like a winner.

Then, the day before the deadline, *boing,* a brilliant idea hit me.

I thought of Peter and his LAFFF machine.

I rushed over to the Lus' garage and, just as I had hoped, Peter was there, tinkering with his machine.

"I've got this great idea for winning the story contest," I told him breathlessly. "You see, to be certain of winning, I have to write the story that would be the winner."

"That's obvious," Peter said dryly. "In fact, you're going around in a circle."

"Wait, listen!" I said. "I want to use LAFFF and go forward to the time when the next issue of the school magazine is out. Then I can read the winning story."

After a moment Peter nodded. "I see. You plan to write down the winning story after you've read it and then send it in to the contest."

I nodded eagerly. "The story would *have* to win, because it's the winner!"

Peter began to look interested. "I've got LAFFF to the point where I can stay in the future for seven minutes now. Will that be long enough for you?"

"I'll just have to work quickly," I said.

Peter smiled. It wasn't his scary Lu Manchu smile, but a nice smile. He was getting as excited as I was. "Okay, Angela. Let's go for it."

He led me to the stool. "What's your destination?" he asked. "I mean, *when's* your destination?"

Suddenly I was nervous. I told myself that Peter had made many time trips, and he looked perfectly healthy.

Why not? What have I got to lose—except time?

I took a deep breath. "I want to go forward three weeks in time." By then I'd have a copy of the new school magazine in my room.

"Ready, Angela?" asked Peter.

"As ready as I'll ever be," I whispered.

Bleep, cheep, and *gurgle.* Suddenly Peter disappeared.

What went wrong? Did Peter get sent by mistake, instead of me?

Then I realized what had happened. Three weeks later in time, Peter might be somewhere else. No wonder I couldn't see him.

There was no time to be lost. Rushing out of Peter's garage, I ran over to our house and entered through the back door.

Mother was in the kitchen. When she saw me, she stared. "Angela! I thought you were upstairs taking a shower!"

"Sorry!" I panted. "No time to talk!"

I dashed up to my room. Then I suddenly had a strange idea. What if I met *myself* in my room? Argh! It was a spooky thought.

There was nobody in my room. Where was I? I mean, where was the I of three weeks later?

Wait. Mother had just said she thought I was taking a shower. Down the hall, I could hear the water running in the bathroom. Okay. That meant I wouldn't run into me for a while.

I went to the shelf above my desk and frantically pawed through the junk piled there. I found it! I found the latest issue of the school magazine, the one with the winning stories printed in it.

How much time had passed? Better hurry.

The shower had stopped running. This meant the other me was out of the bathroom. Have to get out of here!

Too late. Just as I started down the stairs, I heard Mother talking again. "Angela! A minute ago you were all dressed! Now you're in your robe again and your hair's all wet! I don't understand."

I shivered. It was scary, listening to Mother talking to myself downstairs. I heard my other self answering something, then the sound of her—my—steps coming up the stairs. In a panic, I dodged into the spare room and closed the door.

I heard the steps—my steps—go past and into my room.

The minute I heard the door of my room close, I rushed out and down the stairs.

Mother was standing at the foot of the stairs. When she saw me, her mouth dropped. "But . . . but . . . just a minute ago you were in your robe and your hair was all wet!"

"See you later, Mother," I panted. And I ran.

Behind me I heard Mother muttering, "I'm going mad!"

I didn't stop and try to explain. I might go mad, too.

It would be great if I could just keep the magazine with me. But, like the spring roll, it would get carried back to its own time after a few minutes. So the next best thing was to read the magazine as fast as I could.

It was hard to run and flip through the magazine at the same time. But I made it back to Peter's garage and plopped down on the stool.

At last I found the story: the story that had won the contest in our grade. I started to read.

Suddenly I heard *bleep, cheep,* and *gurgle,* and Peter loomed up in front of me. I was back in my original time again.

But I still had the magazine! Now I had to read the story before the magazine popped back to the future. It was hard to concentrate with Peter jumping up and down impatiently, so different from his usual calm, collected self.

I read a few paragraphs, and I was beginning to see how the story would shape up. But before I got any further, the magazine disappeared from my hand.

So I didn't finish reading the story. I didn't reach the end, where the name of the winning writer was printed.

That night I stayed up very late to write down what I remembered of the story. It had a neat plot, and I could see why it was the winner.

I hadn't read the entire story, so I had to make up the ending myself. But that was okay, since I knew how it should come out.

The winners of the writing contest would be announced at the school assembly on Friday. After we had filed into the assembly hall and sat down, the principal gave a speech. I tried not to fidget while he explained about the contest.

Suddenly I was struck by a dreadful thought. Somebody in my class had written the winning story, the one I had copied. Wouldn't that person be declared the winner, instead of me?

The principal started announcing the winners. I chewed my knuckles in an agony of suspense, as I waited to see who would be announced as the winner in my class. Slowly, the principal began with the lowest grade. Each winner walked in slow motion to the stage, while the principal slowly explained why the story was good.

At last, at last, he came to our grade. "The winner is . . ." He stopped, slowly got out his handkerchief, and slowly blew his nose. Then he cleared his throat. "The winning story is 'Around and Around,' by Angela Tang."

I sat like a stone, unable to move. Peter nudged me. "Go on, Angela! They're waiting for you."

I got up and walked up to the stage in a daze. The principal's voice seemed to be coming from far, far away as he told the audience that I had written a science fiction story about time travel.

The winners each got a notebook bound in imitation leather for writing more stories. Inside the cover of the notebook was a ballpoint pen. But the best prize was having my story in the school magazine with my name printed at the end.

Then why didn't I feel good about winning?

After assembly, the kids in our class crowded around to congratulate me. Peter formally shook my hand. "Good work, Angela," he said, and winked at me.

That didn't make me feel any better. I hadn't won the contest fairly. Instead of writing the story myself, I had copied it from the school magazine.

That meant someone in our class—one of the kids here— had actually written the story. Who was it?

My heart was knocking against my ribs as I stood there and waited for someone to complain that I had stolen his story.

Nobody did.

As we were riding the school bus home, Peter looked at me. "You don't seem very happy about winning the contest, Angela."

"No, I'm not," I mumbled. "I feel just awful."

"Tell you what," suggested Peter. "Come over to my house and we'll discuss it."

"What is there to discuss?" I asked glumly. "I won the contest because I cheated."

"Come on over, anyway. My mother bought a fresh package of humbow in Chinatown."

I couldn't turn down that invitation. Humbow, a roll stuffed with barbecued pork, is my favorite snack.

Peter's mother came into the kitchen while we were munching, and he told her about the contest.

Mrs. Lu looked pleased. "I'm very glad, Angela. You have a terrific imagination, and you deserve to win."

"I like Angela's stories," said Peter. "They're original."

It was the first compliment he had ever paid me, and I felt my face turning red.

After Mrs. Lu left us, Peter and I each had another humbow. But I was still miserable. "I wish I had never started this. I feel like such a jerk."

Peter looked at me, and I swear he was enjoying himself. "If you stole another student's story, why didn't that person complain?"

"I don't know!" I wailed.

"Think!" said Peter. "You're smart, Angela. Come on, figure it out."

Me, smart? I was so overcome to hear myself called smart by a genius like Peter that I just stared at him.

He had to repeat himself. "Figure it out, Angela!"

I tried to concentrate. Why was Peter looking so amused?

The light finally dawned. "Got it," I said slowly. "*I'm* the one who wrote the story."

"The winning story is your own, Angela, because that's the one that won."

My head began to go around and around. "But where did the original idea for the story come from?"

"What made the plot so good?" asked Peter. His voice sounded unsteady.

"Well, in my story, my character used a time machine to go forward in time . . ."

"Okay, whose idea was it to use a time machine?"

"It was mine," I said slowly. I remembered the moment when the idea had hit me with a *boing.*

"So you s-stole f-from yourself!" sputtered Peter. He started to roar with laughter. I had never seen him break down like that. At this rate, he might wind up being human.

When he could talk again, he asked me to read my story to him.

I began. "'In movies, geniuses have frizzy white hair, right? They wear thick glasses and have names like Dr. Zweistein . . .'"

Rip Van Winkle

by Washington Irving

Rip Van Winkle

Posthumous Writing of Diedrich Knickerbocker

By Woden, God of Saxons,
From whence comes Wensday, that is Wodensday,
Truth is a thing that ever I will keep
Unto thylke day in which I creep into
My sepulchre—

Cartwright

The following Tale was found among the papers of the late Diedrich Knickerbocker, an old gentleman of New York, who was very curious in the Dutch history of the province and the manners of the descendants from its primitive settlers. His historical researches, however, did not lie so much among books as among men, for the former are lamentably scanty on his favorite topics, whereas he found the old burghers, and still more their wives, rich in that legendary lore so invaluable to true history. Whenever, therefore, he happened upon a genuine Dutch family, snugly shut up in its low-roofed farmhouse, under a spreading sycamore, he looked upon it as a little clasped volume of black letter and studied it with the zeal of a bookworm.

The result of all these researches was a history of the province during the reign of the Dutch governors, which he published some years since. There have been various opinions as to the literary character of his work, and, to tell the truth, it is not a whit better than it should be. Its chief merit is its scrupulous accuracy, which indeed was a little questioned on its first appearance, but has since been completely established, and it is now admitted into all historical collections as a book of unquestionable authority.

The old gentleman died shortly after the publication of his work, and now that he is dead and gone, it cannot do much harm to his memory to say that his time might have been much better employed in weightier labors. He, however, was apt to ride his hobby his own way; and though it did now and then kick up the dust a little in the eyes of his neighbors and grieve the spirit of some friends, for whom he felt the truest deference and affection, yet his errors and follies are remembered "more in sorrow than in anger," and it begins to be suspected that he never intended to injure or offend. But however his memory may be appreciated by critics, it is still held dear by many folks, whose good opinion is well worth having; particularly by certain biscuit bakers, who have gone so far as to imprint his likeness on their new-year cakes, and have thus given him a chance for immortality, almost equal to being stamped on a Waterloo Medal, or a Queen Anne's Farthing.]

Whoever has made a voyage up the Hudson must remember the Kaatskill Mountains. They are a dismembered branch of the great Appalachian family, and are seen away to the west of the river, swelling up to a noble height and lording it over the surrounding country. Every change of season, every change of weather, indeed, every hour of the day produces some change in the magical hues and shapes of these mountains, and they are regarded by all the good wives, far and near, as perfect barometers. When the weather is fair and settled, they are clothed in blue and purple, and print their bold outlines on the clear evening sky but, sometimes, when the rest of the landscape is cloudless, they will gather a hood of gray vapors about their summits, which, in the last rays of the setting sun, will glow and light up like a crown of glory.

At the foot of these fair mountains, the voyager may have described the light smoke curling up from a village, whose shingle roofs gleam among the trees, just where the blue tints of the upland melt away into the fresh green of the nearer landscape. It is a little village of great antiquity, having been founded by some of the Dutch colonists in the early times of the province, just about the beginning of the government of the good Peter Stuyvesant (may he rest in peace!), and there were some of the houses of the original settlers standing within a few years, built of small yellow bricks brought from Holland, having latticed windows and gable fronts, surmounted with weathercocks.

In that same village, and in one of these very houses (which, to tell the precise truth, was sadly time-worn and weather-beaten), there lived many years since, while the country was yet a province of Great Britain, a simple, good-natured fellow of the name of Rip Van Winkle. He was a descendant of the Van Winkles who figured so gallantly in the chivalrous days of Peter Stuyvesant, and accompanied him to the siege of Fort Christina. He inherited, however, but little of the martial character of his ancestors. I have observed that he was a simple, good-natured man; he was, moreover, a kind neighbor, and an obedient, hen-pecked husband. Indeed, to the latter circumstance might be owing that meekness of spirit which gained him such universal popularity, for those men are most apt to be obsequious and conciliating abroad who are under the discipline of shrews at home. Their tempers, doubtless, are rendered pliant and mal-leable in the fiery furnace of domestic tribulation, and a curtain lecture is worth all the sermons in the world for teaching the virtues of patience and long-suffering. A termagant wife may, therefore, in some respects, be considered a tolerable blessing and if so, Rip Van Winkle was thrice blessed.

Certain it is that he was a great favorite among all the good wives of the village, who, as usual with the amiable sex, took his part in all family squabbles and never failed, whenever they talked those matters over in their evening gossipings, to lay all the blame on Dame Van Winkle. The children of the village, too, would shout with joy whenever he approached. He assisted at their sports, made their playthings, taught them to fly kites and shoot marbles, and told them long stories of ghosts, witches, and Indians. Whenever he went dodging about the village, he was surrounded by a troop of them, hanging on his skirts, clambering on his back, and playing a thousand tricks on him with impunity; and not a dog would bark at him throughout the neighborhood.

The great error in Rip's composition was an insuperable aversion to all kinds of profitable labor. It could not be from the want of assiduity or perseverance, for he would sit on a wet rock, with a rod as long and heavy as a Tartar's lance, and fish all day without a murmur, even though he should not be encouraged by a single nibble. He would carry a fowling piece on his shoulder for hours together, trudging through woods and swamps and up hill and down dale to shoot a few squirrels or wild pigeons. He would never refuse to assist a neighbor even in the roughest toil, and was a foremost man at all country frolics for husking Indian corn or building stone fences; the women of the village, too, used to employ him to run their errands and to do such little odd jobs as their less obliging husbands would not do for them. In a word, Rip was ready to attend to anybody's business but his own; but as to doing family duty and keeping his farm in order, he found it impossible.

In fact, he declared it was of no use to work on his farm; it was the most pestilent little piece of ground in the whole country; everything about it went wrong, and would go wrong, in spite of him. His fences were continually falling to pieces; his cow would either go astray or get among the cabbages; weeds were sure to grow quicker in his fields than anywhere else; the rain always made a point of setting in just as he had some outdoor work to do; so that though his patrimonial estate had dwindled away under his management, acre by acre, until there was little more left than a mere patch of Indian corn and potatoes, yet it was the worst-conditioned farm in the neighborhood.

His children, too, were as ragged and wild as if they belonged to nobody. His son Rip, an urchin begotten in his own likeness, promised to inherit the habits, with the old clothes, of his father. He was generally seen trooping like a colt at his mother's heels, equipped in a pair of his father's cast-off galligaskins, which he had much ado to hold up with one hand as a fine lady does her train in bad weather.

Rip Van Winkle, however, was one of those happy mortals of foolish, well-oiled dispositions who take the world easy, eat white bread or brown, whichever can be got with least thought or trouble, and would rather starve on a penny than work for a pound. If left to himself, he would have whistled life away in perfect contentment, but his wife kept continually dinning in his ears about his idleness, his carelessness, and the ruin he was bringing on his family. Morning, noon, and night, her tongue was incessantly going, and everything he said or did was sure to produce a torrent of household eloquence. Rip had but one way of replying to all lectures of the kind, and that, by frequent use, had grown into a habit. He shrugged his shoulders, shook his head, cast up his eyes, but said nothing. This, however, always provoked a fresh volley from his wife, so that he was fain to draw off his forces and take to the outside of the house—the only side which, in truth, belongs to a henpecked husband.

Rip's sole domestic adherent was his dog, Wolf, who was as much henpecked as his master, for Dame Van Winkle regarded them as companions in idleness, and even looked upon Wolf with an evil eye as the cause of his master's going so often astray. True it is, in all points of spirit befitting an honorable dog, he was as courageous an animal as ever scoured the woods—but what courage can withstand the ever-during and all-besetting terrors of a woman's tongue? The moment Wolf entered the house his crest fell, his tail drooped to the ground, or curled between his legs, he sneaked about with a gallows air, casting many a sidelong glance at Dame Van Winkle, and at the least flourish of a broomstick or ladle he would fly to the door with yelping precipitation.

Times grew worse and worse with Rip Van Winkle as years of matrimony rolled on; a tart temper never mellows with age, and a shad tongue is the only edged tool that grows keener with constant use. For a long while he used to console himself, when driven from home, by frequenting a kind of perpetual club of the sages, philosophers, and other idle personages of the village, which held its sessions on a bench before a small inn, designated by a rubicund portrait of His Majesty George the Third. Here they used to sit in the shade through a long, lazy summer's day, talking listlessly over village gossip or telling endless sleepy stories about nothing. But it would have been worth any statesman's money to have heard the profound discussions that sometimes took place when by chance an old newspaper fell into their hands from some passing traveler. How solemnly they would listen to the contents, as drawled out by Derrick Van Bummel, the schoolmaster, a dapper, learned little man who was not to be daunted by the most gigantic word in the dictionary; and how sagely they would deliberate upon public events some months after they had taken place.

The opinions of this junto were completely controlled by Nicholas Vedder, a patriarch of the village and landlord of the inn, at the door of which he took his seat from morning till night, just moving sufficiently to avoid the sun and keep in the shade of a large tree, so that the neighbors could tell the hour by his movements as accurately as by a sundial. It is true he was rarely heard to speak, but smoked his pipe incessantly. His adherents, however (for every great man has his adherents), perfectly understood him, and knew how to gather his opinions.

When anything that was read or related displeased him, he was observed to smoke his pipe vehemently and to send forth short, frequent, and angry puffs; but when pleased, he would inhale the smoke slowly and tranquilly and emit it in light and placid clouds, and sometimes, taking the pipe from his mouth and letting the fragrant vapor curl about his nose, would gravely nod his head in token of perfect approbation.

From even this stronghold the unlucky Rip was at length routed by his termagant wife, who would suddenly break in upon the tranquillity of the assemblage and call the members all to naught; nor was that august personage, Nicholas Vedder himself, sacred from the daring tongue of this terrible virago, who charged him outright with encouraging her husband in habits of idleness.

Poor Rip was at last reduced almost to despair, and his only alternative, to escape from the labor of the farm and clamor of his wife, was to take gun in hand and stroll away into the woods. Here he would sometimes seat himself at the foot of a tree and share the contents of his wallet with Wolf, with whom he sympathized as a fellow sufferer in persecution. "Poor Wolf," he would say, "thy mistress leads thee a dog's life of it; but never mind, my lad, whilst I live thou shalt never want a friend to stand by thee!" Wolf would wag his tail, look wistfully in his master's face, and if dogs can feel pity, I verily believe he reciprocated the sentiment with all his heart.

In a long ramble of the kind of a fine autumnal day, Rip had unconsciously scrambled to one of the highest parts of the Kaatskill Mountains. He was after his favorite sport of squirrel shooting, and the still solitudes had echoed and reechoed with the reports of his gun. Panting and fatigued, he threw himself, late in the afternoon, on a green knoll, covered with mountain herbage, that crowned the brow of a precipice. From an opening between the trees he could overlook all the lower country for many a mile of rich woodland. He saw at a distance the lordly Hudson, far, far below him, moving on its silent but majestic course, with the reflection of a purple cloud or the sail of a lagging bark here and there sleeping on its glassy bosom, and at last losing itself in the blue highlands.

On the other side he looked down into a deep mountain glen, wild, lonely, and shagged, the bottom filled with fragments from the impending cliffs, and scarcely lighted by the reflected rays of the setting sun. For some time Rip lay musing on this scene. Evening was gradually advancing; the mountains began to throw their long blue shadows over the valleys. He saw that it would be dark long before he could reach the village, and he heaved a heavy sigh when he thought of encountering the terrors of Dame Van Winkle.

As he was about to descend, he heard a voice from a distance, hallooing, "Rip Van Winkle! Rip Van Winkle!" He looked around, but could see nothing but a crow winging its solitary flight across the mountain. He thought his fancy must have deceived him, and turned again to descend, when he heard the same cry ring through the still evening air: "Rip Van Winkle! Rip Van Winkle!" At the same time Wolf bristled up his back and, giving a low growl, skulked to his master's side, looking fearfully down into the glen. Rip now felt a vague apprehension stealing over him; he looked anxiously in the same direction and perceived a strange figure slowly toiling up the rocks, and bending under the weight of something he carried on his back. He was surprised to see any human being in this lonely and unfrequented place, but supposing it to be someone of the neighborhood in need of his assistance, he hastened down to yield it.

On nearer approach he was still more surprised at the singularity of the stranger's appearance. He was a short, square-built old fellow, with thick, bushy hair and a grizzled beard. His dress was of the antique Dutch fashion—a cloth jerkin strapped around the waist and several pairs of breeches, the outer one of ample volume, decorated with rows of buttons down the sides and bunches at the knees. He bore on his shoulder a stout keg that seemed full of liquor, and made signs for Rip to approach and assist him with the load. Though rather shy and distrustful of this new acquaintance, Rip complied with his usual alacrity, and mutually relieving one another, they clambered up a narrow gully, apparently the dry bed of a mountain torrent. As they ascended, Rip every now and then heard long rolling peals, like distant thunder, that seemed to issue out of a deep ravine, or rather cleft, between lofty rocks, toward which their rugged path conducted. He paused for an instant, but supposing it to be the muttering of one of those transient thunder showers which often take place in mountain heights, he proceeded. Passing through the ravine, they came to a hollow, like a small amphitheatre, surrounded by perpendicular precipices, over the brinks of which impending trees shot their branches, so that you only caught glimpses of the azure sky and the bright evening cloud. During the whole time, Rip and his companion had labored on in silence, for though the former marveled greatly what could be the object of carrying a keg of liquor up this wild mountain, yet there was something strange and incomprehensible about the unknown that inspired awe and checked familiarity.

On entering the amphitheatre, new objects of wonder were to be seen. On a level spot in the center was a company of odd-looking personages playing at ninepins. They were dressed in a quaint, outlandish fashion; some wore short doublets, others jerkins, with long knives in their belts, and most of them had enormous breeches, of similar style with that of the guide's. Their visages, too, were peculiar; one had a large beard, broad face, and small piggish eyes; the face of another seemed to consist entirely of nose and was surmounted by a white sugar-loaf hat set off with a little red cock's tail. They all had beards, of various shapes and colors. There was one who seemed to be the commander. He was a stout old gentleman, with a weather-beaten countenance; he wore a laced doublet, broad belt and hanger, high-crowned hat and feather, red stockings, and high-heeled shoes, with roses in them. The whole group reminded

Rip of the figures in an old Flemish painting, in the parlor of Dominie Van Shaick, the village parson, and which had been brought over from Holland at the time of the settlement.

What seemed particularly odd to Rip was that though these folks were evidently amusing themselves, yet they maintained the gravest faces, the most mysterious silence, and were, withal, the most melancholy party of pleasure he had ever witnessed. Nothing interrupted the stillness of the scene but the noise of the balls, which, whenever they were rolled, echoed along the mountains like rumbling peals of thunder.

As Rip and his companion approached them, they suddenly desisted from their play and stared at him with such fixed, statuelike gaze and such strange, uncouth, lackluster countenances that his heart turned within him and his knees smote together. His companion now emptied the contents of the keg into large flagons and made signs to him to wait upon the company. He obeyed with fear and trembling; they quaffed the liquor in profound silence and then returned to their game.

By degrees Rip's awe and apprehension subsided. He even ventured, when no eye was fixed upon him, to taste the beverage, which he found had much of the flavor of excellent Hollands. He was naturally a thirsty soul and was soon tempted to repeat the draught. One taste provoked another; and he reiterated his visits to the flagon so often that at length his senses were overpowered, his eyes swam in his head, his head gradually declined, and he fell into a deep sleep.

On waking, he found himself on the green knoll whence he had first seen the old man of the glen. He rubbed his eyes—it was a bright, sunny morning. The birds were hopping and twittering among the bushes, and the eagle was wheeling aloft and breasting the pure mountain breeze. "Surely," thought Rip, "I have not slept here all night." He recalled the occurrences before he fell asleep. The strange man with a keg of liquor—the mountain ravine—the wild retreat among the rocks—the woebegone party at ninepins—the flagon—"Oh! That flagon! That wicked flagon!" thought Rip. "What excuse shall I make to Dame Van Winkle?"

He looked around for his gun, but in place of the clean, well-oiled fowling piece he found an old firelock lying by him, the barrel encrusted with rust, the lock falling off, and the stock worm-eaten. He now suspected that the grave roysters of the mountain had put a trick upon him, and, having dosed him with liquor, had robbed him of his gun. Wolf, too, had disappeared, but he might have strayed away after a squirrel or partridge. He whistled after him and shouted his name, but all in vain; the echoes repeated his whistle and shout, but no dog was to be seen.

He determined to revisit the scene of the last evening's gambol, and if he met with any of the party, to demand his dog and gun. As he rose to walk, he found himself stiff in the joints and wanting in his usual activity. "These mountain beds do not agree with me," thought Rip, "and if this frolic should lay me up with a fit of the rheumatism, I shall have a blessed time with Dame

Van Winkle." With some difficulty he got down into the glen; he found the gully up which he and his companion had ascended the preceding evening, but to his astonishment a mountain stream was now foaming down it, leaping from rock to rock and filling the glen with babbling murmurs. He, however, made shift to scramble up its sides, working his toilsome way through thickets of birch, sassafras, and witch hazel, and sometimes tripped up or entangled by the wild grapevines that twisted their coils or tendrils from tree to tree and spread a kind of network in his path.

At length he reached to where the ravine had opened through the cliffs to the amphitheatre, but no traces of such opening remained. The rocks presented a high, impenetrable wall over which the torrent came tumbling in a sheet of feathery foam and fell into a broad, deep basin, black from the shadows of the surrounding forest. Here, then, poor Rip was brought to a stand. He again called and whistled after his dog; he was only answered by the cawing of a flock of idle crows, sporting high in air about a dry tree that overhung a sunny precipice, and who, secure in their elevation, seemed to look down and scoff at the poor man's perplexities. What was to be done? The morning was passing away, and Rip felt famished for want of his breakfast. He grieved to give up his dog and gun and he dreaded to meet his wife, but it would not do to starve among the mountains. He shook his head, shouldered the rusty firelock, and, with a heart full of trouble and anxiety, turned his steps homeward.

As he approached the village he met a number of people, but none whom he knew, which somewhat surprised him, for he had thought himself acquainted with everyone in the country around. Their dress, too, was of a different fashion from that to which he was accustomed. They all stared at him with equal marks of surprise, and whenever they cast their eyes upon him invariably stroked their chins. The constant recurrence of this gesture induced Rip, involuntarily, to do the same, when, to his astonishment, he found his beard had grown a foot long!

He had now entered the skirts of the village. A troop of strange children ran at his heels, hooting after him and pointing at his gray beard. The dogs, too, not one of which he recognized for an old acquaintance, barked at him as he passed. The very village was altered; it was larger and more populous. There were rows of houses which he had never seen before, and those which had been his familiar haunts had disappeared. Strange names were over the doors—strange faces at the windows—everything was strange. His mind now misgave him; he began to doubt whether both he and the world around him were not bewitched. Surely this was his native village, which he had left but the day before. There stood the Kaatskill Mountains—there ran the silver Hudson at a distance—there was every hill and dale precisely as it had always been. Rip was sorely perplexed. "That flagon last night," thought he, "has addled my poor head sadly!"

It was with some difficulty that he found the way to his own house, which he approached with silent awe, expecting every moment to hear the shrill voice of Dame Van Winkle. He found the house gone to decay—the roof fallen in, the windows shattered, and the doors off the hinges. A half-starved dog that looked like Wolf was skulking about it. Rip called him by name, but the cur snarled, showed his teeth, and passed on. This was an unkind cut indeed. "My very dog," sighed poor Rip, "has forgotten me!"

He entered the house, which, to tell the truth, Dame Van Winkle had always kept in neat order. It was empty, forlorn, and apparently abandoned. This desolateness overcame all his connubial fears—he called loudly for his wife and children; the lonely chambers rang for a moment with his voice, and then all again was silence.

He now hurried forth and hastened to his old resort, the village inn—but it too was gone. A large, rickety, wooden building stood in its place, with great gaping windows, some of them broken and mended with old hats and petticoats, and over the door was painted, "the Union Hotel, by Jonathan Doolittle." Instead of the great tree that used to shelter the quiet little Dutch inn of yore, there now was reared a tall, naked pole, with something on the top that looked like a red nightcap, and from it was fluttering a flag, on which was a singular assemblage of stars and stripes—all this was strange and incomprehensible. He recognized on the sign, however, the ruby face of King George, under which he had smoked so many a peaceful pipe;

but even this was singularly metamorphosed. The red coat was changed for one of blue and buff, a sword was held in the hand instead of a scepter, the head was decorated with a cocked hat, and underneath was painted in large characters, GENERAL WASHINGTON.

There was, as usual, a crowd of folk about the door, but none that Rip recollected. The very character of the people seemed changed. There was a busy, bustling, disputatious tone about it, instead of the accustomed phlegm and drowsy tranquillity. He looked in vain for the sage Nicholas Vedder, with his broad face, double chin, and fair long pipe, uttering clouds of tobacco smoke instead of idle speeches; or Van Bummel, the schoolmaster, doling forth the contents of an ancient newspaper. In place of these, a lean, bilious-looking fellow, with his pockets full of handbills, was haranguing vehemently about rights of citizens—elections—members of congress—liberty—Bunker's Hill—heroes of 'seventy-six—and other words, which were a perfect Babylonish jargon to the bewildered Van Winkle.

The appearance of Rip, with his long, grizzled beard, his rusty fowling piece, his uncouth dress, and an army of women and children at his heels, soon attracted the attention of the tavern politicians. They crowded around him, eyeing him from head to foot with great curiosity. The orator bustled up to him and, drawing him partly aside, inquired "on which side he voted?" Rip stared in vacant stupidity. Another short but busy little fellow pulled him by the arm, and, rising on tiptoe, inquired in his ear, "whether he was Federal or Democrat?" Rip was equally at a loss to comprehend the question; when a knowing, self-important old gentleman in a sharp cocked hat made his way through the crowd, putting them to the right and left with his elbows as he passed, and, planting himself before Van Winkle, with one arm akimbo, the other resting on his cane, his keen eyes and sharp hat penetrating, as it were, into his very soul, demanded in an austere tone, "what brought him to the election with a gun on his shoulder, and a mob at his heels, and whether he meant to breed a riot in the village?" "Alas! Gentlemen," cried Rip, somewhat dismayed, "I am a poor, quiet man, a native of the place, and a loyal subject of the king, God bless him!"

Here a general shout burst from the bystanders. "A tory! A tory! A spy! A refugee! Hustle him! Away with him!" It was with great difficulty that the self-important man in the cocked hat restored order; and, having assumed a tenfold austerity of brow, demanded again of the unknown culprit what he came there for and whom he was seeking. The poor man humbly assured him that he meant no harm, but merely came there in search of some of his neighbors, who used to keep about the tavern.

"Well—who are they? Name them."

Rip bethought himself a moment, and inquired, "Where's Nicholas Vedder?"

There was a silence for a little while, when an old man replied, in a thin, piping voice, "Nicholas Vedder! Why, he is

dead and gone these eighteen years! There was a wooden tomb-
stone in the churchyard that used to tell about him, but that's
rotten and gone too."

"Where's Brom Dutcher?"

"Oh, he went off to the army in the beginning of the war;
some say he was killed at the storming of Stony Point—others
say he was drowned in a squall at the foot of Antony's Nose. I
don't know—he never came back again."

"Where's Van Bummel, the schoolmaster?"

"He went off to the wars, too, was a great militia general,
and is now in congress."

Rip's heart died away at hearing of these sad changes in his
home and friends, and finding himself thus alone in the world.
Every answer puzzled him, too, by treating of such enormous
lapses of time and of matters which he could not understand:
war—congress—Stony Point. He had no courage to ask after
any more friends, but cried out in despair, "Does nobody here
know Rip Van Winkle?"

"Oh, Rip Van Winkle!" exclaimed two or three. "Oh, to be
sure! That's Rip Van Winkle yonder, leaning against the tree."

Rip looked, and beheld a precise counterpart of himself as
he went up the mountain: apparently as lazy, and certainly as
ragged. The poor fellow was now completely confounded. He
doubted his own identity, and whether he was himself or another man. In the midst of his bewilderment, the man in the
cocked hat demanded who he was, and what was his name?

"God knows," exclaimed he, at his wit's end. "I'm not myself—I'm somebody else—that's me yonder—no—that's somebody else got into my shoes—I was myself last night, but I fell asleep on the mountain, and they've changed my gun, and everything's changed, and I'm changed, and I can't tell what's my name, or who I am!"

The bystanders began now to look at each other, nod, wink significantly, and tap their fingers against their foreheads. There was a whisper also about securing the gun and keeping the old fellow from doing mischief, at the very suggestion of which the self-important man in the cocked hat retired with some precipitation. At this critical moment a fresh, comely woman pressed through the throng to get a peep at the gray-bearded man. She had a chubby child in her arms, which, frightened at his looks, began to cry. "Hush, Rip," cried she, "hush, you little fool; the old man won't hurt you." The name of the child, the air of the mother, the tone of her voice, all awakened a train of recollections in his mind. "What is your name, my good woman?" asked he.

"Judith Gardenier."

"And your father's name?"

"Ah, poor man, Rip Van Winkle was his name, but it's twenty years since he went away from home with his gun, and never has been heard of since—his dog came home without him; but whether he shot himself, or was carried away by the Indians, nobody can tell. I was then but a little girl."

Rip had but one question more to ask; but he put it with a faltering voice:

"Where's your mother?"

"Oh, she too had died but a short time since; she broke a blood vessel in a fit of passion, at a New England pedlar."

There was a drop of comfort, at least, in this intelligence. The honest man could contain himself no longer. He caught his daughter and her child in his arms. "I am your father!" cried he. "Young Rip Van Winkle once—old Rip Van Winkle now! Does nobody know poor Rip Van Winkle?"

All stood amazed, until an old woman, tottering out from among the crowd, put her hand to her brow and, peering under it in his face for a moment, exclaimed, "Sure enough! It is Rip Van Winkle—it is himself! Welcome home again, old neighbor. Why, where have you been these twenty long years?"

Rip's story was soon told, for the whole twenty years had been to him but as one night. The neighbors stared when they heard it; some were seen to wink at each other and put their tongues in their cheeks, and the self-important man in the cocked hat, who, when the alarm was over, had returned to the field, screwed down the corners of his mouth and shook his head—upon which there was a general shaking of the head throughout the assemblage.

It was determined, however, to take the opinion of old Peter Vanderdonk, who was seen slowly advancing up the road. He was a descendant of the historian of that name, who wrote one of the earliest accounts of the province. Peter was the most ancient inhabitant of the village, and well versed in all the wonderful events and traditions of the neighborhood. He recollected Rip at once and corroborated his story in the most satisfactory manner. He assured the company that it was a fact, handed down from his ancestor the historian, that the Kaatskill Mountains had always been haunted by strange beings. That it was affirmed that the great Hendrick Hudson, the first discoverer of the river and country, kept a kind of vigil there every twenty years, with his crew of the *Half Moon,* being permitted in this way to revisit the scenes of his enterprise and keep a guardian eye upon the river and the great city called by his name. That his father had once seen them in their old Dutch dresses playing at ninepins in a hollow of the mountain, and that he himself had heard, one summer afternoon, the sound of their balls, like distant peals of thunder.

To make a long story short, the company broke up and returned to the more important concerns of the election. Rip's daughter took him home to live with her; she had a snug, well-furnished house, and a stout, cheery farmer for a husband, whom Rip recollected for one of the urchins that used to climb upon his back. As to Rip's son, and heir, who was the ditto of himself, seen leaning against the tree, he was employed to work on the farm, but evinced a hereditary disposition to attend to anything else but his business.

Rip now resumed his old walk and habits; he soon found

many of his former cronies, though all rather the worse for the wear and tear of time, and preferred making friends among the rising generation, with whom he soon grew into great favor.

Having nothing to do at home, and being arrived at that happy age when a man can be idle with impunity, he took his place once more on the bench at the inn door and was reverenced as one of the patriarchs of the village, and a chronicle of the old times "before the war." It was some time before he could get into the regular track of gossip, or could be made to comprehend the strange events that had taken place during his torpor. How that there had been a revolutionary war—that the country had thrown off the yoke of old England—and that, instead of being a subject of his Majesty George the Third, he was now a free citizen of the United States. Rip, in fact, was no politician—the changes of states and empires made but little impression on him; but there was one species of despotism under which he had long groaned, and that was—petticoat government. Happily that was at an end; he had got his neck out of the yoke of matrimony and could go in and out whenever he pleased, without dreading the tyranny of Dame Van Winkle. Whenever her name was mentioned, however, he shook his head, shrugged his shoulders, and cast up his eyes, which might pass either for an expression of resignation to his fate or joy at his deliverance.

He used to tell his story to every stranger that arrived at Mr. Doolittle's hotel. He was observed, at first, to vary on some points every time he told it, which was, doubtless, owing to his having so recently awaked. It at last settled down precisely to the Tale I have related, and not a man, woman, or child in the neighborhood but knew it by heart. Some always pretended to doubt the reality of it, and insisted that Rip had been out of his head, and that this was one point on which he always remained flighty. The old Dutch inhabitants, however, almost universally gave it full credit. Even to this day they never hear a thunderstorm of a summer afternoon about the Kaatskill but they say Hendrick Hudson and his crew are at their game of ninepins; and it is a common wish of all henpecked husbands in the neighborhood, when life hangs heavy on their hands, that they might have a quieting draught out of Rip Van Winkle's flagon.

Note

The foregoing Tale, one would suspect, had been suggested to Mr. Knickerbocker by a little German superstition about the Emperor Frederick *der Rothbart* and the Kypphaüser mountain. The subjoined note, however, which he had appended to the Tale, shows that it is an absolute fact, narrated with his usual fidelity:

The story of Rip Van Winkle may seem incredible to many, but nevertheless I give it my full belief, for I know the vicinity of our old Dutch settlements to have been very subject to marvelous events and appearances. Indeed, I have heard many stranger stories than this, in the villages along the Hudson, all of which were too well authenticated to admit of a doubt. I have even talked with Rip Van Winkle myself, who, when last I saw him, was a very venerable old man and so perfectly rational and consistent on every other point that I think no conscientious person could refuse to take this into the bargain; nay, I have seen a certificate on the subject taken before a country justice and signed with a cross, in the justice's own handwriting. The story, therefore, is beyond the possibility of doubt.

D. K.

Postscript

The following are traveling notes from a memorandum book of Mr. Knickerbocker:

The Kaatsberg, or Catskill Mountains, have always been a region full of fable. The Indians considered them the abode of spirits who influenced the weather, spreading sunshine or clouds over the landscape, and sending good or bad hunting seasons. They were ruled by an old squaw spirit, said to be their mother. She dwelt on the highest peak of the Catskills and had charge of the doors of day and night, to open and shut them at the proper hour. She hung up the new moons in the skies and cut up the old ones into stars. In times of drought, if properly propitiated, she would spin light summer clouds out of cobwebs and morning dew and send them off from the crest of the mountain, flake after flake, like flakes of carded cotton, to float in the air; until, dissolved by the heat of the sun, they would fall in gentle showers, causing the grass to spring, the fruits to ripen, and the corn to grow an inch an hour. If displeased, however, she would brew up clouds black as ink, sitting in the midst of them like a bottle-bellied spider in the midst of its web; and when these clouds broke, woe betide the valleys!

In old times, say the Indian traditions, there was a kind of Manitou or Spirit, who kept about the wildest recesses of the Catskill Mountains, and took a mischievous pleasure in wreaking all kinds of evils and vexations upon the red men. Sometimes he would assume the form of a bear, a panther, or a deer, lead the bewildered hunter a weary chase through tangled forests and among ragged rocks, and then spring off with a loud ho! ho! leaving him aghast on the brink of a beetling precipice or raging torrent.

The favorite abode of this Manitou is still shown. It is a great rock or cliff on the loneliest part of the mountains, and, from the flowering vines which clamber about it and the wildflowers which abound in its neighborhood, is known by the name of the Garden Rock. Near the foot of it is a small lake, the haunt of the solitary bittern, with water snakes basking in the sun on the leaves of the pond lilies which lie on the surface. This place was held in great awe by the Indians, insomuch that the boldest hunter would not pursue his game within its precincts. Once upon a time, however, a hunter who had lost his way penetrated to the Garden Rock, where he beheld a number of gourds placed in the crotches of trees. One of these he seized and made off with, but in the hurry of his retreat he let it fall among the rocks, when a great stream gushed forth, which washed him away and swept him down precipices, where he was dashed to pieces, and the stream made its way to the Hudson and continues to flow to the present day; being the identical stream known by the name of the Kaaters-kill.

Nuts

by Natalie Babbitt

One day the Devil was sitting in his throne room, eating walnuts from a large bag and complaining, as usual, about the terrible nuisance of having to crack the shells, when all at once he had an idea. "The best way to eat walnuts," he said to himself, "is to trick someone else into cracking them for you."

So he fetched a pearl from his treasure room, opened the next nut very carefully with a sharp knife so as not to spoil the shell, and put the pearl inside along with the meat. Then he glued the shell back together. "Now all I have to do," he said, "is give this walnut to some greedy soul who'll find the pearl in it and insist on opening the lot to look for more!"

So he dressed himself as an old man with a long beard and

went up into the World, taking along his nutcracker and the bag of walnuts with the special nut right on top. And he sat himself down by a country road to wait.

Pretty soon a farm wife came marching along.

"Hey, there!" said the Devil. "Want a walnut?"

The farm wife looked at him shrewdly and was at once suspicious, but she didn't let on for a minute. "All right," she said. "Why not?"

"That's the way," said the Devil, chuckling to himself. And he reached into the bag and took out the special walnut and gave it to her.

However, much to his surprise, she merely cracked the nut open, picked out the meat and ate it, and threw away the shell without a single word or comment. And then she went on her way and disappeared.

"That's strange," said the Devil with a frown. "Either she swallowed my pearl or I gave her the wrong walnut to begin with."

He took out three more nuts that were lying on top of the pile, cracked them open, and ate the meat, but there was no pearl to be seen. He opened and ate four more. Still no pearl. And so it went, on and on all afternoon, till the Devil had opened every walnut in the bag, all by himself after all, and had made a terrible mess on the road with the shells. But he never did find the pearl, and in the end he said to himself, "Well, that's that. She swallowed it." And there was nothing for it but to go back down to Hell. But he took along a stomachache from eating all those nuts, and a temper that lasted for a week.

In the meantime the farm wife went on to market, where she took the pearl out from under her tongue, where she'd been saving it, and she traded it for two turnips and a butter churn and went on home again well pleased.

We are not all of us greedy.

Flight of the Swan

by Marian Flandrick Bray

"Antonio!"

His mother stood on the back porch, her long skirts swirling around her ankles. Antonio thought she looked like one of the angels etched in the stained windows at church. But unlike the way he'd respond to an angel, he ignored her and finished buckling a freshly clean bridle.

She called his name again and he thought of running away. But something in her voice spoke of a certain oakwood branch leaning in the corner of the kitchen. So he wrapped the bridle and reins around his waist and ran across the barnyard, hopping around the biddies and their chicks.

He halted before her. "Firewood gone?" he asked, pawing at the ground like a stud colt.

"No, *mi hijo*," she said and handed him a piece of paper with words scrawled on it. "Put this in your pocket. Papa forgot the list. You run down to the store and give it to him."

Antonio folded it carefully and shoved it in his back pocket. From the barn a horse whinnied, and as Mama turned, Antonio grabbed her skirts.

"If I take the mare, I will get there faster, no?"

"You and that horse. At least put your boots on." She smiled gently, but it was lost as Antonio fled into the house, grabbed his soft, calf leather boots, and yanked them on.

Spring had a gentle hand in the Sacramento Valley, and the barn was as cool as a mountain dawn. Bottom, the old gelding, thrust his bony head over the stall door and whickered to Antonio. The boy ignored him and trotted to the end of the barn. A mare, black as a night without stars, snorted and struck the stall door with a narrow hoof. When he held out his hand, empty, she drew back, disappointed.

"Sorry. No tortilla this time." He slipped into the stall and she turned her haunches toward him. "No you don't, you silly, beautiful mare." He put his hand on her hip, trusting her. She switched her tail—hard—then didn't move. He walked to her head.

"Black Swan," he murmured. Her ears fluttered like young birds, as she listened to him whisper to her in kind Spanish words.

She was Australian-bred. From a land of sand and heat. She was a Thoroughbred, the first in California. Most men thought she was worthless, a skinny beast, not fit for much, but Papa liked her enough to purchase her. And Antonio, well, he loved her.

He wasn't sure why exactly, because Papa had bought other horses equally as beautiful. Perhaps it had to do with her seeming so lost after her long boat trip to California, and the way she would press her nose against his arm as if he reminded her of someone in her home barn, thousands of miles away.

She was a racehorse. But she had lost her races—including a race for five thousand pesos last year. Antonio bit his lip. That was a lot of money.

Antonio bridled Black Swan with the freshly cleaned head-stall and led her out into the slanted light. He sprang up onto her back. Wriggling close to her curved neck, he nudged her side with his heels, carefully, and they slipped out onto the road like a smooth-running river.

At the store, Antonio carefully tied the mare to a post, being sure to leave her enough rope to stretch, but not enough to tangle up in. He burst through the store door. Several men looked up from sitting around a wooden barrel. Antonio ran up to Papa and handed him the list. "You forgot," he said. Papa drew him to his side.

"Have you seven-league boots to arrive so quickly?" asked Papa.

Antonio smiled. "*Sí.* Only this one has four-league boots."

Papa and the men chuckled.

"The mare is fast," said Papa firmly, as if he'd been saying it for some time. The men listened politely because his papa was Don Andreas Sepulveda. They always listened to him. The heavy, sweet scent of candy twisted with the salty broken crackers crumbled in the barrels, and Antonio wished he had some licorice to suck on. He would save some for Black Swan, too; she had a fondness for sugar.

"In fact," Papa was saying, "my mare can outrun your Sarco." Even Antonio was surprised at that. Everyone stared at Governor Don Pio Pico, Sarco's owner.

"Your mare, she lost to Ito last year, no? And he was a gelding. Sarco is a stallion. Very hot-blooded."

Papa tightened. "Only a bad day. The mare is young. She looks better all the time."

"If she's so fast," piped up a thin, wiry man, his hand in the cracker barrel, "how can she have such a long body and narrow bones? It's the horse with many big muscles that runs best." Antonio almost believed him, because he was a trainer of fine horses—horses that could jump over six feet, horses that could herd cattle without the help of people.

Papa smiled. "And can you do a good day's work, my slender friend?"

Lots of laughter at that. Then Papa said, "Black Swan has as many muscles as a racehorse. Only hers are stretched out like a dancer's. You don't see them until she uses them."

The men snickered, and one said, "Who wants a dancer? I want a fast horse."

Don Pico smoothed back his sleek hair. Antonio liked Don Pico. He often ate supper at their house, and had taught Antonio how to tie trick knots and make coins vanish into thin air.

"My mare against your stallion," said Papa. "Five thousand pesos."

The storekeeper slammed down his broom and shouted, "A thousand of your finest cattle, Andreas. Everyone knows about your fine cattle, but horses? Hmm, we shall see."

Papa and Don Pico gazed at each other, Antonio between them, staring at one, then at the other. They were like dogs about to fight. He marveled. He almost expected them to growl.

"One thousand cattle and five thousand pesos," said Papa.

Don Pico nodded and the men shook hands.

"Name the course," said Papa.

"Up a ladder," said the storekeeper. The men laughed, and the thin, wiry one pretended to throw the storekeeper out the door. Antonio laughed with them as they tussled a moment, then abruptly broke apart, sweating like yearlings at play.

When the men settled down, Antonio watched Don Pico's face as he considered the course. Antonio knew his father's friend had bred his stallion for distance; Sarco could run all day.

His pure Spanish blood pulsed in him, wild and strong. Antonio had often petted the golden stallion and watched him fling his silky, scarlet mane.

"The course," said Don Pico. Antonio held his breath. "From the main road by the lake, back to your house." His black hair shone like a crow's wing, almost blue, in the soft gaslight.

"Nine miles," said Papa. Antonio sat quiet, running through the path in his mind, remembering certain hollows, large rocks, and the parched dryness of the land there. Perhaps Black Swan would think she was home, in Australia, galloping in the hot sand.

"When?" asked Papa.

"Four Sundays from the last," said Don Pico. A horse whinnied outside. "After Mass."

"Four Sundays then," said Papa. The men around the barrel murmured in agreement. "And five thousand pesos to the winner, plus one thousand head of fine-blooded heifers."

"Cattle," insisted Don Pico. "I don't want to wipe you out."

Papa put his head close to his friend's and said in a hard voice, "My Thoroughbred will win." He drew Antonio even closer so the boy smelled Papa's warm scent. "This will be my rider."

Antonio felt himself shiver with joy and fear as Don Pico nodded. "Less weight than her last race. Over a mile it might help, but nine miles? Not likely."

Papa shrugged. "Black Swan would run riderless and win or with much weight on her back and still win."

They had a month to prepare.

At first Papa rode the mare, exercising her, with Antonio following on faithful Bottom. The old gelding groaned and grunted, trying to keep up, but Black Swan always flew far ahead.

"But not fast enough," said Papa as they pulled up one bright morning. Bottom's graying muzzle touched the mare's flank, and she whirled, teeth snapping, eyes livid. The gelding hastily backed up. Antonio smiled at her fury, because she was so beautiful, so proud.

Papa steadied the mare and said, "You ride Black Swan often, no?"

He looked up, his image mirrored in Papa's eyes. "*Sí*, Papa." He dropped his head in fear of having done something wrong.

"How does she gallop for you?"

A bird exploded out of a manzanita bush. Bottom merely wiggled his chin whiskers, but Black Swan gave a gulping whinny and reared straight back. Papa reined her down and she struck the ground heavily. Antonio would have been different with her. He would have touched her neck with kind fingers, asking her to return to the ground like a normal beast and not a bird, because time for flying would come later.

He considered Papa's question, his fingers mixed with

Bottom's thin mane and the reins. "She goes like"—he paused and fussed with the reins, untwisting them—"like her name. A swan in flight."

"And you have seen a swan flying, let alone a black swan?"

Antonio's heart jumped like a caught foal. His father was so serious. "No, Papa, but I can imagine. She moved very well for me."

"Better than she did against Ito?"

Black Swan pawed the hard ground, hearing her name. Her black tail snapped over her hocks.

"*Sí,* better than she did against Ito."

Papa persisted. "Better than she does with me?"

Antonio stared hard at his fingers clutching the braided reins. Each length of leather had been carefully woven. He knew, because he had watched Papa patiently braid them. "*Sí,* Papa," he said softly.

Papa touched his heels to Black Swan. She sprang off her hocks and cantered down the path, Bottom galloping behind. "Good," said Papa. "You will exercise her from now on. No need to round up the heifers."

Antonio sat on Bottom's back, his mouth a circle.

Race Sunday rose like a fledgling, quick and gentle. But by the time Mass was over the sky had hardened into a deep blue.

Papa, astride Bottom, led Black Swan to the lake. Antonio walked behind them, his ebony eyes liquid and large as the mare's eyes, except where his were gentle, worried, hers were stretched, the whites showing. She knew. She was bred to know instinctively when a race was to occur. So she pranced and jiggled and Antonio smiled, watching Papa trying to contain her.

He heard a sound behind them and turned to see the governor on his stallion.

"Here comes Don Pico," called Antonio. Black Swan turned at his voice, and at the sight of the stallion she wrought the air with neighs.

Sarco remained silent, but his eyes bulged. Don Pico grinned at Antonio and caught up with Papa. The men talked and laughed while Antonio studied the stallion. He was a brilliant dun, with gold flecks parading over his coat. His muscles bunched under him as if he were about to leap at any moment. Antonio turned and looked at Black Swan again. She was so different from Sarco—a head taller, leaner, more streamlined. Even her crinkly black tail was longer. Antonio chuckled as she turned her narrow face to snap at the stallion.

When they reached the small lake, Antonio was surprised to see so many people. Horses and riders darkened the shore and muddied the water. A few days before, Papa had shown Antonio newspaper articles that told of the race. As far south as Los Angeles, people were betting great amounts, even whole ranches, on Sarco and the foreign mare, but mostly on Sarco.

The thought seeped into Antonio that most of the men were sympathetic, but most thought Black Swan would lose. Again.

His mouth tightened with anger. She would not lose. Not if he could help it.

His anger vanished like a startled bird as Papa lifted him by the seat of his pants onto the mare. She turned her head and nuzzled his boot. The men would be surprised when she won.

The mare lifted her head, her scythe-shaped ears flickering. Hadn't he crouched over her neck when they overtook fleet mule deer in the hills? Hadn't they galloped faster than Papa's hunting dogs as they pursued rabbits? Surprised. The men would be surprised.

Papa put his square hand on Antonio's thigh. "The path is narrow, so try to get in front immediately. Then slow her down to conserve her strength. If Don Pico moves off the path to pass, you stay parallel with him. If he does get ahead, you stay on his heels. Remember, this is a nine-mile race, Antonio. Don't push her beyond what she can do. We know she is the fastest, but you must be the smartest."

Antonio nodded. His hands were clammy on the reins. But the wind would whip them dry once the mare ran. His stomach trembled like a mare's before she foals.

The storekeeper, long stick in his hand, drew a deep line in the dirt. Dust ruffled up in the still, hot air. "Line up!" he shouted. Papa released the reins and Antonio gathered them in his shaking hands. He watched Papa walk away, then turned the mare to face the starting line.

Sarco strode up. His coat gleamed golden brown like Mama's tortillas. Don Pico sat astride him, deep in his silver-trimmed saddle. Sarco nickered very low to the mare. Her ears flashed back and she bared her teeth at them.

"No saddle, little one?" asked Don Pico.

Antonio shook his head and twisted his fingers deep in Black Swan's mane. A saddle didn't allow one to feel the horse. Antonio wanted to feel her every move. She pulled at the curb bit, but his hands spoke to her: *Not yet. Only wait but a moment.*

"Ready?" asked the storekeeper. Antonio and Don Pico nodded. "Remember," he added, "the race starts when the gun goes off. I know you'll both be fair and stay true to the course." He aimed his pistol skyward. "On your mark, get set—" The words drew out like a piece of elastic.

Antonio tightened his legs. Black Swan came up against the bit, quivering. Antonio stared out over the empty path.

"Go!" The gun went off and the stallion and mare leaped. Sarco sang into the lead, his golden tail flipping in Black Swan's face.

The path narrowed as it crested the hill.

Riding hard on Sarco's heels, Antonio wondered briefly if Papa was worried. Perhaps he prayed. Who was the patron saint of horses? He should have asked before this race. Then he firmly guided his thoughts to the race.

The path was familiar to him and the mare. She often grazed

along it with Papa's cattle. And she frequently carried Antonio to many of his secret hideouts.

The mare breathed lightly, but he felt the warm prickliness of her sweat through his pants. Two more hills were tackled and overcome. Still no place to pass Sarco safely. They would have to wait for a draw. Until then he guided the big mare on Sarco's tail, choking on the stallion's dust.

The sun was fierce, unyielding. The mare was sweating more, little rivulets trickling down her neck and shoulders. Antonio was getting tired of seeing the stallion's golden haunches and having rocks strike his face. They would pass. Soon.

A small wash tumbled down from a hill, crossing their path and running alongside them. This was where he could pass.

"Gallop," he said. Black Swan flicked her ears back and lengthened her stride. Antonio remembered what Don Pico had said last night when the grownups thought he was asleep. He'd listened, crouched beside his bedroom door. The man had said, "The mare is attractive. Clean legs. She and Sarco could produce a fine colt." Antonio had heard his papa grunt in agreement. But the boy had been furious. Black Swan didn't need a colt to prove herself. She was enough.

He leaned over her shoulders and guided her off the path and into the wash. The sand was deep and she had to lift her hooves high, but she still flew past the stallion who snorted and the man whose eyes opened wider.

Antonio and the mare drew ahead and onto the path. The mare's long tail snapped in Sarco's face.

As Papa had said, Antonio slowed Black Swan down. The mare fought the bit a moment, then yielded. "To save your strength, little bird," he said and felt his heart fill because he was in charge of her. He would help her win.

Each time Don Pico attempted to guide Sarco off the path, Antonio dug his heels into Black Swan's ribs and she kicked ahead. Antonio heard Don Pico swearing and he laughed at each word. It was like a seesaw. The stallion would begin to surge, and Black Swan would meet the challenge and the stallion would fall back.

The miles thundered away.

As they crested the knoll near home, Antonio knew everyone could see them now. The crowd milled around his home. The chickens would be upset, he thought. All the noise and confusion.

Black Swan didn't care about the chickens or the crowds, so she stretched herself out, her quick gaze keeping her from tripping. Sarco roared beside them, Don Pico leaning over his neck and shouting abuse. The whip rose and fell beside them. The golden body gleamed as shoulders, ribs, flanks, and tail feathered by.

Antonio spoke quietly to Black Swan: "Gallop."

And she did.

Her narrow face pushed out and her wide nostrils flared red. She reached mightily and he strained with her. The barn flew by. He heard the chickens squawking, upset as he thought they'd be, and wondered if Mama was on the porch, watching.

He saw the finish line and Sarco ahead.

Quickly he brought the ends of the reins against Black Swan's shoulders—hard. She leaped, almost out from under him, her breath screaming. The golden hide of Sarco went by again, only in reverse: tail, flanks, ribs, shoulders. Black Swan smoothed faster and Antonio struck her once more, to be sure they didn't see the stallion again.

They didn't.

The finish line, deeply drawn in the dirt, exploded under the mare's hooves.

He allowed her to gallop down the road a bit and then pulled her up. She protested once, yanked at the bit, but realized the race was over. He sat stiff, upright, wondering what next, her sweat soaking his legs.

Don Andreas Sepulveda appeared beside them on Bottom, and Antonio slid off Black Swan into his father's arms. Black Swan tossed her head, the reins flying, and minced over to the side of the road. She began to graze. Nineteen minutes and twenty seconds of racing had left her hungry. Antonio smiled at the sound of her teeth clicking.

"Black Swan." Antonio found his voice. "Black Swan, look what I brought you." Still on Bottom and in Papa's arms, he drew out a tortilla, round and fresh, and held it out. The mare lifted her head, ignored them, and flattened her ears as Sarco and Don Pico rode past. Then she walked over and neatly took the tortilla. She ate it and shook her head, showering foam over Antonio and Papa, who smiled and smiled into her skinny Thoroughbred face.

A famous moon!
Tonight the crabs even
Proclaim their Taira birth.
　　　　　—Issa

Ho-ichi the Earless

by Rafe Martin

For almost one hundred years, the Heike family, also known as the Taira, ruled Japan with an iron fist. But after a time they grew complacent and no longer maintained the strength and vigor with which they had gained power. Another family, the Genji, began to challenge the Heike family for control. They fought terrible battles and finally, off the coast of Dan-no-ura, the two great clans faced each other in two fleets of ships for a confrontation.

As the ships sailed closer and closer, archers stood on the decks in their black armor, bowstrings drawn tight. Suddenly the air was filled with arrows. Men fell, pierced and screaming, into the sea. Ships crashed together, masts splintered and broke. Flames leapt everywhere.

The nursemaid of the baby emperor, seeing defeat all around her, took up the child emperor in her arms, walked to the prow of the ship, and, holding the royal child in her arms, leapt into the sea, her robes flapping around her. She and the child disappeared down into the bloody water and were never seen again.

The Heike family was destroyed, and after that, strange things began to happen along that coastline.

If ships tried to sail through those waters they'd be stopped, as if bony fingers were scraping along the bottoms of the hulls. Only with great effort could the oarsmen break away.

If swimmers were so foolish as to swim out from shore they were dragged down and never seen again. At night you had to be especially careful. Ghost fires would burn in the darkness. And if travelers were not wary they could be led by those ghostly lights to step off the cliff's edge and fall to the rocks below.

Even the crabs that crawled up out of the sea were strange. On their backs you could see a design in the shape of a helmeted face, the face of a dead samurai, impressed right in the shell.

By these signs the villagers who lived along that coast knew that the ghosts of the Heike had not found perfect peace. So they built a temple on the hillside over the sea, and behind the temple they built a graveyard. And in that graveyard they set up marker-stones inscribed with the names of each dead nobleman, noblewoman, and samurai. And they built a monument to the baby emperor and to his nursemaid who had carried him from defeat. They made offerings there. And things did quiet down. But strange things still sometimes happened.

One of the strangest involved a blind storyteller named Ho-ichi. He earned his living by going from town to town and accompanying himself on the *biwa,* an instrument like a lute or guitar. He would tell the story of the Heike and in this way he earned a little money or received food, clothing perhaps, and lodging for the night. It was a hard life for a blind man, traveling all alone.

The priest who was in charge of that temple off the coast of Dan-no-ura loved stories. He heard of Ho-ichi's skill and invited him to his temple. "Ho-ichi," he said, "your life is hard; a blind man, traveling alone from town to town. Why not stay here? I love stories. All you'd have to do is tell me a tale now and then. Come, my friend, your life can be easier. In exchange for your stories I'll give you food, clothing, a place to live, and such money as you need. What do you say?"

So Ho-ichi settled down and his life was easier.

One hot summer's night the priest had to leave on some duty. Ho-ichi sat alone on the back deck of the temple. It was a hot, sticky night. Not a breath of air stirred the bushes. Sweat dripped slowly down Ho-ichi's neck into the collar of his robe. Off in the distance a bell struck midnight. *Bong!* The gate swung open—*creeeaak!* And heavy footsteps started down the path toward where Ho-ichi sat.

Ho-ichi could hear the sound of a sword hilt scraping armor and the scratching of the cords that tie on a samurai's helmet. He knew that it wasn't the priest returning, but a fully armed samurai coming toward him.

The footsteps came closer. They stopped just before Ho-ichi, and a voice like iron said, "HO-ICHI!"

"*Hai!* Yes!" Ho-ichi responded.

"Come with me," said the voice. "My lord, a lord of high degree, has heard of your skill in telling the story of the Heike clan, and now you must tell your tale to him. So rise and follow!"

Ho-ichi's heart beat with fear. He knew that to disobey the orders of a samurai could be fatal. Indeed, if a samurai did not like your response to a command, he might take out his sword and *sssssscccchhhhh!* Cut you in half!

"I'm blind," Ho-ichi stammered. "I cannot see to follow."

"Hmm," said the voice, still gruff but more gently, "don't be afraid. Just raise your fist and I will guide you."

So Ho-ichi slung the cord of his *biwa* around his neck and raised his fist. Then a fist like an iron vise was clamped around his fist. He was raised to his feet and led off, down the path, through the yard of the temple, and out the gate, which swung closed behind him. He was guided down the narrow stone stairs that led to the village, through the twisting streets of the village, up a great hill, and then through a huge wooden gate that he did not remember ever having passed through before. They came to two huge barred wooden doors. The samurai pounded upon these doors with his mailed fist. "Open!" he called. "Open, for I have brought Ho-ichi!" The doors were unbarred and swung slowly open. Then Ho-ichi found himself being led into a huge room. Although he was blind he could hear very well. Voices murmured all around him in a refined and courtly tongue. He could hear the rustling of silken robes, and he knew that he was among a most wealthy and noble company. He was led to the center of the room. He kneeled on the mats and placed his *biwa* before him.

Then a woman's voice, rich and elegant, spoke, saying, "Welcome, Ho-ichi. We have heard of your skill in telling the tale of the Heike. Our lord, a lord of high degree, has therefore had you brought here so that you may tell your tale. Now you may begin."

"Oh, Noble Host," Ho-ichi stammered, "the tale of the Heike is so long it takes four whole nights to tell. With which part of the story should I entertain this august company this evening?"

And the woman's voice said, "Tell of the battle at Dan-no-ura, for the pain of that is most bitter—yet most sweet." As she said this there was something in her voice that chilled Ho-ichi's blood and made the hair prickle along his skull.

Then Ho-ichi took up his *biwa*. He strummed upon it and began to chant the story of the battle at Dan-no-ura. And as he did so, it seemed that once again the two fleets of ships faced one another. Once again the archers stood on the decks in their black armor. Once again the bowstrings were drawn tight. Once again the air was filled with arrows as men fell pierced and screaming into the sea. Again the ships crashed together, the masts splintered and broke, and flames leapt everywhere. Then the nursemaid of the baby emperor once more lifted the child up in her arms. She walked to the prow of the ship and, holding the child emperor in her arms, leapt into the sea, her robes flapping around her as she and the infant sank down under the bloody water.

As Ho-ichi played and as he chanted the tale, a wild sobbing, a wailing and crying, rose up around him, and he grew frightened. Never had any listeners responded so strongly to the tale. When he was done he could hear that noble company wiping their eyes on the sleeves of their silken robes. Then the woman's voice spoke again. "Ho-ichi," she said, "we had heard that you were a good storyteller, but we never knew how good. You must come again. Come three more nights and tell the whole tale. And," she added, "when you are done we shall reward you, greatly. BUT," she said, and there was again that something in her voice that chilled his blood, "you must tell no one where you have been! Is that understood?"

Ho-ichi's heart was pounding, but he thought to himself, *This is a noble, a wealthy company. If they like my work my fortune is assured.* And he cast aside his fear.

"Yes," he said, "I shall return. I will come three more nights and I will tell no one."

"Good. Now raise your fist. The samurai will guide you

home. Remember, tell no one, Ho-ichi. And be ready tomorrow at midnight. Until then, farewell."

Once again Ho-ichi raised his fist. Once again a fist like an iron vise was clamped around his fist. Then he was guided to his feet and led out of the huge room. The wooden doors swung closed behind him. The bar was slid into place. Down the hill they went, through the narrow, twisting streets of the village and back up the stone stairs and into the temple yard. There the samurai left him, just as the sun was rising. Ho-ichi knew the dawn had come, for the birds were singing in the trees.

Ho-ichi stumbled to his quarters and slept all through the day, so exhausted was he. But that night, at midnight, he was ready. As the bell struck the hour, once again the samurai came for him and took him to the great palace on the hill. And there Ho-ichi told more of the tale and then returned at dawn, guided by the samurai. But that morning when he entered the temple, the priest was waiting.

"Ho-ichi, where have you been? A blind man out alone through the night. Tell me, my friend. What has happened?"

"It's a personal matter. A private affair. Don't be concerned. I am just very tired and must sleep." And stumbling past the priest, Ho-ichi went to his room, where he collapsed, completely exhausted, and fell at once into a deep sleep.

But the priest did worry. He knew that sometimes the ghosts of the Heike clan returned and did strange things. So that night he had two servants with covered lanterns in their hands waiting behind the low stone wall that ran around the temple yard.

Just before midnight the two men saw Ho-ichi emerge from the temple and seat himself, legs folded beneath him, on the polished wooden deck at the rear of the temple. As the bell struck the hour, lightning flashed! Thunder crashed! Rain poured down. And the two servants, astonished, saw Ho-ichi sling his *biwa* on his back, raise his fist up into the night, and go running off into the darkness, alone!

They raised their lanterns and followed. But by the time they came to the village, Ho-ichi was gone. They had lost him. They knocked on many doors. But no one had seen Ho-ichi. They, with lanterns and eyes, had lost a blind man in a storm! How could it be? They were too ashamed to return and tell the priest. Instead, as the storm raged on, they continued their search for Ho-ichi.

It must have been about three in the morning when they heard a voice singing. They followed. It led to the graveyard. They peered over the wall. And there, seated in the pouring rain, splashed with the mud of the graves, was Ho-ichi playing upon the *biwa* and chanting the tale of the Heike clan! And all around him, dancing and swaying and wavering to that music, were thousands upon thousands of the ghost fires!

The two servants were astonished. And they were scared. Still, they climbed over the low wall, crept up to Ho-ichi, and shook him. "Ho-ichi!" they cried. "Come with us! Come at once with us!"

But Ho-ichi was in some kind of trance. "What are you doing? Let me go! Don't embarrass me before this noble company!"

But the servants wouldn't release him. They held him tight, dragged him through the mud, carried him over the wall, and, teeth chattering with cold and fear, brought him back through the rain and the dark to the temple. There they put dry clothes upon him and gave him something hot to drink. Then the priest questioned Ho-ichi.

"Ho-ichi, what have you been doing? Where have you been going? You must tell me."

Then Ho-ichi, in great distress, told him the whole story. He said that he had been going up to a great palace or temple on a hill. And there he had been telling the story of the Heike clan to a most noble company. "One more night and I should have been greatly rewarded. But your servants have ruined it all. I am lost."

"No, Ho-ichi. No. Perhaps you are saved. For you see, you have not been telling your tale to the living but to the ghosts of the Heike clan themselves." Then he added even more gravely, "Alas, now that they know that you know who they are, when they come for you this night they will surely tear you to pieces. But they would have done something like that in any case. On this final night I am sure they planned to carry you off with them. Let me think. There must be some way. Hmm. I have a plan. Ho-ichi, you must be strong. You must be brave. And you must do just as I say. Now listen. I must leave the temple tonight, not to return until morning. It can't be helped. My servants, however, will paint sacred words over your body which will make you invisible to the ghosts. Then you must sit out alone again on the deck tonight. Only this night, when the ghosts come, do nothing. You must not rise or answer or respond in any way. Is that clear? No matter what they do, just sit unmoved, like a mountain. They will not be able to find you. Then they will leave and you will be free of them forever. But you must be strong and brave. I must leave now, my friend. I will be back in the morning. Farewell."

The priest left. Then his attendants painted over Ho-ichi's body, even on his hands, palms, fingers, his shaven head, face, and eyelids, the words of a sacred text. They led Ho-ichi to the rear deck of the temple and they left him. They slid the door closed and locked it. And they hid themselves in the rooms farthest from the rear of the temple.

It was a hot, sticky night. Not a breath of air stirred the bushes. Sweat gathered under Ho-ichi's eyes. It dripped down his neck into the collar of his robe. Off in the distance a bell struck midnight. *Bonngggggg!* The gate swung open, *crreeeeeeaaak!* And heavy footsteps started down the path toward where Ho-ichi sat. They came closer, closer. He could hear the scraping and jangling of armor, the metallic clang as the sword hilt struck the samurai's mailed side. He could hear, too, the scratching of the cords that tied on the samurai's helmet.

And Ho-ichi's heart began to beat louder and louder. Then like a wave his fear rose up and broke completely over him. His whole body was shaking and his heart began pounding furiously. It seemed so loud now that to Ho-ichi it was as if a drum were pounding in the night. He was sure the ghost samurai would hear it and find him. But he could do nothing. He just sat there and sat there, the sweat pouring down his body and soaking his robe. Then the footsteps stopped just before Ho-ichi, and a voice like iron said, "Ho-ICHI!" But Ho-ichi said nothing. He just sat there and sat there. The footsteps walked all around him. At last they stopped right behind him. "Hmm," said the voice, "I don't see this fellow. Where can he be? Still, I do see two ears. I will bring these ears back to my lord to prove I have done my job."

Then two fists, like iron vises, reached down, took hold of Ho-ichi's ears, and *rrrrrriiiiiiiippp!*

But Ho-ichi didn't cry out! He didn't move! He just sat there and sat there as the warm blood trickled down the sides of his face and soaked into his robe.

The iron footsteps marched off down the path. The gate swung closed. And once again the night was silent.

In the morning the priest returned with a covered lantern in his hand. As he walked along the stone path leading to the rear of the temple, he slipped in something wet. What could it be? He bent down, looked, and saw—blood! "Ho-ichi!" he cried as he hurried forward. "Ho-ichi!" There, on the rear deck of the temple, lay Ho-ichi, covered with blood, his hands pressed to the sides of his head. "Ho-ichi!" the priest cried. "Speak to me!"

When Ho-ichi heard the priest's voice, he sobbed out the whole story.

"It was my fault, my fault," exclaimed the priest in distress. "I should never have left. My servants made a terrible error. They forgot to paint your ears. That is why the ghost warrior could see them. But oh, Ho-ichi, you were strong. You have come through the darkness with courage. You shall be free of these ghosts forever. Your life shall change. Come, let me bandage your wounds."

He took Ho-ichi into the temple and bandaged his wounds. In time those terrible wounds healed. When they did, once again Ho-ichi took up his *biwa* and began to play upon it. And once more he began to tell the story of the Heike clan. But now he also told of his own strange encounter with the ghosts of the Heike. Many great noblemen and samurai came to hear him so that, in time, he did become both rich and famous. But after this he was never known just as Ho-ichi again. He was always known as Ho-ichi the Earless.

The Lady Who Put Salt in Her Coffee

by Lucretia P. Hale

This was Mrs. Peterkin. It was a mistake. She had poured out a delicious cup of coffee, and, just as she was helping herself to cream, she found she had put in salt instead of sugar! It tasted bad. What should she do? Of course she couldn't drink the coffee; so she called in the family, for she was sitting at a late breakfast all alone. The family came in; they all tasted, and looked, and wondered what should be done, and all sat down to think.

At last Agamemnon, who had been to college, said, "Why don't we go over and ask the advice of the chemist?" (For the chemist lived over the way, and was a very wise man.)

Mrs. Peterkin said, "Yes," and Mr. Peterkin said, "Very well," and all the children said they would go, too. So the little boys put on their India rubber boots, and over they went.

Now the chemist was just trying to find out something which should turn everything it touched into gold; and he had a large glass bottle into which he put all kinds of gold and silver, and many other valuable things, and melted them all up over the fire, till he had almost found what he wanted. He could turn things into almost gold. But just now he had used up all the gold that he had round the house, and gold was high. He had used up his wife's gold thimble and his great-grandfather's gold-bowed spectacles; and he had melted up the gold head of his great-great-grandfather's cane; and, just as the Peterkin family came in, he was down on his knees before his wife, asking her to let him have her wedding ring to melt up with all the rest, because this time he knew he should succeed, and should be able to turn everything into gold; and then she could have a new wedding ring of diamonds, all set in emeralds and rubies and topazes, and all the furniture could be turned into the finest of gold.

Now his wife was just consenting when the Peterkin family burst in. You can imagine how mad the chemist was! He came near throwing his crucible—that was the name of his melting pot—at their heads. But he didn't. He listened as calmly as he could to the story of how Mrs. Peterkin had put salt in her coffee.

At first he said he couldn't do anything about it; but when Agamemnon said they would pay in gold if he would only go, he packed up his bottles in a leather case, and went back with them all.

First he looked at the coffee, and then stirred it. Then he put in a little chlorate of potassium, and the family tried it all round; but it tasted no better. Then he stirred in a little bichlorate of magnesia. But Mrs. Peterkin didn't like that. Then he added some tartaric acid and some hypersulphate of lime. But no; it was no better. "I have it!" exclaimed the chemist. "A little ammonia is just the thing!" No, it wasn't the thing at all.

Then he tried, each in turn, some oxalic, cyanic, acetic, phosphoric, chloric, hyperchloric, sulphuric, boracic, silicic, nitric, formic, nitrous nitric, and carbonic acids. Mrs. Peterkin tasted each, and said the flavor was pleasant, but not precisely that of coffee. So then he tried a little calcium, aluminum, barium, and strontium, a little clear bitumen, and a half of a third of a sixteenth of a grain of arsenic. This gave rather a pretty color; but still Mrs. Peterkin ungratefully said it tasted of anything but coffee. The chemist was not discouraged. He put in a little belladonna and atropine, some granulated hydrogen, some potash, and a very little antimony, finishing off with a little pure carbon. But still Mrs. Peterkin was not satisfied.

The chemist said that all he had done ought to have taken out the salt. The theory remained the same, although the experiment had failed. Perhaps a little starch would have some effect. If not, that was all the time he could give. He should like to be paid, and go. They were all much obliged to him, and willing to give him $1.37 ½ in gold. Gold was now 2.69 ¾, so Mr. Peterkin found in the newspaper. This gave Agamemnon a pretty little sum. He sat himself down to do it. But there was the coffee! All sat and thought awhile, till Elizabeth Eliza said, "Why don't we go to the herb woman?" Elizabeth Eliza was the only daughter. She was named after her two aunts—Elizabeth, from the sister of her father; Eliza, from her mother's sister. Now, the herb woman was an old woman who came round to sell herbs, and knew a great deal. They all shouted with joy at the idea of asking her, and Solomon John and the younger children agreed to go and find her, too. The herb woman lived down at the very end of the street; so the boys put on their India rubber boots again, and they set off. It was a long walk through the village, but they came at last to the herb woman's house, at the foot of a high hill. They went through her little garden. Here she had marigolds and hollyhocks, and old maids and tall sunflowers, and all kinds of sweet-smelling herbs, so that the air was full of tansy-tea and elder-blow. Over the porch grew a hop vine, and a brandy-cherry tree shaded the door, and a luxuriant cranberry vine flung its delicious fruit across the window. They went into a small parlor, which smelt very spicy. All around hung little bags full of catnip, and peppermint, and all kinds of herbs; and dried stalks hung from the ceiling; and on the shelves were jars of rhubarb, senna, manna, and the like.

But there was no little old woman. She had gone up into the woods to get some more wild herbs, so they all thought they would follow her—Elizabeth Eliza, Solomon John, and the little boys. They had to climb up over high rocks, and in among huckleberry bushes and blackberry vines. But the little boys had their India rubber boots. At last they discovered the little old woman. They knew her by her hat. It was steeple-crowned, without any vane. They saw her digging with her trowel round a sassafras bush. They told her their story—how their mother had put salt in her coffee, and how the chemist had made it worse instead of better, and how their mother couldn't drink it, and wouldn't she come and see what she could do? And she said she would, and took up her little old apron, with pockets all round, all filled with everlasting and pennyroyal, and went back to her house.

There she stopped, and stuffed her huge pockets with some of all the kinds of herbs. She took some tansy and peppermint, and caraway seed and dill, spearmint and cloves, pennyroyal and sweet marjoram, basil and rosemary, wild thyme and some of the other time—such as you have in clocks—sappermint and oppermint, catnip, valerian, and hop; indeed, there isn't a kind of herb you can think of that the little old woman didn't have done up in her little paper bags, that had all been dried in her little Dutch oven. She packed these all up, and then went back with the children, taking her stick.

Meanwhile Mrs. Peterkin was getting quite impatient for her coffee.

As soon as the little old woman came she had it set over the fire, and began to stir in the different herbs. First she put in a little hop for the bitter. Mrs. Peterkin said it tasted like hop tea, and not at all like coffee. Then she tried a little flagroot and snakeroot, then some spruce gum, and some caraway and some dill, some rue and rosemary, some sweet marjoram and sour, some oppermint and sappermint, a little spearmint and peppermint, some wild thyme, and some of the other tame time, some tansy and basil, and catnip and valerian, and sassafras, ginger, and pennyroyal. The children tasted after each mixture, but made up dreadful faces. Mrs. Peterkin tasted, and did the same. The more the old woman stirred, and the more she put in, the worse it all seemed to taste.

So the old woman shook her head, and muttered a few words, and said she must go. She believed the coffee was bewitched. She bundled up her packets of herbs, and took her trowel, and her basket, and her stick, and went back to her root of sassafras that she had left half in the air and half out. And all she would take for pay was five cents in currency.

Then the family were in despair, and all sat and thought a great while. It was growing late in the day, and Mrs. Peterkin hadn't had her cup of coffee. At last Elizabeth Eliza said, "They say that the lady from Philadelphia, who is staying in town, is very wise. Suppose I go and ask her what is best to be done." To this they all agreed, it was a great thought, and off Elizabeth Eliza went.

She told the lady from Philadelphia the whole story—how her mother had put salt in the coffee; how the chemist had been called in; how he tried everything but could make it no better;

and how they went for the little old herb woman, and how she had tried in vain, for her mother couldn't drink the coffee. The lady from Philadelphia listened very attentively, and then said, "Why doesn't your mother make a fresh cup of coffee?" Elizabeth Eliza started with surprise. Solomon John shouted with joy; so did Agamemnon, who had just finished his sum; so did the little boys, who had followed on. "Why didn't we think of that?" said Elizabeth Eliza; and they all went back to their mother, and she had her cup of coffee.

The Town Cats

by Lloyd Alexander

Valdoro was the smallest town in the farthest corner of the Kingdom of Mondragone. Its people being honest, sensible, and prudent, it boasted no great men of state, scholarship, or military glory. The town council once had given thought to raising a statue of its most distinguished citizen; but, as no accord could be reached on whom this might be, or if indeed there was one, the pedestal in the square stood empty. Valdoro, thus, for many years went happily unknown, unnoticed, and ignored.

One day, however, Ser Basilio, the mayor, received a document from the Directorate of Provincial Affairs. It stated that a Deputy Provincial Commissioner, one Ser Malocchio, would arrive that very afternoon to obtain permanent residence and to supervise all local activities. Henceforth, following the recommendations of the said Deputy Provisional Commissioner, the inhabitants of Valdoro would share the blessings and benefits enjoyed by their fellow subjects throughout the realm.

"He'll skin us alive with taxes!" cried the cloth merchant, after Basilio had read the pronouncement to all the townsfolk gathered in the square. "Better a visit from the seven-year itch!"

"He'll send all our lads into the army!" wailed the barber's daughter.

"He'll set lawyers, clerks, and notaries among us," the baker cried. "Rather a dozen pickpockets than one of them!"

So, the folk of Valdoro, and Ser Basilio no less than anyone, bemoaned this evil day, sure that never again would they call their lives their own.

Now, there was in Valdoro a certain mackerel-striped cat, Pescato by name. Long-tailed, long-legged, with jaunty tufts of fur at the tips of his ears, this Pescato was known to all as the boldest rascal ever on four paws. Glib enough to wheedle his way into any house he chose, he liked better the streets and alleys. Days, he sunned himself on the pedestal; nights, he prowled the byways or perched on a chimney pot, where he sang melodiously until dawn. He was sleek as an otter, for never in his life had he missed a meal. As the folk of Valdoro kept many cats, most of them related to him one way or another, he could always accept hospitality from his kindred. He preferred, however, living by his wits; to Pescato, a neatly swindled chicken wing tasted sweeter than a whole fowl without the sauce of a clever venture.

That morning, while Ser Basilio and the townsfolk wept and wailed, tore their hair, and gnashed their teeth at the disaster soon to overtake them, Pescato sat on the steps of the town hall, calmly observing these doings. At last, he got up, unfurled his tail, stretched himself, and went to the mayor, saying:

"My dear friend Basilio, how foolish to let a trifle spoil such a pleasant day."

"Trifle?" cried Basilio, looking ready to fall to the ground from sheer dismay. "You'll call it a trifle when this Malocchio sets about his poking and prying? Ah, misery of miseries! I can feel those blessings and benefits already, like a hot mustard plaster on my back!"

"Every cat's a kingdom in himself," replied Pescato, "and we rule ourselves better than anyone can rule for us. Alas, the same can't be said for you human creatures."

"Do you think you'll escape?" retorted Basilio. "No, no, my fine fellow. You'll be pinched and squeezed along with the rest of us; and so, too, your kittens, your nephews, nieces, and cousins, and every cat in Valdoro. Will you have table scraps when we can't afford crust or crumb on our tables? If it's to be lean pickings for us, then for you no pickings at all."

"A cat can always make a living in the world," replied Pescato. "However, as you tell it, I recognize certain inconveniences." Then, after a few moments of thought, Pescato added:

"Come, cheer up. This is a simple matter, easily set right."

"So you say," returned Basilio, casting a doubting eye on Pescato, since the mayor had more than once been on the wrong end of the cat's enterprises. As he listened to Pescato's plan, he frowned, shook his head, and declared this would be an impossible endeavor. He soon realized, however, there was no hope otherwise; and admitted the cat's scheme to be better than his own, which was none whatever. So, at last he agreed that all should be done according to Pescato's instruction.

"Very well," said Pescato. "Now, Basilio, fetch me your sash, your ermine cloak and cap, and your chain of office."

The mayor did as the cat required of him, being assured by Pescato that all this regalia would be returned before the day ended.

"Believe me," Pescato said, "I have no desire to be mayor a moment longer than need be. Therefore, the sooner we get about our business, the sooner you shall be once again in office."

So saying, Pescato wrapped the sash around his middle, hung the chain from his neck, and draped the cloak over his shoulders. Thus garbed, and leaving Basilio to certain other duties, Pescato cocked the hat on his head and set off for the bridge he knew Ser Malocchio would be obliged to cross.

There he patiently waited until he glimpsed four horses drawing a gilded coach. As the vehicle clattered over the bridge, Pescato stepped forward and raised a paw. As the coachman, astonished at the sight, hastily pulled up, the occupant, who was none other than Ser Malocchio himself, thrust his bewigged head out the window and stared in both amazement and indignation.

"What mockery is this?" he cried. Ser Malocchio was a lean-faced, lantern-jawed fellow with a high-ridged nose and a mouth that snapped open and shut like a cash box. His cheeks turned as crimson as the jacket of his uniform, and he shook his fist at Pescato:

"A cat! Tricked out in robes and chains! An insult! A damnable impertinence! Out of my way, beast. We shall soon see who put you up to this. Make sport of a royal officer? That will prove a costly game."

In spite of this outburst, Pescato doffed his hat, swept a deep and graceful bow, and courteously replied:

"Excellency, allow me humbly to assure you: Things are not as you might suppose. Mock you? On the contrary, I am here in my official capacity to welcome you to Valdoro, and to convey the most respectful greetings of my townspeople."

"A cat, mayor of a town?" returned Malocchio, still scowling, but a little softened, nevertheless, by Pescato's deference. "You have strange customs in this part of the country."

"Your Honor," answered Pescato, "let me only say again: All is not what it may seem, as I shall presently explain to you. Meantime, forgive me if I am unable to express fully the sensations that stir my heart at your arrival, and the knowledge that our modest village has been deemed worthy of your attention. I could not begin to describe our feelings at the prospect of all the blessings and benefits you must have in store for us; indeed, they are truly unspeakable."

"Intelligent creature!" exclaimed Malocchio, more and more kindly disposed toward Pescato. Never before had his presence offered the occasion for such agreeable words, and he was delighted to accept such a welcome even from a cat. "Small wonder you are mayor of this town; for I perceive in you rare qualities of statesmanship, and a keen appreciation of the nature of civic administration."

"May I say in all modesty," answered Pescato, "no one appreciates it more than I."

"My dear sir," cried Malocchio, "what pleasure it is to hear that. Worthy colleague, do me the honor of joining me in my coach."

"Gladly, Your Worshipful Excellence," said Pescato, climbing in beside him and ordering the coachman to drive in the direction of the town hall. "I am eager and impatient to learn of your plans for Valdoro, and trust you will reveal them to me without delay. In addition, I have certain suggestions of my own which I earnestly hope you will allow me to offer you."

"Initiative on the part of His Majesty's subjects is always highly esteemed," replied Malocchio, "depending, of course, on the degree to which it enhances His Majesty's treasury."

"And perhaps your own, as well?" said Pescato, with a wink. "For it seems to me, worthy Ser Malocchio, that your efforts on behalf of our town should be generously, though discreetly, compensated."

"How clearly statesmen understand each other," replied Malocchio, grinning with all his teeth. "It gratifies me to antici- pate that we shall conjoin to our mutual advantage."

"Like two rogues at a town fair," said Pescato, adding quickly, "an old country expression we use in this corner of the world. Now, to the business at hand. First, I suggest and beseech you to consider establishing a garrison of militia, constabulary, and watchmen. Naturally, for this luxury, our citizens would be overjoyed to pay their wages—through your good offices, of course, leaving the matter of disbursement entirely in your hands."

"Exactly the manner in which it should be done," returned Malocchio. "Nothing is more efficacious and economical, and saves burdensome record-keeping."

"You should also know," Pescato went on, "that I am hardly able to restrain the men of our town, especially the lame, the halt, and the blind, from their eagerness not to serve in one of the royal regiments. So I suggest that their heroic impulses be expressed through payment of a fee; and, so that all may be just and equitable, the greater their ardor, the larger the sum."

"What nicety!" cried Malocchio. "What a delicate discern- ment!"

"Your official residence is not quite prepared," continued Pescato. "Until it is, I trust you will do me the honor of being my guest. The elegance of my establishment, if I myself dare say so, is no less than you deserve. I assure you I live exactly as I choose; which, in my opinion, is rather well indeed."

"I sense, dear colleague, that you are one who enjoys the finer things of life," said Malocchio. "I should not dream of denying you the pleasure of sharing them with me."

The coach by now had only passed through the outskirts of the town when the coachman suddenly reined up. Vexed at the delay, Malocchio peered out to discover the cause. Stammering, he fell back onto his seat.

In the middle of the street, crouching on all fours, naked as radishes, were Taddeo the barber and Mascolo the butcher. Hissing, spitting, yelling in frenzy, they scuttled back and forth, circling, darting to one side then the other. Next instant, Taddeo shot out his hand and fetched Mascolo a smack on the head; at the same time, Mascolo fetched Taddeo a cuff on the ear. In a trice, barber and butcher went at it hammer and tongs, rolling over the cobbles, grappling, kicking, and miauling at the top of their voices.

"Can I believe my eyes?" cried Malocchio. "Who, sir, are they? Your village idiots?"

"Bobtail and Whitepaw?" replied Pescato. "They mean each other no harm. Those two cats are forever squabbling."

"Cats?" exclaimed Malocchio. "Cats, you say? Those? But—but you, yourself—"

Pescato shook his head and raised a paw to his lips. "There

are, dear friend, certain, shall I say, local conditions. But they are better discussed in private."

Ser Malocchio had managed to accommodate himself to the notion of dealing with a cat as mayor; but now, having heard two unquestionable men referred to as cats, all began turning topsy-turvy in his head. However, before he could ask further, the coach rattled into the square and, at Pescato's command, drew up in front of the town hall. Pescato beckoned for the bewildered functionary to descend and follow him into the building. And if Ser Malocchio had been taken aback at the sight of the barber and butcher, he gaped all the more at what he presently observed.

For here were some dozen townsfolk scattered throughout the square, perched on barrels, curled on steps, or drowsing on window ledges. In Taddeo's barber shop, one of Pescato's cousins, garbed in a white apron, had mounted a high stool and was busy snipping away at the whiskers of one of Pescato's nephews. In the tailor shop, as one cat measured another for a waistcoat, his assistant, a young orange and white cat, unrolled a bolt of cloth, while the human tailor sat cross-legged in a corner, toying with a spool of thread. By the fish market, the fishwife scurried after her three little ones to snatch them up and lick their ears. The greengrocer sped past on all fours, in hot pursuit of a mouse. From the upper windows of the houses, cats and kittens in dust caps and ribbons peered down and waved their paws in welcome.

"What manner of town is this?" babbled Malocchio, following Pescato into the mayor's chambers. There, Malocchio clapped hands to his head; for, stretched full length on the council table, was Ser Basilio.

"Naughty creature," Pescato chided, shaking a finger at the mayor. "How often have I told you never to sleep on official papers!"

In response, Basilio rolled over on his back, waving hands and feet in the air. Pescato, clicking his tongue in fond reproach, tickled the mayor under the chin.

"Good fellow," said Pescato, while Basilio purred and wriggled with delight. "But enough now. Off you go! Behave yourself and you'll have a fine bit of mackerel for your supper."

The mayor sprang from the table and loped out the door, while Malocchio's jaws snapped open and shut as though he were trying vainly to disgorge the words stuck like so many fishbones in his gullet.

"You were about to say that I spoil him?" remarked Pescato. "Yes, no doubt I do. But we must indulge our pets for the sake of the pleasure they give us. Now, a moment of pleasure for ourselves before considering our affairs," he continued, settling himself in the mayor's high-backed chair. Taking up a little silver bell, he rang it briskly.

"Ah—ah, Honorable Mayor, colleague—" Malocchio at last was able to stammer, squirming uneasily on the seat Pescato had indicated. "Before all else, you must explain to me—"

That moment, Pescato's uncle, a stately gray cat with a steward's key hanging from his neck, came bearing a tray of food and a goblet of wine. Bowing solemnly, he presented this refreshment to Malocchio, who gratefully seized the goblet in trembling hands and immediately gulped down most of its contents.

"You appear a little distracted, my dear friend," said Pescato. "The result, no doubt, of your long journey. And I quite understand you may have been somewhat unsettled by our particular condition. I assure you, we no longer consider it in the least way disturbing. We go about our business as usual, as you have seen for yourself."

"As usual?" cried Malocchio. "Great merciful heavens, whatever has befallen you?"

"The situation you may have noticed," said Pescato, "has come upon us quite recently. I might even say with a degree of suddenness." Here, Pescato made a show of reluctance to speak further; but, after some hesitation, he continued:

"Needless to say, I rely on your absolute discretion. If so much as a whisper should reach the Provincial Directorate as to the cause of our transformation—you can foresee the consequences. No one would ever set foot in Valdoro, or have anything whatever to do with us."

"What are you hiding?" burst out Malocchio. "An epidemic? An infestation? Has some horrible disease made your cats look like people, and your people cats?"

"Disease?" replied Pescato. "Indeed, sir, never have I felt

better in my life. I confess it was discomfiting at first. But one quickly grows accustomed, and even comes to enjoy it. As you will."

"I?" shouted Malocchio, springing to his feet. "I? What are you telling me?"

"Yes, you too, since you shall be living among us," replied Pescato. "After the peculiar occurrence, we made every effort to determine the cause. We concluded it was the wine."

"Wine?" choked Malocchio, spewing out the last mouthful he had taken, and flinging away the goblet.

"Calm yourself," said Pescato. "We soon understood it was not our wine, since not all of us drink it. And so we judged it must be the food."

"Food?" cried Malocchio, sweeping aside the tray of refreshments. "Poison!"

"Be at ease," Pescato assured him. "Eat your fill. It was not the food, nor the water. We examined both and found no fault with either."

Malocchio heaved a sigh of relief. But Pescato continued:

"No, none of these things. In the firm opinion of the town physician, the apothecary, and all our learned individuals: beyond any doubt, it is the air."

"Air?" sputtered Malocchio. "Did you say air?"

"The very air you are breathing at this instant," said Pescato.

Hearing this, Malocchio gave a shriek of horror, emptied his lungs in a great gust, clapped one hand over his mouth and the other over his nose. Stifling his gasps, terrified to draw so much as another breath, he dashed from the chamber. While his face turned at first red, then lavender, then purple for want of air, he threw himself into the coach, buried his head under the seat cushions, and went galloping out of town, never stopping and scarcely breathing until he reached the capital.

Never again was Valdoro troubled with any Provincial Commissioners. Nor did Ser Malocchio reveal what he had seen, lest his superiors think him altogether out of his wits. Instead, he claimed that a terrible pestilence had stricken the town and not one human being remained. So Valdoro was removed from the maps and blotted from the archives, and a special directive was issued declaring the town had never existed in the first place. Yet, ever after, Ser Malocchio was continually scrutinizing his face in the mirror, fearful that he might at any moment sprout cat's whiskers or grow fur from his ears.

And so the folk of Valdoro happily resumed their former ways. Pescato was proclaimed Town Cat; and the mayor and the council unanimously voted to raise a bronze figure of him. Pescato, however, declined this honor, seeing no reason to give up his comfortable spot on the pedestal for the sake of a mere statue.

Zlateh the Goat

by Isaac Bashevis Singer

Translated by the author and Elizabeth Shub

At Hanukkah time the road from the village to the town is usually covered with snow, but this year the winter had been a mild one. Hanukkah had almost come, yet little snow had fallen. The sun shone most of the time. The peasants complained that because of the dry weather there would be a poor harvest of winter grain. New grass sprouted, and the peasants sent their cattle out to pasture.

For Reuven the furrier it was a bad year, and after long hesitation he decided to sell Zlateh the goat. She was old and gave little milk. Feivel the town butcher had offered eight gulden for her. Such a sum would buy Hanukkah candles, potatoes and oil for pancakes, gifts for the children, and other holiday necessaries for the house. Reuven told his oldest boy Aaron to take the goat to town.

Aaron understood what taking the goat to Feivel meant, but had to obey his father. Leah, his mother, wiped the tears from her eyes when she heard the news. Aaron's younger sisters, Anna and Miriam, cried loudly. Aaron put on his quilted jacket and a cap with earmuffs, bound a rope around Zlateh's neck, and took along two slices of bread with cheese to eat on the road. Aaron was supposed to deliver the goat by evening, spend the night at the butcher's, and return the next day with the money.

While the family said goodbye to the goat, and Aaron placed the rope around her neck, Zlateh stood as patiently and good-naturedly as ever. She licked Reuven's hand. She shook her small white beard. Zlateh trusted human beings. She knew that they always fed her and never did her any harm.

When Aaron brought her out on the road to town, she seemed somewhat astonished. She'd never been led in that direction before. She looked back at him questioningly, as if to say, "Where are you taking me?" But after a while she seemed to come to the conclusion that a goat shouldn't ask questions. Still, the road was different. They passed new fields, pastures, and huts with thatched roofs. Here and there a dog barked and came running after them, but Aaron chased it away with his stick.

The sun was shining when Aaron left the village. Suddenly the weather changed. A large black cloud with a bluish center appeared in the east and spread itself rapidly over the sky. A cold wind blew in with it. The crows flew low, croaking. At first it looked as if it would rain, but instead it began to hail as in summer. It was early in the day, but it became dark as dusk. After a while the hail turned to snow.

In his twelve years Aaron had seen all kinds of weather, but he had never experienced a snow like this one. It was so dense it shut out the light of the day. In a short time their path was completely covered. The wind became as cold as ice. The road to town was narrow and winding. Aaron no longer knew where he was. He could not see through the snow. The cold soon penetrated his quilted jacket.

At first Zlateh didn't seem to mind the change in weather. She, too, was twelve years old and knew what winter meant. But when her legs sank deeper and deeper into the snow, she began to turn her head and look at Aaron in wonderment. Her mild eyes seemed to ask, "Why are we out in such a storm?" Aaron hoped that a peasant would come along with his cart, but no one passed by.

The snow grew thicker, falling to the ground in large, whirling flakes. Beneath it Aaron's boots touched the softness of a plowed field. He realized that he was no longer on the road. He had gone astray. He could no longer figure out which was east or west, which way was the village, the town. The wind whistled, howled, whirled the snow about in eddies. It looked as if white imps were playing tag on the fields. A white dust rose above the ground. Zlateh stopped. She could walk no longer.

Stubbornly she anchored her cleft hooves in the earth and bleated as if pleading to be taken home. Icicles hung from her white beard, and her horns were glazed with frost.

Aaron did not want to admit the danger, but he knew just the same that if they did not find shelter they would freeze to death. This was no ordinary storm. It was a mighty blizzard. The snowfall had reached his knees. His hands were numb, and he could no longer feel his toes. He choked when he breathed. His nose felt like wood, and he rubbed it with snow. Zlateh's bleating began to sound like crying. Those humans in whom she had so much confidence had dragged her into a trap. Aaron began to pray to God for himself and for the innocent animal.

Suddenly he made out the shape of a hill. He wondered what it could be. Who had piled snow into such a huge heap? He moved toward it, dragging Zlateh after him. When he came near it, he realized that it was a large haystack, which the snow had blanketed.

Aaron realized immediately that they were saved. With great effort he dug his way through the snow. He was a village boy and knew what to do. When he reached the hay, he hollowed out a nest for himself and the goat. No matter how cold it may be outside, in the hay it is always warm. And hay was food for Zlateh. The moment she smelled it she became contented and began to eat. Outside, the snow continued to fall. It quickly covered the passageway Aaron had dug. But a boy and an animal need to breathe, and there was hardly any air in their hideout.

Aaron bored a kind of a window through the hay and snow and carefully kept the passage clear.

Zlateh, having eaten her fill, sat down on her hind legs and seemed to have regained her confidence in man. Aaron ate his two slices of bread and cheese, but after the difficult journey he was still hungry. He looked at Zlateh and noticed her udders were full. He lay down next to her, placing himself so that when he milked her he could squirt the milk into his mouth. It was rich and sweet. Zlateh was not accustomed to being milked that way, but she did not resist. On the contrary, she seemed eager to reward Aaron for bringing her to a shelter whose very walls, floor, and ceiling were made of food.

Through the window Aaron could catch a glimpse of the chaos outside. The wind carried before it whole drifts of snow. It was completely dark, and he did not know whether night had already come or whether it was the darkness of the storm. Thank God that in the hay it was not cold. The dried hay, grass, and field flowers exuded the warmth of the summer sun. Zlateh ate frequently; she nibbled from above, below, from the left and right. Her body gave forth an animal warmth, and Aaron cuddled up to her. He had always loved Zlateh, but now she was like a sister. He was alone, cut off from his family, and wanted to talk. He began to talk to Zlateh. "Zlateh, what do you think about what has happened to us?" he asked.

"Maaaa," Zlateh answered.

"If we hadn't found this stack of hay, we would both be frozen stiff by now," Aaron said.

"Maaaa" was the goat's reply.

"If the snow keeps on falling like this, we may have to stay here for days," Aaron explained.

"Maaaa," Zlateh bleated.

"What does 'maaaa' mean?" Aaron asked. "You'd better speak up clearly."

"Maaaa, maaaa," Zlateh tried.

"Well, let it be 'maaaa' then," Aaron said patiently. "You can't speak, but I know you understand. I need you and you need me. Isn't that right?"

"Maaaa."

Aaron became sleepy. He made a pillow out of some hay, leaned his head on it, and dozed off. Zlateh, too, fell asleep.

When Aaron opened his eyes, he didn't know whether it was morning or night. The snow had blocked up his window. He tried to clear it, but when he had bored through to the length of his arm, he still hadn't reached the outside. Luckily he had his stick with him and was able to break through to the open air. It was still dark outside. The snow continued to fall and the wind wailed, first with one voice and then with many. Sometimes it had the sound of devilish laughter. Zlateh, too, awoke, and when Aaron greeted her, she answered, "Maaaa." Yes, Zlateh's language consisted of only one word, but it meant many things. Now she was saying, "We must accept all that God gives us—heat, cold, hunger, satisfaction, light, and darkness."

Aaron had awakened hungry. He had eaten up his food, but Zlateh had plenty of milk.

For three days Aaron and Zlateh stayed in the haystack. Aaron had always loved Zlateh, but in these three days he loved her more and more. She fed him with her milk and helped him keep warm. She comforted him with her patience. He told her many stories, and she always cocked her ears and listened. When he patted her, she licked his hand and his face. Then she said, "Maaaa," and he knew it meant, I love you, too.

The snow fell for three days, though after the first day it was not as thick and the wind quieted down. Sometimes Aaron felt that there could never have been a summer, that the snow had always fallen, ever since he could remember. He, Aaron, never had a father or mother or sisters. He was a snow child, born of the snow, and so was Zlateh. It was so quiet in the hay that his ears rang in the stillness. Aaron and Zlateh slept all night and a good part of the day. As for Aaron's dreams, they were all about warm weather. He dreamed of green fields, trees covered with blossoms, clear brooks, and singing birds. By the third night the snow had stopped, but Aaron did not dare to find his way home in the darkness. The sky became clear and the moon shone, casting silvery nets on the snow. Aaron dug his way out and looked at the world. It was all white, quiet, dreaming dreams of heavenly splendor. The stars were large and close. The moon swam in the sky as in a sea.

On the morning of the fourth day Aaron heard the ringing of sleigh bells. The haystack was not far from the road. The peasant who drove the sleigh pointed out the way to him—not to the town and Feivel the butcher, but home to the village. Aaron had decided in the haystack that he would never part with Zlateh.

Aaron's family and their neighbors had searched for the boy and the goat but had found no trace of them during the storm. They feared they were lost. Aaron's mother and sisters cried for him; his father remained silent and gloomy. Suddenly one of the neighbors came running to their house with the news that Aaron and Zlateh were coming up the road.

There was great joy in the family. Aaron told them how he had found the stack of hay and how Zlateh had fed him with her milk. Aaron's sisters kissed and hugged Zlateh and gave her a special treat of chopped carrots and potato peels, which Zlateh gobbled up hungrily.

Nobody ever again thought of selling Zlateh, and now that the cold weather had finally set in, the villagers needed the services of Reuven the furrier once more. When Hanukkah came, Aaron's mother was able to fry pancakes every evening, and Zlateh got her portion, too. Even though Zlateh had her own pen, she often came to the kitchen, knocking on the door with her horns to indicate that she was ready to visit, and she was always admitted. In the evening Aaron, Miriam, and Anna played dreidel. Zlateh sat near the stove watching the children and the flickering of the Hanukkah candles.

Once in a while Aaron would ask her, "Zlateh, do you remember the three days we spent together?"

And Zlateh would scratch her neck with a horn, shake her white bearded head, and come out with the single sound which expressed all her thoughts, and all her love.

To Starch a Spook

by Andrew Benedict

Grownups are so strange. I mean, how can you ever understand them? For one thing, they worry so much. They worry about the stock market and the lawn and the price of building materials— Dad is an architect—and Europe and Asia and Africa and the world situation and just everything.

They even worry about ghosts! I just discovered that this week. How old-fashioned can you get? Why, worrying about ghosts is prehistoric! But I suppose it's a symptom of getting old.

The other evening I was studying my math and Mom was making a braided rug out of old nylon stockings. All of a sudden Dad rushed in, looking pale, his eyes big and his hair practically on end.

At first Mom was sure he'd been in an accident. But it wasn't that. After Dad had had a cup of strong coffee to calm him down—it wasn't really coffee, but I'm not going to tattle about Dad even to you—he was able to tell us what had happened.

"By George, Mary!" he said—Mary is Mom—"Harry Gerber has a haunted house on his hands. I just came from the place with him. It's absolutely crawling with ghosts. He's so upset, he almost wrecked us getting back to town. I don't blame him! We saw some of the spooks and—"

At that point Dad needed some more coffee. Of course, I was all ears. I'll just put down the simple details as Dad told them to us.

As I said, Dad is an architect, and Mr. Gerber, the big real estate man—he's very fat and also he owns a lot of real estate—had hired him for a job.

On the edge of town there is a grand old mansion, built to imitate an English castle. It's made of stone and timber and has about fifty rooms. It was put up way back when, by a very rich man named Mr. Ferguson. After Mrs. Ferguson, who lived to be ninety-nine, lost Mr. Ferguson, she stayed right on living in the big house in spite of high taxes and the cost of help these days.

But when finally Mrs. Ferguson went, too, the old house stayed empty for a long time. Dad said it was a shame, because they don't build houses like that anymore. But nobody wanted it, the taxes were so high. Then Dad had an idea. It could be remodeled into a retirement home for elderly people who like nice surroundings.

Dad persuaded Mr. Gerber to buy Ferguson's Castle, as the house is called by just about everybody, and hire him to remodel it. They were out looking the property over, lingered until after dark, and suddenly had a terrible shock when a positive parade of phantoms started appearing.

To quote Dad, he and Mr. Gerber got out of there fast. Now, and I'm quoting him again—grownups use such prehistoric language—the fat was in the fire. Mr. Gerber blamed Dad for ever getting him into the deal. In fact, Mr. Gerber was coming over soon to see what ideas Dad had for de-spooking Ferguson's Castle, and if Dad didn't have any, Mr. Gerber was going to get nasty.

Dad was drinking his third cup of coffee when Mr. Gerber burst in. I mean he really did. Just stormed in and threw his hat on the floor and shouted.

"Carter, you've ruined me! You got me to invest two hundred thousand dollars in a hotel for haunts, and I hold you personally responsible!"

His manners were simply terrible. But then, what can you expect of the older generation these days?

Dad gave Mr. Gerber some coffee, and by and by they were able to talk without anybody shouting.

"I've done some fast checking, Carter," Mr. Gerber said. "I've learned where those ghosts in Ferguson's Castle came from. Every single one of them is imported."

"Imported?" Mom asked. "What do you mean?"

"The Fergusons were great travelers," Mr. Gerber sighed. "And Mrs. Ferguson was psychic. She could get in touch with spirits. See them. Talk to them. Naturally, being a lady, she never made it public. I learned about this from a daughter of her former maid."

"Go on," Dad urged him. "Do I understand that Mrs. Ferguson, in her travels abroad, used to meet up with ghosts and bring them back home with her?"

"That's exactly what she did. She and her husband wanted a collection that would be unique, something no one, no matter how rich, could match. So they collected ghosts. They didn't stop until they had one for every room in the place, including the main entrance hall. That Thing that chased us out of there is an authentic Japanese dragon ghost from the fifth century, and we were right—it *was* breathing fire at us!"

He shuddered so hard that in order not to spill his coffee he had to drink it all. Then he said in a hollow voice:

"Do you understand, Carter? Every single room in that confounded place is haunted!"

I thought it was a wonderful idea myself. Mr. and Mrs. Ferguson must have been very unusual grownups to think of collecting ghosts.

"You realize what this means, Carter," Mr. Gerber said. "I can never house retirement guests in that castle. One sight of one of those spooks and half a dozen might have fatal attacks. I could be sued for millions!"

"I realize that." Dad sounded very gloomy. I certainly felt bad for his sake. On top of worrying about everything grownups worry about, now he had to worry about a haunted house, too.

"Also," Mr. Gerber continued, "just let one word get out that the place is haunted and I can never hope to unload it—I mean resell it. I'm stuck. Just stuck!"

His little eyes in his big red face glared at Dad in a very mean way.

"Carter, I hold you responsible. You talked me into this. Now just how do you propose to get that place de-haunted?"

Dad suggested sending to England, where they have lots of haunted castles and are very familiar with the problem, to get a psychic expert. He also suggested exorcism by churchly rites and—but Mr. Gerber wouldn't even let him finish.

"Too expensive!" he barked. "Too time-consuming! Too much publicity! Don't you realize, Carter, that if we do any of those things we as much as admit we have a haunted house on our hands? The story will get into every newspaper in the country!"

Dad poured some more coffee and looked even gloomier.

"I'd give a thousand dollars to be rid of those ghosts," Mr. Gerber rumbled. "If it could be done quickly and quietly. Yes sir, a thousand dollars!"

That was when I had my inspiration.

"If you mean that, Mr. Gerber," I said, putting away my math, "I'll get rid of them for you."

Mr. Gerber stared at me. Dad stared at me. Mom stared at me. Why are grownups always staring at you? I mean, as if they'd never seen you before when you've been part of the family for positively years?

"This is no joking matter, young lady," Mr. Gerber said severely. "And I hope you aren't going to be telling about what you have just heard in school tomorrow."

He stuck out his jaw at me—I told you he has terrible manners. I just smiled my extra-sweet smile.

"I'm not joking, Mr. Gerber, and I won't tell anyone. That is, I'll just tell one other person because I have to have a helper. But he won't tell anyone."

Dad started to say something but Mom signaled him to silence. Mom can be very understanding sometimes. Even though she is almost thirty-five.

"Very well, young lady," Mr. Gerber said. "I'm going to take you up on that. You have the job of de-ghosting Ferguson Castle. How long do you think it will take you?"

I knew he was just having fun with me, but I didn't let him know I knew.

"I can't tell until I have surveyed the job," I said, using language I had heard Dad use. I looked at the clock. It was only nine. Quite early, actually. "I'll survey the situation tonight and give you an estimate." I turned to Mom. "If I can stay out a little extra late," I said.

Dad looked bewildered and Mom looked baffled—poor things, grownups are bewildered or baffled so much of the time.

"I think we can trust Sue to at least try whatever she has in mind," Mom told Dad. He nodded. Mr. Gerber started to ask me what I planned but stopped. He wouldn't give me the satisfaction of taking me seriously. I told Mom I would need all the old nylon hose she had collected for making her braided rugs and, after blinking, she put them into a bag for me.

I got my sweater and a flashlight, told them all I'd be back as soon as I could, went out and got my bike, and bicycled three blocks to Bill Arnold's home. Bill was the helper I'd decided I needed.

I found Bill where I thought I would—out in his family's garage, which he has turned into his own laboratory. Bill is tall and very intellectual. He also plays football.

"What's up, Sue?" he asked as I walked in. The door was open for ventilation—some of his experiments generate a lot of bad smells.

"Bill, do you believe in ghosts?"

"Sure," he said. "Why not?"

"Some people don't," I told him. "Do you know what they are?"

"The ghosts? No. But that doesn't prove anything. The world is full of things people don't understand. Take the modern transistor in the transistor radio. Thirty years ago even Einstein couldn't have understood it. Ghosts are a natural phenomenon we'll probably understand someday, even if we don't now."

You can see why I admire Bill. He has a clear, logical mind.

"Well, I want to catch some ghosts," I told him. "Will you help me?"

As he wiped his hands, he asked me how I planned to do it. I got out the nylon hose Mom had given me.

"Ghosts are very insubstantial," I told him. "They can go through keyholes and underneath doors. But I figure that there must be something they can't get through, and if there is, that something is fine nylon hose. I thought we'd take all these stockings and sew them together into a ghost-catching net."

Bill just stood there, thinking. I used the time while he was thinking to fill him in on the ghost situation at Ferguson Castle. At the end of two minutes, he nodded twice and shook his head once.

"Good idea, Sue," he said. "But it'll take too long to sew the stockings together. Mr. Henderson."

Sometimes Bill is a little enigmatic. But I knew Mr. Henderson was the biology teacher at school, and that Bill had thought of something. To tell the truth, I had been counting on Bill to think of something.

Bill has a driver's license, so he went in and got permission to use the family car. Then we drove over to Mr. Henderson's house.

When we rang, Mr. Henderson, a small man with large glasses, came to the door, blinking inquiringly.

"Good evening, Mr. Henderson," Bill said. "Could I borrow your largest specimen-collecting net, the one with the fine mesh?"

Mr. Henderson didn't seem surprised. Bill was always working on two or three scientific experiments. Mr. Henderson just went in and came back with a big net on a long handle. It was made of nylon almost as fine as sheer hose. He also had a big jar.

"Going after some rare specimen, Bill?" he asked, handing Bill the net and me the jar. "If so you'll need a jar for it."

"Yes, sir." Bill always believes in telling the truth. "We're after a ghost."

"A ghost moth?" Mr. Henderson asked. "I didn't know they could be found around here."

But we were already halfway back to the car. Ten minutes later we were outside Ferguson's Castle.

Well, it did look as if it should be haunted, but that was just because there weren't any lights on. Bill and I had flashlights and we went up the stone steps and into the entrance hall.

It was a beautiful entrance hall, lined with fine carved chairs and tapestries. But we didn't spend much time looking at them because we'd hardly got inside before the Japanese dragon ghost Mr. Gerber had mentioned appeared.

It stood on the stairs, a real dragon at least ten feet long—a ghost of a real dragon, I ought to say—and it stared at us. We stared back at it. It had curly horns and a pug-nosed snout and little legs with big clawy toes, and a tail with a tip like the head of an arrow. It was adorable!

"Oh, Bill!" I said. "Isn't it cute!"

"No wonder Mrs. Ferguson brought it back for her collection," Bill said. "Well, here it comes—it's charging us."

After waiting for us to get scared and run, as we would have if we'd been so old we didn't know better, the dragon realized it would have to chase us. So it charged down the steps and came at us, breathing flames from its nostrils. Real flames! They were simply beautiful!

We stepped to one side and Bill swung the specimen-collecting net.

The dragon ghost's head went into it, and the rest of him followed. Apparently ghosts can be squeezed into a very small size when necessary. Anyway, the dragon ghost's charge carried him right into the net, the fine nylon stopped him from going any farther, and his speed sort of collapsed him or condensed him into a small dragon only about two feet long.

Bill quickly swirled the net so that the mouth was closed off, and we'd caught our first ghost!

The poor thing was so frightened; it snorted and snarled inside the net, and breathed flames at us with all its might. Bill put his hand into the flame and reported that the flame had no heat.

"Cold flame, like the light from a firefly," he said. "That's about what I'd expect, otherwise he'd burn down every house he haunted."

"How are we ever going to get it into the specimen jar?" I asked.

But Bill was already twisting the net, making the space inside it smaller and smaller. As he twisted, the dragon ghost got smaller and smaller, too, until it was no bigger than a mouse.

Then I held the specimen jar and Bill quickly pushed the tiny little dragon spook into it. I snapped on the lid and we had him, safe and sound. There wasn't the tiniest crack for him to ooze out of, and, of course, a ghost has to have *some* space to move in, even if it's no bigger than a keyhole.

For a while we watched him run around and around inside the jar, giving off tiny flashes of light with his breathing, like a firefly. But by and by we realized we only had one ghost and there were at least fifty more to catch.

So we went on into the library. The library's ghost was stalking back and forth, making a rattling noise. He was a beauty. He was wearing full armor, which Bill said dated back at least to the sixth century, and when he saw us, he lifted the front of his visor—that's the part that protects his face—and let us see him.

Diary, inside that suit of ghostly armor was a ghostly skeleton! He clashed his teeth at us with the most frightening noise. Bill and I were speechless in admiration.

"Mrs. Ferguson certainly knew quality when she collected phantoms," Bill said.

He swung the collecting net at the armored spook. But this wasn't a dragon with just enough sense to charge. This one ducked. All Bill caught in the net was an armored arm. The rest of the ghost oozed away and clashed his teeth at us some more.

When Bill approached it, it retreated. Finally Bill chased it all around the room, swinging the net in vain. He caught little bits and pieces of the phantom in armor—a foot, a hand, part of his shield—but the main part of the spook always oozed from the net. Finally, the ghost in armor slipped into a crack in the woodwork and got away.

Panting a little bit, Bill and I looked at each other. Bill dumped the ghostly bits and pieces out of the net and they floated over into the woodwork to rejoin the rest of the hiding spook.

"Guess that first one was luck," Bill said. "But we'll see. Let's try the dining room next."

The dining room was a big formal room, and it had a ghost in it that we had to admire just as much as the others. This was the ghost of some medieval headsman, or executioner, complete with a black hood over his head and a huge-bladed ax.

"Probably from Germany," Bill said. "Early sixteenth century, I'd judge."

The phantom headman glided toward us and raised his ax. Bill raised his net. The ax came down and Bill caught it in the net. It broke off in the middle of the handle, and the phantom headsman, seeming very confused, turned the broken handle over several times to look at it. While he was doing this, Bill tried to take him by surprise.

The headsman ducked. Bill's net hit him on the shoulder and Bill got one side of him into the net. But the ghostly executioner was quick. He shot free from the net, grabbing his ax while he was at it, and in no time he'd scooted up a chimney where we couldn't get at him.

"Darn!" Bill said. "They're so insubstantial. They tear apart. I get part of one and the rest just pulls loose."

"Now if only we had some way to stiffen them up a little," I said. "That would help, wouldn't it?"

Bill looked at me. Then he went into one of his silent thinking periods. Then he nodded.

"Sue," he said, "you have some darned good ideas. We'll come back tomorrow night and do it."

I didn't know I'd had an idea, but it was awfully nice of Bill to say so.

Bill drove me back to his house and put the specimen bottle with the phantom dragon on a shelf. He hung up the net and we agreed to meet there same time the next night. Then I biked on home.

Dad and Mom and Mr. Gerber were still sitting there. They looked as if they were waiting for me.

"Well, young lady?" Mr. Gerber rumbled. "Chased all my ghosts away?"

"No, sir," I said. "But I can give you an estimate. We can have Ferguson's Castle de-ghosted by the end of the week."

Mr. Gerber swallowed hard.

"Just what plan of operation do you intend to use?" he asked.

If I'd known I might have told him, just to be polite. But as I didn't know, all I could do was smile mysteriously.

"I'm sorry, Mr. Gerber," I said. "That's a professional secret."

He gave a big snort. Then he got up and jammed on his hat.

"Carter," he said to Dad, "I have to go to New York until Saturday. On Saturday night you and I will inspect Ferguson's Castle. If those ghosts are gone, we proceed. If they're not—"

He left it at that and stamped out. Dad rubbed his jaw.

"Sue," he asked, "would you care to tell me what you are up to?"

I wanted to, but as I didn't know, I couldn't.

"I'm sorry, Dad," I said. "I can't. But don't worry. Bill and I have some ideas. We've already got rid of one ghost."

Dad rubbed his jaw some more. Then he rolled his eyes and looked at Mom.

"Thank heaven for small favors," he said, a remark which I did not understand at all. "Let's go to bed."

Honestly, communication with grownups is so *difficult*.

The next night Dad was working late and Mom didn't object when I biked over to Bill's place. He was in his lab, just filling two plant sprayers—you know, the kind with handles you push in and out to kill bugs—with some kind of gunk.

"Hi, Sue!" he said. "We're taking the delivery truck tonight. Let's go!"

Bill's father owns a big dry cleaning establishment, and Bill had the truck there. Sometimes he drove it on weekends. We rode over to Ferguson's Castle in it, and as we went, Bill told me what I was to do, though he didn't explain.

"If it works, you'll see the results," he said. "And if it doesn't, back to the drawing board!"

We hurried inside, into the library. The skeleton-in-armor phantom was already there, marching up and down. When he saw us, he waved his arms at us and made chattery noises with his skeleton teeth. Either he wasn't afraid of us because we didn't have the net, or he didn't remember us. I suspect that to a ghost people all look alike.

We let him get close, then Bill said, "Now!"

The minute he spoke, I started working my sprayer on the ghost's feet, and Bill started in on his head. We worked our way toward the middle.

In about one second that skeleton in armor was enveloped in a white mist. The white mist seemed to settle right on him— whatever a ghost is made of, it's substantial enough for tiny droplets to cling to—and in another second the spook was standing in front of us, one arm upraised, looking for all the world like a marble statue.

He started to topple over, and Bill and I caught him. He couldn't have weighed more than four ounces altogether. But he was certainly stiff! He was stiffer than a newly starched shirt collar.

"It worked!" Bill acted pleased. "Your idea, Sue. You said we needed to stiffen up these ghosts to catch them. So I put a lot of liquid starch into the sprayers, with some goo to make the starch harden on contact with air.

"We have just starched a spook!"

I marveled at our starched ghost. Every detail of his armor was perfect, right down to the last link on his chain-mail shirt. He was too stiff to risk moving his arms or legs, and every little draught almost blew him away. We finally laid him on the floor and put a very light rug over him to hold him in place.

Then we went into the dining room to tackle the ghostly headsman with the ax.

It was practically a repetition of our success with the skeleton in armor. Two or three puffs from the sprayers, the starch took effect, and we had a snow white statue of a starched spook, with his ax upraised in a most fearsome manner.

We weighted him down and went on to the next rooms.

In quick succession we bagged fifteen more. I'd like to describe them to you, but it would take too long. One was a goblin ghost, small, gnarled, with a long nose, long hair, and long teeth. He was just *beautifully* ugly.

After we had starched so many spooks and were a little tired of pumping on those sprayers, we had to stop. Anyway, it was getting late. I wondered what we would do with them, but Bill was all prepared. In the delivery truck he had a lot of those big plastic bags dry cleaning companies put over your overcoat. He got them, and we slipped each starched spook into a neat plastic bag and tied the end. Then all we had to do was carry them to the truck and stow them in, being careful not to crush any of them.

They were so light, the only hard part was that they kept trying to blow out of our hands.

When we got back to Bill's place, we stored the ghosts in the old stables that still stand in his backyard. As a matter of fact, when we were smaller, Bill owned a couple of ponies. But the stable is empty now, except for some old hay up in the loft, and we laid our starched spooks out in a row up there.

Poor things. I felt rather sorry for them. All their lives they had been able to slide through keyholes, and now they couldn't so much as quiver an eyelash.

When I got home, Dad was still away and Mom was working on her braided rug—I had given her back the old nylon hose.

"It's okay, Mom," I told her. "Bill and I are making just terrific progress. Dad doesn't have a thing to worry about."

Mom gave a stifled sob. Deciding for the ninetieth time that you just can't understand grownups, I went to bed.

The next night we starched and stored twenty spooks, and last night, Friday, we finished off the rest. Ferguson's Castle was positively de-ghosted, and we had a hayloft crammed to overflowing with starched spooks, which I, for one, didn't know what to do with.

I really hadn't seen Dad for three days, what with my school and his work. But Saturday I saw him as he was starting for the office.

"It's all right, Dad," I told him. "You can take Mr. Gerber out to Ferguson's Castle now and you won't find as much as a ghost mouse."

Dad gave me a weak smile.

"I'm keeping my fingers crossed," he said. "He's coming in on the eight o'clock plane, and he phoned he wants to examine the castle first thing. So I won't be home to dinner."

Poor Mom was on pins and needles all during dinner. I was calm because of course I knew Ferguson's Castle was totally de-ghosted. Sure enough, a little after nine, Dad and Mr. Gerber came in and they were both grinning.

"Well!" Mr. Gerber said, slapping Dad on the back. "Funny, isn't it, what two grown men can think they see? That place isn't haunted and never was! It was all in our imagination."

Well, how do you like that? I was highly indignant, but I kept my voice low and sweet.

"There were fifty-one ghosts in it, Mr. Gerber," I said. "Bill and I counted them carefully."

Mr. Gerber's round, red face split in a grin just like a jack-o'-lantern.

"Wonderful!" he chuckled. "Wonderful sense of humor your

daughter has, Carter! Well, you can start the renovations first thing Monday morning. Now I have to get back to my house. Little poker game going on. Important people going to be there. Might mean some big contracts!"

He started to go, but I called to him.

"Mr. Gerber!" I said. "You haven't forgotten, have you? About the thousand-dollar fee for getting rid of your ghosts?"

He didn't grin now. He scowled.

"Young lady," he said. "A joke is a joke, but you youngsters must learn not to carry one too far. Just because your father and I had a slight brain lapse and thought we saw some ghosts, when of course there weren't any—as you no doubt realized— you mustn't overdo it by actually trying to get money out of me! I'm Gerber the builder, and I don't like such tactics!"

He slammed on his hat and marched out. Well, honestly, you see what I mean about grownups? Some are—I hate to say it— but they're *sneaky*.

Dad put his arm around me.

"You're my girl, Sue," he said, "and I love you. But Gerber's right. Of course there weren't any ghosts. I'm sure you tried, though. What did you do, go out there with Bill and recite an incantation or something?"

"Something like that, Dad," I told him. I couldn't let him know I was boiling inside. After all, grownups have so many troubles that I hate to add to them.

"It's all right," I said. "But if Mr. Gerber wants any more

ghosts got rid of, even one teeny little one, the price is doubled. May I go over and see Bill for a few minutes?"

Well, it was Saturday night, so that part was all right, and I biked over to Bill's lab. He was there, working, but this time he was working at his little printing press.

"Hi, Sue!" he said. "Look! I haven't finished yet but this will give you the idea."

He inked some type and drew off a quick proof of what he had been setting.

It said:

OFFERED FOR SALE

Petrified Phantoms

Our petrified phantoms are of the finest imported quality, suitable for institutions or private collectors.

Only a few of the available models are listed below.
Many more in stock!

Skeleton in Armor (Fifth Century)	$250.00
Goblin (Probably from Harz Mts.)	150.00
Headsman with Ax (Sixteenth Century)	225.00
Fire-breathing Japanese Dragon	450.00

"You see," he said, "I feel sorry for those poor ghosts. After all, they were just being themselves. Any one of them would be fine to haunt a museum, and if a private collector wants an imported ghost, we have the best stock in this country. They can keep them starched, or, by adding water, restore them to their normal, phantasmal shape. By selling them we can make enough to send us both through college. And with the thousand we're getting from Mr. Gerber—"

That reminded me. I had been so overwhelmed by Bill's brilliance, I had forgotten Mr. Gerber. Now I told Bill just what Mr. Gerber had said.

Bill went into one of his thinking periods. Then he nodded.

"The trouble is, he doesn't believe anymore," he said. "His faith in phantoms must be restored. You say he is playing poker at home tonight?"

I nodded.

"Okay, Sue. You go on home. I'll handle it from here."

I biked home. As I left, I could see Bill already getting the truck out.

I stayed in my room, waiting for developments. Mom and Dad were downstairs, reading. I'd been so quiet they'd forgotten about me. I certainly hoped Bill—

There! There was a lot of excitement downstairs! Mr. Gerber just arrived and he was absolutely frothing at the mouth. I mean, he was *wild*. It seems that in the middle of his card game, three ghosts from Ferguson's Castle showed up. And they were all hopping mad!

The skeleton in armor raced around the room, gnashing his teeth at the guests. The phantom headsman swung his ax and did his best to behead Senator Jones. The senator fainted and knocked over Mr. Gerber's antique cabinet full of rare dishes and did a thousand dollars' worth of damage. Assemblyman Smith had a slight fit and had to be carried out. The others simply ran for their cars and left as fast as they could.

Gerber followed them. As he left, the goblin ghost was making magic spells with his fingers and turning all the expensive food for refreshments into—yes, honestly—garbage!

Mr. Gerber begged and pleaded with me to do something. I reminded him he didn't believe in ghosts, and he said now he did, he certainly did, cross his heart. I acted very unconcerned about the whole thing, until he not only promised me two thousand dollars to de-ghost his house but wrote out the check and handed it to Dad.

Then I agreed. Reluctantly. I do think that when grownups misbehave, they should be disciplined, but perhaps Mr. Gerber had been punished enough.

I saw Bill's car out in the driveway, so I slipped out to speak to him. What he had done, he told me, was just to take three of the ghosts in their plastic bags in the car to Mr. Gerber's big expensive home. Then he took them out and sprayed water on them.

The water softened the starch, the ghosts were able to move again, and they immediately slipped into the nearest house.

Mr. Gerber's house.

Mr. Gerber left to go to a motel and I promised him we'd have his house de-ghosted by morning. Bill is waiting for me with the big sprayers full of his special solution.

So excuse me.

I have to go starch a spook.

The Night of the Pomegranate

by Tim Wynne-Jones

Harriet's solar system was a mess. She had made it—the sun and its nine planets—out of rolled-up balls of the morning newspaper. It was mounted on a sheet of green Bristol board. The Bristol board had a project about Austria on the other side. Harriet wished the background were black. Green was all wrong.

Everything about her project was wrong. The crumpled paper was coming undone. Because she had used the last of the Scotch tape on Saturn's rings, the three remaining planets had nothing to keep them scrunched up. Tiny Pluto was already bigger than Jupiter and growing by the minute. She had also run out of glue, so part of her solar system was stuck together with grape chewing gum.

Harriet's big brother, Tom, was annoyed at her because Mom had made him drive her to school early with her stupid project. Dad was annoyed at her for using part of the business section. Mostly she had stuck to the want ads, but then an advertisement printed in red ink in the business section caught her eye, and she just had to have it for Mars. Harriet had a crush on Mars; that's what Tom said. She didn't even mind his saying it.

Mars was near the earth this month. The nights had been November cold but clear as glass, and Harriet had been out to see Mars every night, which was why she hadn't gotten her solar system finished, why she was so tired, why Mom made Tom drive her to school. It was all Mars's fault.

She was using the tape on Ms. Krensky's desk when Clayton Beemer arrived with his dad. His solar system came from the hobby store. The planets were Styrofoam balls, all different sizes and painted the right colors. Saturn's rings were clear plastic painted over as delicately as insect wings.

Harriet looked at her own Saturn. Her rings were drooping despite all the tape. They looked like a limp skirt on a . . . on a ball of scrunched-up newspaper.

Harriet sighed. The wires that supported Clayton's planets in their black box were almost invisible. The planets seemed to float.

"What d'ya think?" Clayton asked. He beamed. Mr. Beemer beamed. Harriet guessed that *he* had made the black box with its glittery smears of stars.

She had rolled up her own project protectively when Clayton entered the classroom. Suddenly one of the planets came unstuck and fell on the floor. Clayton and Mr. Beemer looked at it.

"What's that?" asked Clayton.

"Pluto, I think," said Harriet, picking it up. She popped it into her mouth. It tasted of grape gum. "Yes, Pluto," she said. Clayton and Mr. Beemer walked away to find the best place to show off their project.

Darjit arrived next. "Hi, Harriet," she said. The project under her arm had the planets' names done in bold gold lettering. Harriet's heart sank. Pluto tasted stale and cold.

But last night Harriet had tasted pomegranates. Old Mrs. Pond had given her one while she busied herself putting on layer after layer of warm clothing and gathering the things they would need for their Mars watch.

Mrs. Pond lived in the country. She lived on the edge of the woods by a meadow that sloped down to a marsh through rough frost-licked grass and prickly ash and juniper. It was so much darker than town; good for stargazing.

By eleven p.m. Mars was directly above the marsh, which was where Harriet and Mrs. Pond set themselves up for their vigil. They found it just where they had left it the night before: in the constellation Taurus between the Pleiades and the Hyades. But you didn't need a map to find Mars these nights. It shone like rust, neither trembling nor twinkling as the fragile stars did.

Mrs. Pond smiled and handed Harriet two folding chairs. "Ready?" she asked.

"Ready, class?" said Ms. Krensky. Everyone took a seat. Harriet placed the green Bristol board universe in front of her. It was an even worse mess than it had been when she arrived. Her solar system was ravaged.

It had started off with Pluto and then, as a joke to make Darjit laugh, she had eaten Neptune. Then Karen had come in, and Jodi and Nick and Scott.

"The planet taste test," Harriet had said, ripping off a bit of Mercury. "Umm, very spicy." By the time the bell rang, there wasn't much of her project left.

Kevin started. He stood at the back of the classroom holding a green and blue marble.

"If this was earth," he said, "then the sun would be this big—" He put the earth in his pocket and pulled a fat squishy yellow beach ball from a garbage bag. Everybody hooted and clapped. "And it would be at the crosswalk," he added. Everyone looked confused, so Ms. Krensky helped Kevin explain the relative distances between the earth and the sun. "And Pluto would be fifty miles away from here," said Kevin. But then he wasn't sure about that, so Ms. Krensky worked it out at the board with him.

Meanwhile, using Kevin's example, the class was supposed to figure out where other planets in the solar system would be relative to the green and blue marble in Kevin's pocket. Harriet sighed.

Until last night, Harriet had never seen the inside of a pomegranate before. As she opened the hard rind, she marveled at the bright red seeds in their cream-colored fleshy pouches.

"It's like a little secret universe all folded in on itself," said Mrs. Pond.

Harriet tasted it. With her tongue, she popped a little red bud against the roof of her mouth. The taste startled her, made her laugh.

"Tonight," Mrs. Pond said, "Mars is only forty-five million miles away." They drank a cocoa toast to that. Then she told Harriet about another time when Mars had been even closer on its orbit around the sun. She had been a girl then, and had heard on the radio the famous broadcast of *The War of the Worlds*. An actor named Orson Welles had made a radio drama based on a story about Martians attacking the world, but he had presented it in a series of news bulletins and reports, and a lot of people had believed it was true.

Harriet listened to Mrs. Pond and sipped her cocoa and stared at the earth's closest neighbor and felt deliciously chilly and warm at the same time. Mars was wonderfully clear in the telescope, but even with the naked eye she could imagine canals and raging storms. She knew there weren't really Martians, but she allowed herself to imagine them anyway. She imagined one of them preparing for his invasion of the earth, packing his laser gun, a thermos of cocoa, and a folding chair.

"What in heaven's name is this?" Ms. Krensky was standing at Harriet's chair, staring down at the green Bristol board. There was only one planet left.

"Harriet says it's Mars." Darjit started giggling.

"And how big is Mars?" asked Ms. Krensky. Her eyes said Unsatisfactory.

"Compared to Kevin's marble earth, Mars would be the size of a pomegranate seed, including the juicy red pulp," said Harriet. Ms. Krensky walked to the front of the class. She turned at her desk. Was there the hint of a smile on her face?

"And where is it?" she asked, raising an eyebrow.

Harriet looked at the calculations she had done on a corner of the green Bristol board. "If the sun was at the crosswalk," said Harriet, "then Mars would be much closer. Over there." She pointed out the window at the slide in the kindergarten playground. Some of the class actually looked out the window to see if they could see it.

"You *can* see Mars," said Harriet. "Sometimes." Now she was sure she saw Ms. Krensky smile.

"How many of you have seen Mars?" the teacher asked. Only Harriet and Randy Pilcher put up their hands. But Randy had only seen it in the movie *Total Recall.*

"Last night was a special night, I believe," said Ms. Krensky, crossing her arms and leaning against her desk. Harriet nodded. "Tell us about it, Harriet," said the teacher.

So Harriet did. She told them all about Mrs. Pond and the Mars watch. She started with the pomegranate.

The Librarian and the Robbers

by Margaret Mahy

One day Serena Laburnum, the beautiful librarian, was carried off by wicked robbers. She had just gone for a walk in the woods at the edge of the town, when the robbers came charging at her and carried her off.

"Why are you kidnapping me?" she asked coldly. "I have no wealthy friends or relatives. Indeed I am an orphan with no real home but the library."

"That's just it," said the Robber Chief. "The City Council will pay richly to have you restored. After all, everyone knows that the library does not work properly without you."

This was especially true because Miss Laburnum had the library keys.

"I think I ought to warn you," she said, "that I spent the

weekend with a friend of mine who has four little boys. Everyone in the house had the dread disease of Raging Measles."

"That's all right!" said the Robber Chief, sneering a bit. "I've had them."

"But I haven't!" said the robber at his elbow, and the other robbers looked at Miss Laburnum uneasily. None of them had had the dread disease of Raging Measles.

As soon as the robbers' ransom note was received by the City Council there was a lot of discussion. Everyone was anxious that things should be done in the right way.

"What is it when our librarian is kidnapped?" asked a councilor. "Is it staff expenditure or does it come out of the cultural fund?"

"The Cultural Committee meets in a fortnight," said the mayor. "I propose we let them make a decision on this."

But long before that, all the robbers (except the Robber Chief) had Raging Measles.

First of all they became very irritable and had red sniffy noses.

"I *think* a hot bath brings out the rash," said Miss Laburnum doubtfully. "Oh, if only I were in my library I would be able to look up measles in my *Dictionary of Efficient and Efficacious Home Nursing.*"

The Robber Chief looked gloomily at his gang.

"Are you sure it's measles?" he said. "That's a very undignified complaint for a robber to suffer from. There are few people who are improved by spots, but for robbers they are disastrous. Would you take a spotty robber seriously?"

"It is no part of a librarian's duty to take any robber seriously, spotty or otherwise," said Miss Laburnum haughtily. "And, anyhow, there must be no robbing until they have got over the Raging Measles. They are in quarantine. After all you don't want to be blamed for spreading measles everywhere, do you?"

The Robber Chief groaned.

"If you will allow me," said Miss Laburnum, "I will go back to my library and borrow *The Dictionary of Efficient and Efficacious Home Nursing.* With the help of that invaluable book I shall try to alleviate the sufferings of your fellows. Of course I shall only be able to take it out for a week. It is a special reference book, you see."

The groaning of his fellows suffering from Raging Measles was more than the Robber Chief could stand.

"All right," he said. "You can go and get that book, and we'll call off the kidnapping for the present. Just a temporary measure."

In a short time Miss Laburnum was back with several books.

"A hot bath to bring out the rash!" she announced reading clearly and carefully. "Then you must have the cave darkened, and you mustn't read or play cards. You have to be careful of your eyes when you have measles."

The robbers found it very dull, lying in a darkened cave. Miss Laburnum took their temperatures and asked them if their ears hurt.

"It's very important that you keep warm," she told them, pulling blankets up to their robberish beards, and tucking them in so tightly that they could not toss or turn. "But to make the time go quickly I will read to you. Now, what have you read already?"

These robbers had not read a thing. They were almost illiterate. "Very well," said Miss Laburnum, "we shall start with Peter Rabbit and work our way up from there."

Never in all their lives had those robbers been read to. In spite of the fever induced by Raging Measles they listened intently and asked for more. The Robber Chief listened too, though Miss Laburnum had given him the task of making nourishing broth for the invalids.

"Tell us more about that Br'er Rabbit!" was the fretful cry of the infectious villains. "Read to us about Alice in Wonderland."

Robin Hood made them uneasy. He was a robber, as they were, but full of noble thoughts such as giving to the poor. These robbers had not planned on giving to the poor, but only on keeping for themselves.

After a few days the spots began to disappear, and the robbers began to get hungry. Miss Laburnum dipped into her *Dictionary of Efficient and Efficacious Home Nursing,* and found some tempting recipes for the convalescent. She wrote them out for the Robber Chief. Having given up the idea of kidnapping Miss Laburnum, the Robber Chief now had the idea of kidnapping the book, but Miss Laburnum wouldn't let him have it.

"It is used by a lot of people who belong to the library," she said. "But, of course, if you want to check up on anything later you may always come to the library and consult it."

Shortly after this the robbers were quite recovered and Miss Laburnum, with her keys, went back to town. It seemed that robbers were a thing of the past. *The Dictionary of Efficient and Efficacious Home Nursing* was restored to the library shelves. The library was open once more to the hordes who had been starved for literature during the days of Miss Laburnum's kidnapping.

Yet, about three weeks after all these dramatic events, there was more robber trouble!

Into the library, in broad daylight, burst none other than the Robber Chief.

"Save me!" he cried. "A policeman is after me."

Miss Laburnum gave him a cool look.

"You had better give me your full name," she said. "Quickly!"

The Robber Chief sprang back, an expression of horror showing through his black tangled beard.

"No, no!" he cried. "Anything but that!"

"Quickly," repeated Miss Laburnum, "or I won't have time to help you."

The Robber Chief leaned across the desk and whispered his name to her . . . "Salvation Loveday."

Miss Laburnum could not help smiling a little bit. It certainly went very strangely with those wiry whiskers.

"They used to call me Sally at school," cried the unhappy robber. "It's that name that has driven me to a life of crime. But hide me, dear Miss Laburnum, or I shall be caught."

Miss Laburnum stamped him with a number, as if he were a library book, and put him into a bookshelf with a lot of books whose authors had surnames beginning with "L." He was in strict alphabetical order. Alphabetical order is a habit with librarians.

The policeman who had been chasing the Robber Chief burst into the library. He was a good runner, but he had fallen over a little boy on a tricycle, and this had slowed him down.

"Miss Laburnum," said the policeman, "I have just had occasion to pursue a notable Robber Chief into your library. I can see him there in the bookshelves among the 'L's.' May I take him out please?"

"Certainly!" said Miss Laburnum pleasantly. "Do you have your library membership card?"

The policeman's face fell.

"Oh dear," he said. "No . . . I'm afraid it's at home marking the place in my *Policeman's Robber-Catching Compendium*."

Miss Laburnum gave a polite smile.

"I'm afraid you can't withdraw anything without your membership card," she said. "That Robber Chief is Library Property."

The policeman nodded slowly. He knew it was true: you

weren't allowed to take anything out of the library without your library card. This was a strict library rule. "I'll just tear home and get it," he said. "I don't live very far away."

"Do that," said Miss Laburnum pleasantly. The policeman's strong police boots rang out as he hurried from the library.

Miss Laburnum went to the "L" shelf and took down the Robber Chief. "Now, what are you doing *here?*" she said severely. However, the Robber Chief was not fooled—she was really very pleased to see him.

"Well," he replied, "the fact is, Miss Laburnum, my men are restless. Ever since you read them those stories they've been discontented in the evening. We used to sit around our campfire singing rumbustical songs and indulging in rough humor, but they've lost their taste for it. They're wanting more *Br'er Rabbit,* more *Treasure Island,* and more stories of kings and clowns. Today I was coming to join the library and take some books out for them. What shall I do? I daren't go back without books, and yet that policeman may return. And won't he be very angry with you when he finds I'm gone?"

"That will be taken care of," said Miss Laburnum, smiling to herself. "What is your number? Ah yes. Well, when the policeman returns I will tell him someone else has taken you out, and it will be true, for you are now issued to me."

The Robber Chief gave Miss Laburnum a very speaking look.

"And now," said Miss Laburnum cheerfully, "you must join

the library yourself and take out some books for your poor robbers."

"If I am a member of the library myself, perhaps I could take you out," said the Robber Chief with robberish boldness. Miss Laburnum quickly changed the subject, but she blushed as she did so.

She sent the Robber Chief off with some splendid story-books.

He had only just gone when the policeman came back.

"Now," said the policeman, producing his membership card, "I'd like to take out that Robber Chief, if I may."

He looked so expectant, it seemed a pity to disappoint him. Miss Laburnum glanced toward the "L's."

"Oh," she said, "I'm afraid he has already been taken out by someone else. You should have reserved him."

The policeman stared at the shelf very hard. Then he stared at Miss Laburnum.

"May I put my name down for him?" he asked after a moment.

"Certainly," said Miss Laburnum, "though I ought to warn you that you may have a long wait ahead of you. There could be a long waiting list."

After this the Robber Chief came sneaking into town regularly to change books. It was dangerous, but he thought it was worth it.

As the robbers read more and more, their culture and philosophy deepened, until they were the most cultural and philosophic band of robbers one could wish to encounter. As for Miss Laburnum, there is no doubt that she was aiding and abetting robbers; not very good behavior in a librarian, but she had her reasons.

Then came the day of the terrible earthquake. Chimneys fell down all over town. Every building creaked and rattled. Out in the forest the robbers felt it and stood aghast as trees swayed and pinecones came tumbling around them like hailstones. At last the ground was still again. The Robber Chief went pale.

"The library!" he called. "What will have happened to Miss Laburnum and the books?"

Every other robber turned pale, too. You never saw such a lot of pale-faced robbers at one and the same time.

"Quickly!" they shouted. "To the rescue! Rescue! Rescue Miss Laburnum. Save the books."

Shouting such words as these they all ran down the road out of the forest and into town.

The policeman saw them, but when he heard their heroic cry he decided to help them first and arrest them afterward.

"Save Miss Laburnum!" he shouted. "Rescue the books."

What a terrible scene in the library! Pictures had fallen from the walls and the flowers were upset. Boxes of stamps were overturned and mixed up all over the floor. Books had fallen from their shelves like autumn leaves from their trees, and lay all over the floor in helpless confusion.

There was no sign of Miss Laburnum that anyone could see.

Actually Miss Laburnum had been shelving books in the old store—the shelves where they put all the battered old books—when the earthquake came. Ancient, musty encyclopedias showered down upon her. When the earthquake was over she was still alive, but so covered in books that she could not move.

"Pulverized by literature," thought Miss Laburnum. "The ideal way for a librarian to die."

She did not feel very pleased about it, but there was nothing she could do to save herself. Then she heard a heroic cry!

"Serena, Serena Laburnum!" a voice was shouting. Someone was pulling books off her. It was the Robber Chief.

"Salvation is a very good name for you," said Miss Laburnum faintly.

Tenderly he lifted her to her feet and dusted her down.

"I came as soon as I could," he said. "Oh, Miss Laburnum, this may not be the best time to ask you, but as I am giving up a life of crime and becoming respectable, will you marry me? You need someone to lift the books off you, and generally rescue you from time to time. It would make things so much simpler if you would marry me."

"Of course I will," said Miss Laburnum simply. "After all, I did take you out with my library membership card. I must have secretly admired you for a long time."

Out in the main room of the library there was great activity. Robbers and councilors, working together like brothers, were sorting the mixed-up stamps, filing the spilled cards, reshelving the fallen books. The policeman was hanging up some of the pictures. They all cheered when the Robber Chief appeared with Miss Laburnum, bruised but still beautiful.

"Ahem," said the Robber Chief. "I am the happiest man alive. Miss Laburnum has promised to marry me."

A great cheer went up from everyone.

"On one condition," said Miss Laburnum. "That all you robbers give up being robbers and become librarians instead. You weren't very good at being robbers, but I think as librarians you might be excellent. I have come to feel very proud of you all."

The robbers were struck to breathless silence. Never when they were mere inefficient robbers in the forest had they dreamed of such praise. Greatly moved by these sentiments, they then and there swore that they would cease to be villains and become librarians instead.

It was all very exciting. Even the policeman wept with joy.

So, ever after, that particular library was remarkably well run. With all the extra librarians they suddenly had, the council was able to open a children's library with story readings and adventure plays every day. The robber librarians had become very good at such things practicing around their campfires in the forest.

Miss Laburnum, or Mrs. Loveday as she soon became, sometimes suspected that the children's library in their town was— well—a little wilder, a little more humorous, than many other fine libraries she had seen, but she did not care. She did not mind that the robber librarians all wore wiry black whiskers still, or that they took down all the notices saying "Silence" and "No talking in the library."

Perhaps she herself was more of a robber at heart than anyone ever suspected . . . except, of course, Robber Chief and First Library Assistant Salvation Loveday, and he did not tell anyone.

The Woman in the Snow

by Patricia McKissack

Grady Bishop had just been hired as a driver for Metro Bus Service. When he put on the gray uniform and boarded his bus, nothing mattered, not his obesity, not his poor education, not growing up the eleventh child of the town drunk. Driving gave him power. And power mattered.

One cold November afternoon, Grady clocked in for the three-to-eleven shift. "You've got Hall tonight," Billy, the route manager, said matter-of-factly.

"The Blackbird Express." Grady didn't care who knew about his nickname for the route. "Not again." He turned around, slapping his hat against his leg.

"Try the *Hall Street Express*," Billy corrected Grady, then hurried on, cutting their conversation short. "Snow's predicted. Try to keep on schedule, but if it gets too bad out there, forget it. Come on in."

Grady popped a fresh stick of gum into his mouth. "You're the boss. But tell me. How am I s'posed to stay on schedule? What do those people care about time?"

Most Metro drivers didn't like the Hall Street assignment in the best weather, because the road twisted and turned back on itself like a retreating snake. When slick with ice and snow, it was even more hazardous. But Grady had his own reason for hating the route. The Hall Street Express serviced black domestics who rode out to the fashionable west end in the mornings and back down to the lower east side in the evenings.

"You know I can't stand being a chauffeur for a bunch of colored maids and cooks," he groused.

"Take it or leave it," Billy said, walking away in disgust.

Grady started to say something but thought better of it. He was still on probation, lucky even to have a job, especially during such hard times.

Snow had already begun to fall when Grady pulled out of the garage at 3:01. It fell steadily all afternoon, creating a frosted wonderland on the manicured lawns that lined West Hall. But by nightfall the winding, twisting, and bending street was a driver's nightmare.

The temperature plummeted, too, adding a new challenge to the mounting snow. "Hurry up! Hurry up! I can't wait all day," Grady snapped at the boarding passengers. "Get to the back of the bus," he hustled them on impatiently. "You people know the rules."

The regulars recognized Grady, but except for a few muffled groans they paid their fares and rode in sullen silence out to the east side loop.

"Auntie! Now, just why are you taking your own good time getting off this bus?" Grady grumbled at the last passenger.

The woman struggled down the wet, slippery steps. At the bottom she looked over her shoulder. Her dark face held no clue of any emotion. "Auntie? Did you really call me *Auntie*?" she said, laughing sarcastically. "Well, well, well! I never knew my brother had a white son." And she hurried away, chuckling.

Grady's face flushed with surprise and anger. He shouted out the door, "Don't get uppity with me! Y'all know *Auntie* is what we call all you old colored women." Furious, he slammed the door against the bitter cold. He shook his head in disgust. "It's a waste of time trying to be nice," he told himself.

But one look out the window made Grady refocus his attention to a more immediate problem. The weather had worsened. He checked his watch. It was a little past nine. Remarkably, he was still on schedule, but that didn't matter. He had decided to close down the route and take the bus in.

That's when his headlights picked up the figure of a woman running in the snow, without a hat, gloves, or boots. Although she'd pulled a shawl over the lightweight jacket and flimsy dress she was wearing, her clothing offered very little protection against the elements. As she pressed forward against the driving snow and wind, Grady saw that the woman was very young, no more than twenty. And she was clutching something close to her body. What was it? Then Grady saw the baby, a small bundle wrapped in a faded pink blanket.

"These people," Grady sighed, opening the door. The woman stumbled up the steps, escaping the wind that mercilessly ripped at her petite frame.

"Look here. I've closed down the route. I'm taking the bus in."

In big gulping sobs the woman laid her story before him. "I need help, please. My husband's gone to Memphis looking for work. Our baby's sick, real sick. She needs to get to the hospital. I know she'll die if I don't get help."

"Well, I got to go by the hospital on the way back to the garage. You can ride that far." Grady nodded for her to pay. The woman looked at the floor. "Well? Pay up and get on to the back of the bus so I can get out of here."

"I—I don't have the fare," she said, quickly adding, "but if you let me ride, I promise to bring it to you in the morning."

"Give an inch, y'all want a mile. You know the rules. No money, no ride!"

"Oh, please!" the young woman cried. "Feel her little head. It's so hot." She held out the baby to him. Grady recoiled.

Desperately the woman looked for something to bargain

with. "Here," she said, taking off her wedding ring. "Take this. It's gold. But please don't make me get off this bus."

He opened the door. The winds howled savagely. "Please," the woman begged.

"Go on home, now. You young gals get hysterical over a little fever. Nothing. It'll be fine in the morning." As he shut the door the last sounds he heard were the mother's sobs, the baby's wail, and the moaning wind.

Grady dismissed the incident until the next morning, when he read that it had been a record snowfall. His eyes were drawn to a small article about a colored woman and child found frozen to death on Hall Street. No one seemed to know where the woman was going or why. No one but Grady.

"That gal should have done like I told her and gone on home," he said, turning to the comics.

It was exactly one year later, on the anniversary of the record snowstorm, that Grady was assigned the Hall Street Express again. Just as before, a storm heaped several inches of snow onto the city in a matter of hours, making driving extremely hazardous.

By nightfall Grady decided to close the route. But just as he was making the turnaround at the east side loop, his headlight picked up a woman running in the snow—the same woman he'd seen the previous year. Death hadn't altered her desperation. Still holding on to the blanketed baby, the small-framed woman pathetically struggled to reach the bus.

Grady closed his eyes but couldn't keep them shut. She was still coming, but from where? The answer was too horrible to consider, so he chose to let his mind find a more reasonable explanation. From some dark corner of his childhood he heard his father's voice, slurred by alcohol, mocking him. *It ain't the same woman, dummy. You know how they all look alike!*

Grady remembered his father with bitterness and swore at the thought of him. This *was* the same woman, Grady argued with his father's memory, taking no comfort in being right. Grady watched the woman's movements breathlessly as she stepped out of the headlight beam and approached the door. She stood outside the door waiting . . . waiting.

The gray coldness of Fear slipped into the driver's seat. Grady sucked air into his lungs in big gulps, feeling out of control. Fear moved his foot to the gas pedal, careening the bus out into oncoming traffic. Headlights. A truck. Fear made Grady hit the brakes. The back of the bus went into a sliding spin, slamming into a tree. Grady's stomach crushed against the steering wheel, rupturing his liver and spleen. *You've really done it now, lunkhead.* As he drifted into the final darkness he heard a woman's sobs, a baby wailing—or was it just the wind?

Twenty-five years later, Ray Hammond, a war hero with two years of college, became the first black driver Metro hired. A lot of things had happened during those two and a half decades to pave the way for Ray's new job. The military had integrated its forces during the Korean War. In 1954 the Supreme Court had ruled that segregated schools were unequal. And one by one, unfair laws were being challenged by civil rights groups all over the South. Ray had watched the Montgomery bus boycott with interest, especially the boycott's leader, Dr. Martin Luther King, Jr.

Ray soon found out that progress on the day-to-day level can be painfully slow. Ray was given the Hall Street Express.

"The white drivers call my route the Blackbird Express," Ray told his wife. "I'm the first driver to be given that route as a permanent assignment. The others wouldn't take it."

"What more did you expect?" his wife answered, tying his bow tie. "Just do your best so it'll be easier for the ones who come behind you."

In November, Ray worked the three-to-eleven shift. "Snow's predicted," the route manager barked one afternoon. "Close it down if it gets bad out there, Ray."

The last shift on the Hall Street Express.

Since he was a boy, Ray had heard the story of the haunting of that bus route. Every first snowfall passengers and drivers testified that they'd seen the ghost of Eula Mae Daniels clutching her baby as she ran through the snow.

"Good luck with Eula Mae tonight," one of the drivers said, snickering.

"I didn't know white folk believed in haints," Ray shot back.

But parked at the east side loop, staring into the swirling snow mixed with ice, Ray felt tingly, as if he were dangerously close to an electrical charge. He'd just made up his mind to close down the route and head back to the garage when he saw her. Every hair on his head stood on end.

He wished her away, but she kept coming. He tried to think, but his thoughts were jumbled and confused. He wanted to look away, but curiosity fixed his gaze on the advancing horror.

Just as the old porch stories had described her, Eula Mae Daniels was a small-framed woman frozen forever in youth. "So young," Ray whispered. "Could be my cousin Carolyn in a few more years." He watched as the ghost came around to the doors. She was out there, waiting in the cold. Ray heard the baby crying. "There but for the grace of God goes one of mine," he said, compassion overruling his fear. "Nobody deserves to be left out in this weather. Ghost or not, she deserves better." And he swung open the doors.

The woman had form but no substance. Ray could see the snow falling *through* her. He pushed fear aside. "Come on, honey, get out of the cold," Ray said, waving her on board.

Eula Mae stood stony still, looking at Ray with dark, questioning eyes. The driver understood. He'd seen that look before, not from a dead woman but from plenty of his passengers. "It's okay. I'm for real. Ray Hammond, the first Negro to drive for Metro. Come on, now, get on," he coaxed her gently.

Eula Mae moved soundlessly up the steps. She held the infant to her body. Ray couldn't remember ever feeling so cold, not even the Christmas he'd spent in a Korean foxhole. He'd seen so much death, but never anything like this.

The ghost mother consoled her crying baby. Then with her head bowed she told her story in quick bursts of sorrow, just as she had twenty-six years earlier. "My husband is in Memphis looking for work. Our baby is sick. She'll die if I don't get help."

"First off," said Ray, "hold your head up. You got no cause for shame."

"I don't have any money," she said. "But if you let me ride, I promise to bring it to you tomorrow. I promise."

Ray sighed deeply. "The rule book says no money, no ride. But the book doesn't say a word about a personal loan." He took a handful of change out of his pocket, fished around for a dime, and dropped it into the pay box. "You're all paid up. Now, go sit yourself down while I try to get this bus back to town."

Eula Mae started to the back of the bus.

"No you don't," Ray stopped her. "You don't have to sit in the back anymore. You can sit right up front."

The ghost woman moved to a seat closer, but still not too close up front. The baby fretted. The young mother comforted her as best she could.

They rode in silence for a while. Ray checked in the rear-view mirror every now and then. She gave no reflection, but when he looked over his shoulder she was there, all right. "Nobody will ever believe this," he mumbled. "*I* don't believe it.

"Things have gotten much better since you've been . . . away," he said, wishing immediately that he hadn't opened his mouth. Still he couldn't—or wouldn't—stop talking.

"I owe this job to a little woman just about your size named Mrs. Rosa Parks. Down in Montgomery, Alabama, one day, Mrs. Parks refused to give up a seat she'd paid for just because she was a colored woman."

Eula Mae sat motionless. There was no way of telling if she had heard or not. Ray kept talking. "Well, they arrested her. So the colored people decided to boycott the buses. Nobody rode for over a year. Walked everywhere, formed carpools, or just didn't go, rather than ride a bus. The man who led the boycott was named Reverend King. Smart man. We're sure to hear more about him in the future . . . You still with me?" Ray looked around. Yes, she was there. The baby had quieted. It was much warmer on the bus now.

Slowly Ray inched along the icy road, holding the bus steady, trying to keep the back wheels from racing out of control. "Where was I?" he continued. "Oh yeah, things changed after that Montgomery bus boycott. This job opened up. More changes are on the way. Get this: They got an Irish Catholic running for president. Now, what to do you think about that?"

About that time Ray pulled the bus over at Seventeenth Street. The lights at Gale Hospital sent a welcome message to those in need on such a frosty night. "This is it."

Eula Mae raised her head. "You're a kind man," she said. "Thank you."

Ray opened the door. The night air gusted up the steps and nipped at his ankles. Soundlessly, Eula May stepped off the bus with her baby.

"Excuse me," Ray called politely. "About the bus fare. No need for you to make a special trip . . . back. Consider it a gift."

He thought he saw Eula Mae Daniels smile as she vanished into the swirling snow, never to be seen again.

The Binnacle Boy

by Paul Fleischman

1

When the brig *Orion,* three weeks out from Havana, appeared off her home port of New Bethany, Maine, Miss Evangeline Frye was just parting her bed curtains, formally banishing night.

While those who'd chanced to spy the sails wondered why the ship hadn't fired a salute, Miss Frye was combing her coarse gray hair. While the *Orion* drifted unexpectedly about, at last presenting her stern to the harbor, Miss Frye was blowing the hearth fire into being. And while the harbor pilot's drowsy son rowed his father out to the ship, to return in a frenzy, eyes wide and hands trembling, Miss Frye was stationed at her parlor window, awaiting the sight of Sarah Peel.

She peered down the length of Bartholomew Street. Straight-spined as a mast and so tall that her gaze was aimed out through the top row of windowpanes, Miss Frye eyed the clock on the town hall next door. It was eight-fifteen. The girl was late—and plenty of scrubbing and spinning to be done.

She pursed her lips, lowered her eyes, and looked out upon her flower garden. It was nearly Independence Day—tansy was thriving, pinks were in bloom, marigolds were budding on schedule. But the poppy seeds she'd bought from a rogue of a peddler, and gullibly planted with care, still hadn't sent up a single shoot. And probably never would, she reflected. In memory, she heard her mother's voice: "Girls take after their mothers, Evangeline. Men take after the Devil." She regarded the bare stretch of soil below, sneering at this latest confirmation.

The door knocker sounded. Miss Frye opened up and was surprised to find not Sarah Peel, but her ten-year-old younger sister, Tekoa.

"I've come to do chores, ma'am."

Miss Frye cocked her head. "But where is Sarah?"

"In bed, ma'am. Taken ill." The girl spoke softly, tucking a strand of straw-blond hair under her kerchief.

"Well then." Miss Frye motioned her in and closed the door behind her. "I suppose you've had practice scouring pewter."

Tekoa stood in the hallway, silent.

Miss Frye blinked her eyes. Was this some impertinence?

Then at once she recalled what Sarah had told her—that the girl had been left deaf by a fever and was able to listen only with her eyes, by reading the words on others' lips.

Miss Frye passed Tekoa, then turned to face her.

"You can begin with the pewter."

"Yes, ma'am," said the girl.

Miss Frye led her down the hall to the kitchen. "And what manner of illness has seized poor Sarah?"

"Her jaws," said Tekoa. "They won't come open."

Miss Frye appeared startled. "And when did this happen?"

"This morning, just after the news of the *Orion*."

Miss Frye's eyebrows jerked. "The *Orion*? What news?" Among the crew of New Bethany boys was Miss Frye's adopted son, Ethan.

"She appeared offshore this morning, ma'am," Tekoa calmly replied.

At once Miss Frye rushed to the window.

"All of the crew were found to be dead."

2

Bells were tolled. Trunks were opened and mourning clothes solemnly exhumed. The crew of the brig *Orion* was buried. And yet the matter remained unfinished.

No evidence of attack had been found. There was no sign of scurvy, no shortage of food. When the ship was boarded the crew was discovered to be lying about the decks as if hexed, with no witness to bear the tale to the living. None, that is, except the binnacle boy.

He alone remained standing, the life-sized carving of a sailor boy holding the iron binnacle, the housing for the ship's compass. Straight backed, sober lipped, in his jacket and cap, he stood resolutely before the helm, his lacquered eyes shining chicory blue. And after the ship's sails had been furled and her cargo of molasses unloaded, the binnacle boy was laid in a wagon and, like the seventeen sailors before him, slowly borne up the road to the top of the cliff upon which New Bethany stood. And there, before the town hall, the pinewood statue was mounted, still bearing the ship's compass, a memorial to the *Orion's* crew.

Upon him the families of the dead gazed for hours, convinced he'd somehow reveal the nature of the catastrophe he'd witnessed. Mothers kept watch on his ruddy lips, expecting each moment to see them move. Fathers stared into his painted eyes, waiting to catch them in the act of blinking. Children cocked their ears to the wind as it moaned eerily over the boy, and believed they heard the sound of his voice.

Yet the binnacle boy clung to his secret. The mystery of the *Orion* remained, and gradually, as the summer progressed, those who stood and awaited the boy's words were replaced by those who'd come instead to leave him with secrets of their own, knowing his steadfast lips to be sealed.

At first it was children who took up the practice. After whispering into his chiseled ear, they ran off, or studied his stouthearted features as if expecting a nod of acknowledgment. Soon their elders took after them, and before long the binnacle boy became the repository for all that couldn't be safely spoken aloud in New Bethany.

Lovers opened their hearts to him. Hurrying figures sought him out in the night. Those who felt their lives running out entrusted him with their final confessions.

It was one of these last, a long-winded farmer, whom Miss Frye was observing from her parlor one morning when she noticed three women with parasols filing down the walk toward her door.

"Tekoa," she addressed her helper. "I believe we have company."

The brass door knocker sounded three times. Tekoa set down her feather duster, opened the door, and showed into the parlor Miss Bunch, Miss Mayhew, and Mrs. Stiggins.

"Good day to you, Miss Frye," chirped Miss Bunch. Without asking, she plopped herself down on a chair, a trespass that drew a stare from her hostess. Affirming her sovereign powers, Miss Frye regally motioned the others to be seated.

"It's some time since you've been seen about," said Miss Bunch. "So we decided to come on our own." She dabbed at the sweat on her brow with a handkerchief, adjusted her bonnet, and opened her fan. "To express our condolences, that is. About your son, Ethan."

"Indeed," said Miss Mayhew.

"You're very kind," replied Miss Frye. She noted that, like herself, Mrs. Stiggins was attired in a black mourning dress.

"I believe that your Ethan and my Jeroboam were *dear* companions," Mrs. Stiggins spoke up. "Aye, and full of mischief, as well."

"All boys be apprenticed to the Devil," said Miss Frye.

Tekoa entered with a pitcher of cider.

"And tell me, child," Miss Bunch addressed her. "How does your sister Sarah progress?"

"She's able to open her mouth, ma'am, and eat. But she's weak still, and refuses to speak to a soul."

"Truly now!" Miss Bunch lamented. "Come, child—sit down and visit with us."

Tekoa turned her eyes toward her mistress, who was glaring across at Miss Bunch in dismay.

"If you're fully caught up with your work," said Miss Frye, "you may take a chair, Tekoa, and join us."

The girl found herself a seat in the corner. And in the midst of the conversation Miss Bunch noticed Tekoa looking out the window.

She touched the girl's shoulder. "What do you see, child?"

"Excuse me, ma'am. Nothing of importance, ma'am."

"Nothing?" Miss Bunch lowered her voice. "You were eyeing the binnacle boy, I warrant. Watching the ones that speak in his ear—same as *I'd* be doing myself if I knew the trick of reading lips." She glanced at Miss Mayhew and the two traded smiles.

"In truth, I was watching the swallows, ma'am."

"Swallows!" Miss Bunch commenced to chuckle. "*Any* fool can see swallows, child. But perhaps you'd put your eyes to use—and tell us what you next see spoken into the statue's ear."

Miss Mayhew's own dim eyes lit up.

"Really!" protested Miss Frye. "That's not proper!"

"Purely to help pass the time," said Miss Bunch. "To take our minds from our grief for a spell."

Tekoa stared at the women uneasily.

"And naturally," Miss Mayhew piped up, "with the curtains drawn, only she'll know who's speaking."

"And she'll *not* disclose the name," Miss Bunch added.

Miss Frye looked over at Mrs. Stiggins. Both knew that the matter wasn't right. And yet they too were curious as to what was said to the binnacle boy. After all, they themselves wouldn't actually be eavesdropping. And the name of the speaker would remain a mystery, never to be revealed.

"You may humor Miss Bunch's wishes, Tekoa," Miss Frye announced after deliberation.

"Yes, ma'am," said the girl.

The curtains were closed, dimming the light. Tekoa reluctantly took up her post, while Miss Bunch and Miss Mayhew looked on in suspense.

The church bell declared it to be eleven. Then noon. Impatiently the women fanned themselves, squirming about like children in church. Then suddenly Tekoa drew back from the window.

"Did you spy someone?" Miss Bunch burst out. And suddenly it occurred to her that some sharp-eyed soul might reveal the fact that one of the various false teeth she wore had originally belonged to a dog.

"Yes, ma'am, I did."

Miss Mayhew grinned eagerly. "Well then—and what was spoken, child?"

The girl swallowed.

"Come now—speak up! Let us hear it word for word."

"Yes, ma'am."

Tekoa lowered her gaze. She studied her hands, and breathed in deeply.

"'I know what killed the *Orion*'s crew.'"

3

After her three visitors had gone and Tekoa had finished her chores and left, Miss Frye climbed to the top of the stairs, and then, as she hadn't in weeks, turned right. Tekoa's revelation still rang in her head as she walked down the hall, came to a halt—and opened the door to Ethan's room.

She stood there in the doorway a moment. The room was

musty, the light dim. She passed his bed, opened the curtains, and gazed out his window at the indigo sea, musing on all he might have been.

Miss Frye turned around. Surveying the cobwebs, she recalled that both her natural sons had occupied the room as well. But they'd grown up wild, and long ago had left, following their father to sea, and like him gaining a fondness for the rum they freighted across the waters. When the schooner on which all three had shipped went down in a gale off the Georgia coast, Miss Frye had been neither surprised nor sorry, and had returned with relief to her maiden name. Her mother, herself abandoned by her husband, regarded the sinking as a fitting judgment. "Men," she'd summed up, "are a stench in God's nostrils."

Miss Frye paced slowly about the room. She found herself staring at Ethan's washstand, recalling the chill October day she'd gone mushroom picking, miles from home, and discovered an infant wrapped in a flour sack, left at a crossroads, dead. Or so she'd feared, till she'd gradually warmed him, holding the bundle next to her skin—and felt him slowly begin to squirm. Astonished, she hadn't known what to do, until suddenly something her mother had long ago told her leaped into memory: "If you save a creature's life, Evangeline, you're responsible for its every deed afterward." Unwilling to entrust his raising to another, she'd borne him home, burnt the flour sack, bathed him thoroughly, and named him Ethan.

Miss Frye walked up to his mahogany desk. The lamp by

which he'd worked was dusty. His goose-quill pen and his ink bottle waited. She opened the primer he'd used, and recalled the pleasures of shaping his youthful mind.

A freethinker in religious matters, she'd refused to take the child to church and had taught him a catechism of her own devising. Shunning New Bethany's public school, Miss Frye had been his only tutor as well. She'd vowed that Ethan would turn out a gentleman, cultured and refined, an exception to his sex. No weed would be allowed to take root in the boy, no unwanted notion would enter his head. She would tend the child like a seedling tree, encouraging one branch and cutting another, keeping the image of its final shape fixed firmly in her mind. After all, she reasoned, God had meant him to die; by granting him life she'd assumed His role. The boy was thenceforward her private domain, whose growing body she marveled at as if it were her own work.

Tekoa's words came suddenly to mind and Miss Frye emerged from her reverie. She closed the curtains, shut the door, and marched downstairs to the parlor again.

It was dusk. She stood watch on the binnacle boy, hoping to catch someone seeking his ear, desperate to know whom Tekoa had seen.

When the light at last failed she gave up her vigil and slowly sipped down a bowl of bean soup. She wondered if Tekoa might have made up the message she'd reported—then quickly put the thought out of her head. There wasn't a speck of deceit in the girl, and Miss Frye wondered what Tekoa must think of a mistress who ordered her to eavesdrop.

She broke through the crust of a cold plum tart and considered the girl's ways. She performed her duties competently enough, and yet there was something distant about her. The others had hopped to Miss Frye's commands and striven anxiously to please her. They'd always been afraid of her, as Tekoa's sister Sarah had been—little wonder, since of all the town, Miss Frye alone did not go to church. She rarely went out, and was rarely visited. Yet in her presence quiet Tekoa seemed to be calmly detached.

Hoping to break through the girl's silence, and frantic to know whom she'd seen at the statue, she called Tekoa from her work the next morning and set her to watching the binnacle boy. She felt a need to win the girl to her and hoped she was appreciative of this respite from her chores. Doggedly, she attempted to kindle a conversation with the girl, in vain. Thereafter Miss Frye sat in silence, studying Tekoa's pale features, hoping the speaker she'd seen might return.

For an hour Tekoa watched from the window. Then glancing over to her left she sighted Miss Bunch and her two companions, traveling under the portable shade of their parasols, bustling down the walk.

"Dear child—how good to see you," Miss Bunch addressed Tekoa at the door. "And good day to you as well, Miss Frye. As you're no doubt lonely without your dear son, we felt it to be our solemn duty to lend you our company once again."

"You're most kind," Miss Frye curtly replied.

"And while we're here," Miss Mayhew added, while Miss Frye led them into the parlor, "we thought Tekoa might be allowed to read out the secrets spoken to the statue."

"In quest of the truth concerning the *Orion*," Mrs. Stiggins sternly declared.

Miss Frye declined to mention the fact that she'd already had the girl doing just that. Ashamed to engage in the practice so openly, she decided to set Tekoa to spinning—when she glimpsed a woman crossing the street and heading toward the binnacle boy.

"Yes, of course!" she stammered. "Why—we owe it to the town!"

She hurried Tekoa back to her seat. A few moments later the girl turned around.

"Well?" asked Miss Frye. "Have you something to report?"

"Yes, ma'am," the girl gravely replied.

Mrs. Stiggins leaned forward. "Let us hear it, then, child!"

Tekoa lowered her eyes in embarrassment. "'Miss Pike put no money in the collection plate at church, but only rattled the coins.'"

Miss Bunch and Miss Mayhew gaped at each other. A blush spread over Mrs. Stiggins.

"You may return to the window now, Tekoa," Miss Frye informed the girl.

In silence, the women fanned themselves. Mrs. Stiggins looked across at Miss Frye.

"My dear Jeroboam always spoke *most* highly of your Ethan."

Miss Frye gazed blankly, lost in thought. "He might have been a scholar. Or a poet, perhaps."

Slowly, Tekoa drew back from the window.

Miss Frye's eyes flashed.

"What is it? Something spoken?"

"Yes, ma'am."

"Well then—speak it out, Tekoa!"

The girl glanced down at the hardwood floor.

"'Tonight we meet. Under the elm tree.'"

Miss Bunch gasped for breath. "*Which* elm tree, child?"

"Didn't say, ma'am," Tekoa replied.

Miss Bunch and Miss Mayhew sighed in unison. Again they waited while Tekoa watched.

"My Jeroboam had just turned fourteen," Mrs. Stiggins said. "And your Ethan?"

"Fourteen as well," Miss Frye replied.

Mrs. Stiggins released a sigh.

An hour passed. The church bell rang twelve. Miss Bunch yawned and reached for her parasol.

"Perhaps we should go."

"Indeed," said Miss Mayhew.

Suddenly, Tekoa turned. Her eyes appeared glazed, her features stiff.

"What is it?" Miss Frye demanded. "A message?"

"Yes, ma'am," the girl reluctantly replied.

"Gracious sakes, child—let us hear it then!"

Tekoa swallowed. She gazed absently before her.

"'One of the tins of tea snuck among the *Orion*'s provisions— was poisoned.'"

"Poisoned?" shrieked Mrs. Stiggins. "The tea?"

Miss Frye jumped up. "Is there more, Tekoa?"

"That's all of it, ma'am."

Mrs. Stiggins shot forward. "I insist you reveal the speaker," she cried, taking hold of Tekoa's shoulders.

"But ma'am, the agreement—"

"She's right," said Miss Bunch. "The name of the speaker must not be revealed."

"But my very own Jeroboam—poisoned! The murderer must be brought to justice!"

"Perhaps," said Miss Mayhew, "the speaker is lying."

Slowly, Miss Frye paced the room. "But why would someone lie to the statue?"

"No reason at all," Mrs. Stiggins snapped. She sat back down and wrung her hands. "They must have opened the tea that morning."

"And Lord knows," Miss Mayhew grimly continued, "with all the molasses they sweeten it with, they might have drunk hemlock itself and not known it."

A silence fell over Miss Frye's three visitors. They rose to their feet, bid farewell to Miss Frye, and slowly retraced their steps down the street, avoiding the binnacle boy's eyes in passing, as if this knower of secrets might discover their own with a glance.

4

Miss Frye did not sleep well that night. The next morning Tekoa's revelation still echoed in her ears. When the girl arrived at eight o'clock, Miss Frye set her to mixing up bread dough and stepped outside to the garden.

At a deliberate pace she strolled the paths, searching for comfort in the company of flowers. She smiled to see her larkspur thriving, and lad's-love blooming in its appointed season. She gazed upon her Queen Margrets and mint, and sampled the various scents of her roses.

Sitting on a bench, she inspected her tansy, eyeing the cornmeal yellow petals and recalling how Ethan too had loved flowers. She grinned to remember the morning they'd merrily roamed the cliff, two summers before, collecting posies of hawkweed and chicory—and at once the smile left her lips. For that was the day the loquacious Mrs. Gump had stopped them to chat on their return. The woman's ill-mannered son had appeared, while she jabbered about her watery eye, and the pain in her lungs, and the history of her limp—till Miss Frye turned around to find the boys gone, dashing through Mrs. Gump's melon patch and trampling her corn, playing at pirates.

It was not till weeks later that Miss Frye discovered that Ethan was sneaking off in the evenings, to cavort with Mrs. Gump's son and others. When she'd confronted him he was unrepentant and had openly mocked her in Sarah's presence. Recalling her ship-bred, rum-sodden sons, she'd had no choice but to be stern with the boy, determined he'd bloom according to plan.

And now, she reflected, Ethan was gone, his promise lost forever.

Miss Frye marched indoors and entered the parlor, closed the curtains, and approached Tekoa. The girl was setting her dough to rise, and although Miss Frye knew there was mending to be done, she felt driven to find out if anything further about the *Orion* might come to light.

"Rest yourself awhile," said Miss Frye, "and aim your eyes on the binnacle boy."

The girl sat down and no sooner looked out than Miss Bunch, Miss Mayhew, and Mrs. Stiggins made their way to the door.

"Good day, Tekoa," bubbled Miss Bunch. "And good day to you, my dear Miss Frye. A day *especially* long for one so recently robbed of her child."

"Indeed," said Miss Mayhew. "The very reason we felt bound to help you pass the time."

Miss Frye's lips puckered. "How very thoughtful."

"Perhaps Tekoa could be of assistance," suggested Miss Bunch.

"If she's free," said Miss Mayhew.

Mrs. Stiggins tapped her parasol on the floor. "That justice might be done."

The women seated themselves in the parlor and Tekoa resumed her place at the window.

An hour passed in silent suspense, Miss Frye's three guests providing the barest minimum of their promised companionship.

"Tell me, Tekoa," Miss Bunch spoke up. "How does your precious sister fare?"

"The same, ma'am," the girl replied.

Miss Bunch shook her head and softened her voice. "I've heard it said that Sarah had a sweetheart among the *Orion*'s crew. Simeon Sprigg, they say it was." She glanced from one pair of eyes to the next. "They say the two were seen talking together, and that he's the cause of the girl's affliction."

Her listeners shook their heads in sympathy, then returned their attention once more to Tekoa.

Patiently, the girl looked out, though no one was near the binnacle boy. She trained her gaze on the swirling swallows and watched the swifts career through the sky. She studied a sparrow feeding its young—and suddenly noticed a figure appear, approach the statue, and seek out its ear.

"What is it, Tekoa?" Miss Frye demanded.

"Something spoken, ma'am. To the binnacle boy."

"Naturally, child! But what? Speak it out!"

Tekoa swallowed. She glanced about. Her lips quivered nervously.

"'He wouldn't listen. He wished to roam free—and signed himself aboard the *Orion*.'"

Mrs. Stiggins bolted to her feet. "Quick, child—is this the same speaker as before?"

Gloomily, Tekoa nodded, and Mrs. Stiggins's eyes blazed.

"I *demand* to know who it is at once!"

Seeing the woman charging toward her, Tekoa clasped the curtains shut.

"Away, child!" Mrs. Stiggins ordered, as she grabbed a curtain—and flung it open.

"Sarah!" she gasped. "Sarah Peel!"

The others scrambled at once to the window.

"Protecting her older sister, she was!" Mrs. Stiggins shouted out. "But we'll get to the truth—believe me we will!"

Snatching her parasol, she steamed out the door, with Miss Bunch and Miss Mayhew right behind her.

"Tekoa—stay here and mind the bread!" Miss Frye settled a stern eye on the girl. Then quickly she followed her guests out the door, and found them standing in a circle around Sarah.

"So it's you!" thundered Mrs. Stiggins. "You—who can't get a word out of your lips."

"Except to the binnacle boy," said Miss Mayhew.

"And small wonder that your jaws seized shut." Mrs. Stiggins peered into her eyes. "With a secret like yours perched on your tongue."

Sarah lowered her gaze at once and fingered her long brown hair.

"Namely," Mrs. Stiggins proclaimed, "that it was *you* who murdered the *Orion*'s crew!"

Sarah's eyes opened wide in terror.

"You couldn't bear your sweetheart Simeon Sprigg forsaking you for the sea." Mrs. Stiggins poked the girl's shoe with the tip of her parasol. "So you poisoned him—and his mates as well!"

Speechlessly, Sarah shook her head, desperately denying the charge. Her jaws trembled, her lips twitched. She labored to open her mouth and speak, noticed Miss Frye's eyes upon her—and all of a sudden broke free.

"Seize her!" Mrs. Stiggins screamed.

Panic-stricken, Sarah dashed off, holding the hem of her skirt as she ran.

"She mustn't escape!" Miss Bunch cried out, and the four took after her in pursuit. Down the middle of the street they scurried, gathering the curious to their cause and shouting for those with fleeter feet to catch the girl at once. Panting, the women turned down an alley, and soon trailed the mob they'd called into being. Along the common, past the graveyard, through a field they hurried along, till they crossed a meadow and at last caught up with the rest of the crowd—at the cliff.

"And where's the girl?" Mrs. Stiggins demanded.

A man turned around. "Sarah Peel, ma'am?"

"Of course! And who *else?*" Mrs. Stiggins snapped.

"Fell from the cliff, ma'am. Drowned, she did."

Mrs. Stiggins gasped.

Miss Frye closed her eyes.

"Poor, dear Sarah," she whispered.

Side by side, without speaking a word, the women slowly made their way homeward. Left alone for the final block of her journey, Miss Frye cast a glance at the binnacle boy, turned to her left, and approached his ear.

"Sarah spoke truly—he meant to go to sea. Not Simeon Sprigg, but my Ethan."

She paused for a moment. "Sarah must have seen." She licked her lips and drew closer to the statue. "That it was I who poisoned the *Orion's* crew."

Miss Frye glanced across at her planting of tansy, with whose deadly leaves she'd destroyed her wayward son, and the corrupting crew as well. Dreamily, she stared at the flowers, yellow as the noonday sun—and so failed to notice Tekoa Peel remove her gaze from her mistress's lips, take a step back from the parlor window, and hurry toward the back door.

The Baby in the Night Deposit Box

by Megan Whalen Turner

The Elliotville Bank had just added a secure room to their bank vault and filled it with safety deposit boxes. Things rarely changed around Elliotville, and something new always got people's attention, but to be sure that everyone had heard about the service, the bank rented a billboard near the center of town and put a picture up with the slogan "Your treasure will be safe with us."

The president of the bank, Homer Donnelly, had thought of the slogan himself, and was quite proud of it. More than just the president of the bank, he was the chief executive officer and the chairman of the Board of Trustees. His family had founded the bank. The old-fashioned iron safe they had started with still sat in the lobby.

The people in the town were not what you would call wealthy, but they were prosperous and hard-working and, Homer thought, certain to have a family heirloom that needed safekeeping. If someone had asked, he would have said they had good moral character in Elliotville, so it was something of a shock to come in early one morning, a week after the billboard had gone up, and find that someone had left a baby in the night deposit box.

The night deposit box was actually a slot in the outside wall of the bank with a slide in it, like the one in a mailbox or the public library's book return. When the bank was closed, customers could put their money and a deposit slip into an envelope, pull down on the handle, put their envelope on the slide, and then let go. Their deposit would drop through the wall and into a bin positioned below. There it would stay, safely inside the bank, to be recorded the next day.

Emptying the bin was the first business of the banking day, and because he arrived before the tellers, Homer frequently did the job himself. That's why he was the one that found the baby. She was there, wrapped in a blanket, sleeping peacefully on the stack of deposits.

Homer could not have been more dumbstruck if the bin had been empty and the night deposits had disappeared. With a shaking hand he opened the folded bit of paper pinned to the baby blanket, afraid that he knew what it would read. He did.

In spidery, elegant handwriting it said, "Our treasure, please keep her safe."

Homer moaned and the baby stirred. Silently he backed away. He went to find the security guard who stayed in the building through the night.

"You're fired," he said.

"What?" said the guard.

"Fired," said Homer.

"But . . ."

"But nothing," said Homer. "Fired. Last night while you were reading your magazine, or having your nap, or God only knows what, someone dropped a baby in the night deposit box."

"A what?"

"A BABY," Homer shouted and pointed with his finger, "IN THE NIGHT DEPOSIT BOX!"

"Alive?" asked the guard, blanching.

"OF COURSE!" shouted Homer, and, as if in agreement, a thin cry rose from the bin.

"Oh gosh," said the security guard. "Oh, my gosh." He hurried across the bank and looked into the bin, Homer behind him.

Pepas, the security guard, was older than Homer, the father of three grown children, and the grandfather of five small ones. He flipped the blanket off the baby and looked at it carefully. He lifted the legs and wiggled the arms while the baby howled louder.

"Poor Precious," said Pepas. "Do you have a bump? No, you're not hurt. You look just fine and everything is fine, don't you fuss." Carefully putting his large hand behind the baby's head, he picked it up and settled it on his shoulder. "Yes, Precious," he said, "you come to Poppy," and hearing his deep voice and rocking on his shoulder the baby grew quiet. Its eyes opened and it looked over the guard's shoulder at Homer. Homer felt as if the bank vault had dropped from the ceiling and landed on his head.

"Is she all right?" he asked.

"Just fine," said Pepas. "But you can't tell she's a girl. You never know with babies until you look."

"Of course she's a girl. Any idiot can see that she's a girl. Why is she doing that? What's the matter?"

"She's hungry, I think," said the guard.

"I better call the police," said Homer.

"Call my wife first," said the guard.

Homer called the police, but Mrs. Pepas, who lived two doors down from the bank, beat all four of the town's policemen by a quarter of an hour. She banged at the glass doors at the front of the bank and waved a bottle.

Homer went to let her in.

"Where's the baby?" she asked. "Where's the little treasure?"

"She's over here," said Homer.

"She?" asked Mrs. Pepas, over her shoulder as she hurried across the bank. "Did you look?"

* * * *

Well, it was the first bit of excitement in Elliotville since the truck carrying chicken manure turned over on Main Street. The police showed up at the bank with their lights on and sirens blazing. Mrs. Pepas made the first officer to reach the bank go back outside to turn them off, because they woke the baby, who'd drunk her bottle and fallen asleep. The tellers arrived one by one and all wanted a chance to hold the little girl. She was definitely a girl, about three months old. She had a silver rattle like a tiny barbell with a larger round ball at one end and a smaller ball at the other. She had a teething ring that was also silver, round like a bracelet with intriguing bumps and ridges to suck on. There was no other sign of identification with her except the note. Whoever she was, she seemed unperturbed at having been dropped through a night deposit box. She smiled indiscriminately at the faces all around her. Homer wondered if anyone else felt quite as stunned as he did when he looked into her eyes.

He had tentatively asserted his right to hold the baby and was getting careful instruction from a female police officer when the representative from the Children's Protective Services arrived. She was a tall woman in a crisp business suit with a short skirt and sharply pointed heeled shoes. She plucked the baby out of Homer's arms and after the briefest discussion with a policeman, carried her through the doors of the bank. Homer felt like he'd been robbed. Through the glass doors of the bank he could see the woman fitting the baby into a plastic seat. There was a flash of lightning and a clap of thunder. It had been sunny when Homer walked to the bank, but the day was as dark as night and it began to rain. The CPS woman had to put the baby seat on the pavement beside the open door of the getaway car and kneel down in order to drag the straps over the baby's head. Not that it was a getaway car, Homer reminded himself. And of course the baby wasn't being stolen. It just felt that way.

"Oh," said Mrs. Pepas, "I have her rattle and her teething ring. I better go give them to that woman."

Homer, his eyes still on the crying baby, stopped her with a lifted hand. "I wonder, Mrs. Pepas, if you might just step into the safety deposit room first?" He hustled the protesting Mrs. Pepas past the eighteen-inch-thick door into the vault. "Wait right here," he said and hurried back across the bank and through the front doors.

He snagged the baby out of the car seat with one hand. He forgot whatever it was that the police officer had been telling him about supporting her head. He scooped her up and was pleased to find that she fit right into the crook of his elbow like a football.

"Excuse me," he said to the CPS representative, who was staring up at him in surprise. "We forgot a little something." Feeling just the way he had when he'd scored a winning touchdown in a high school game, Homer swept back through the double doors and into the bank. He hurried across the lobby and into the vault, pulling on the heavy door as he passed. The hinges on the door were huge and the door was carefully balanced. It swung very slowly but steadily with the inertia of its tremendous weight.

Inside the vault, stunned at his own behavior, but still gamely carrying on, Homer handed the baby to Mrs. Pepas. He stepped back out again to face the highly irritated CPS woman.

"Just forgot the rattle," Homer said as the vault door shut behind him with the almost inaudible click of electromagnets. Homer turned. "Oh dear me," he said. "I must have bumped it."

"Mrs. Pepas?" he said, pushing a button next to a small grill set by the door. "Mrs. Pepas, I seem to have shut the vault door by accident. I am terribly sorry. It has a time lock and I will have to override it. It will take a few minutes to get the codes. Will you and the baby be all right? Don't worry about the air, the vault is ventilated. And we put the intercom in just for moments like this." He let go of the button, cutting off Mrs. Pepas's reply.

Homer smiled at the CPS woman. "Terribly sorry. Won't take a minute." And he went off to fetch the instruction booklet for the vault.

Some of the codes were in the booklet, but others, for safety's sake, were elsewhere. Homer had to telephone his aunt to get her part of the code and as it was seven o'clock in the morning she was not pleased. She didn't know the codes off the top of her head. She told Homer she would call him back. Homer had other calls to make, to his mother and his lawyer, and the mayor and his friend who was Elliotville's county judge. It took some time. In between calls, Homer smiled brightly at the CPS woman and the CPS woman fumed, swinging her baby carrier like the Wicked Witch of the West waiting to carry off Toto.

Carrying the instruction manual and pages torn from his memo pad, Homer addressed himself to the vault door. He pushed button after button in careful order, pausing in between to read and reread the instruction manual until finally his lawyer arrived.

"Ah, there we are," said Homer. He rapidly tapped a few more numbers into the keypad and the door clicked obediently.

Mrs. Pepas stepped out with the baby and Homer gently guided her toward his office. "If you will just step this way," he murmured, but they were blocked by the CPS woman, tapping the pointy toe of her high heels.

"If you please, I think we've spent enough time here. I'll take the baby now."

"No," said Homer, and sidled past her.

"What do you mean, *no*?" she asked as she hurried into Homer's office behind the baby and ahead of the lawyer.

"She's going to stay here. We will take good care of her."

"I am afraid that is entirely out of the question, Mr. . . . Mr. . . ." She had forgotten his name. "The infant will need to be seen at the hospital by a pediatrician and checked for malnutrition as well as disease. She'll need a PKU test and a genetic screening. She'll need to be given vaccinations: DPT, MMR, HIB, Hep A, Hep B. She can't stay here."

Homer smiled at the list of horrors and propelled his reluctant lawyer forward. "This is Harvey Bentwell. He'll explain." Homer patted his lawyer on the shoulder, the sort of pat he hoped would remind Harvey that there weren't many accounts that paid as well as the bank's in a town as small as Elliotville. Then he and Mrs. Pepas and the baby went to look for a changing table.

Harvey Bentwell smiled, but the CPS woman didn't, so Harvey pulled himself together with a sigh and began a long incantation in Latin. The most important words of which turned out to be *in loco parentis*. Harvey explained that legally speaking the baby hadn't been abandoned, she'd been turned over to the care of the bank, so the Children's Protective Services, while a fine and noble organization, really wasn't called on to look after her. The bank would do that. He'd already called upon a pediatrician and a pediatric nurse to make a house call, or a bank call, to examine the baby.

CPS said that this was the most ridiculous thing she'd ever heard of. Harvey smiled. "I want that baby," CPS said. Harvey Bentwell shook his head. "I will have that baby." Harvey shook his head again.

Well, you can imagine the fuss, but Harvey Bentwell wasn't just a small-town lawyer, he was a good small-town lawyer, and in the end there wasn't much the Children's Protective Services could do. They couldn't guarantee the baby a better home than the bank would offer, and they couldn't produce any legal reason why a bank couldn't be guardian for a child. The judge insisted that the baby be brought to the hearings and she screamed right through them.

She had good reason. The weather was terrible. The skies had been clear in the morning the day they dressed the baby to take her to the courthouse, but by the time they got to the car there was thunder and lightning and driving rain. The world seemed full of shadows and reasonless disturbances. A stoplight fell into the street just ahead of them. The light bulbs in the street lamps, turned on in the middle of the day, exploded. Walking from the car to the courthouse, Homer felt there were people invisible behind the screen of the rain. He hurried up the stairs and into the building. Once inside, everyone seemed to want to take the baby away from him. Good-natured people offered to hold the crying infant, saying they could soothe her better, offering their experience with children as credentials. "I had three children, I'm a grandmother, I've got a baby of my own." Homer declined more or less politely. He wouldn't let anyone take the baby. He put her car seat down for a moment by his feet while he took off his coat. With one arm still in its sleeve, he looked down in horror as he saw the car seat sliding away from him. He whirled around and caught the CPS woman, who'd crouched behind him, with one hand under the edge of the seat, pulling it across the floor. With a look of mock sheepishness, she lifted the seat up by the handle. "She's crying, I'll just take her a mo—"

But Homer had the other side of the handle. He snatched the baby back and hurried away with his coat hanging from one sleeve and dragging on the marble floor with a slithering sound.

The baby went on screaming. She was inconsolable until she was carried back through the bank doors where she went right to sleep, just like any tired baby. The CPS woman seemed to take it all very personally and she assured Homer that she would be watching carefully.

Homer said he didn't care, she could watch all she wanted, so long as the baby stayed at the bank.

A crib was set up in the safety deposit box room. One of the tellers made a mobile to hang over it with coins and dollar bills hanging from strings. They took turns carrying her in a pack on their chests while they talked to customers and passed out papers and collected deposits and counted money. On their breaks they fed her her bottled formula and burped her. Homer got over his first shyness around babies and let her sit on his lap while he took care of the business of the bank. The judge had insisted that a birth certificate be created for the baby and Homer had filled it in. He named her Precious Treasure Donnelly, but no one ever called her anything but Penny.

In the evenings Mr. and Mrs. Pepas came to work together and Mrs. Pepas made her husband dinner on a hot plate in the employees' break room. After dinner she fed the baby again and tucked her into her crib in the safety deposit room. Then the vault door was sealed and the intercom was turned on so that Mr. Pepas could hear her if she woke during the night. Homer had a video camera installed in the vault so that they could see her as well, but she slept every night as peacefully as a lamb. In the morning Homer came in, or one of the tellers, to wake her and get her ready for the day. There was probably never a baby so closely supervised as the bank's baby, but she seemed to thrive. She never had a runny nose, never had a fussy day or a toothache. She seemed happy and normal with a smile for one and all.

But she never left the bank. The tellers did try taking her out in a stroller they bought for her, but she screamed so that they quickly brought her back and Homer declared that she wasn't to be taken out of the bank again. At first this wasn't so remarkable. There was plenty of room in the bank and plenty of things to amuse her. The town got used to stepping around a tricycle when they came to cash their checks. She had her own pretend teller window and play money. In the afternoons she sat with Homer while he worked. He taught her the combination to the old-fashioned iron safe in the lobby and she liked to put her rattle and her teething ring, which she still played with, into the safe and spin the dials and then take them back out again. She never left them there. She carried them with her wherever she went, like talismans to remind her of her parents who had left their Penny in the bank for safekeeping.

By the time she was supposed to be going to kindergarten, Penny knew her numbers to a thousand as well as her times tables up to nine, she could add and subtract numbers in her head and was already reading on her own. Of course, there's a law that children of a certain age have to be in school, and that's when the Children's Protective Services stepped back in. The woman in her pointy shoes arrived at the door on the first of September and asked why Penny wasn't at school. Homer had to call Harvey Bentwell and Harvey had to come up with a tutor and a pile of forms all carefully filled out that would allow Penny to be home-schooled, though obviously it wasn't home-schooling, it was bank-schooling.

CPS must have thought they had a better case, because they dragged the whole thing back into court, saying that no guardian could legally keep a child incarcerated her entire life. Harvey argued that Penny wasn't incarcerated in the bank; she was home and she liked being there. She didn't want to go outside. CPS said no normal child would choose to stay inside. Harvey said she wasn't a normal child, and that much was true. Watching carefully Homer had concluded that yes, most people were a little stunned the first time they looked into her eyes. She seemed happy and she played like any child, and she raced around the lobby on a two-wheeler after the bank had closed and the path was clear, but when you looked into her eyes you seemed to stare into a well of peace, and, well, the only word Homer had for it was security. At least, when she was in the bank. The only time that Homer saw that serenity clouded was during the court hearings about her custody. She didn't scream through them, the way she had as a baby. She was five years old, after all, and had too much self-possession. She sat in a wooden chair with her feet swinging down and her hands folded in her lap, an unnaturally quiet and mannered little girl with coffee-colored skin and dark hair tightly curled like a lamb's fur.

The judge had insisted that Penny come to the hearings, but Homer in turn insisted that the judge come to the bank to speak to her at least once before ruling on the case. Homer walked the judge from the door of the bank across the lobby to his office, where Penny was waiting. He suggested that Penny stand up and shake hands with the judge and he watched the judge's face carefully as he bent down and looked into her face as he took her hand.

Homer smiled with satisfaction. He quietly closed the office door behind him. He was smiling as he put his arm around the puzzled Harvey's shoulder. "We're all set, Harvey," he said.

The judge emerged twenty minutes later and summoned the concerned parties to his chamber.

"I am considering leaving the child in the sole custody of the bank of Elliotville," he told them. "She seems in every way happy and well cared for."

"Except that she never leaves the bank, Your Honor," said the lawyer for CPS.

"That's true, but I am content that this is in line with the desires of the child and not an imposition."

"Imposition or not, Your Honor, it's unnatural. It's a psychosis. She needs treatment."

Homer sat quietly while the argument went back and forth. He wasn't concerned. Penny had had the desired effect.

The CPS produced a child psychiatrist who said Penny needed medical help, maybe drugs, maybe hospitalization. Harvey Bentwell agreed that it might be an illness, but said that Penny had felt this way since she was a baby and that no court in the world would say that it wasn't the guardian's right to decide on medical treatment for a child. Did the judge have reason to believe that the bank was an inadequate guardian?

"Yes," said the CPS woman, jumping up and interrupting. "The bank is no guardian at all. This child needs a mother and a father. She needs a family to help her deal with her irrational fears of the outside world. Where is her family?"

"We are her family," Homer pointed out gently.

"Are you?" said Ms. CPS. "Show me some instance where you have helped her deal with her fear. As far as I can see, you do nothing but encourage her debility."

"Have you met the child in the bank?"

Ms. CPS had adamantly refused to step into the bank. She hadn't been back inside it since the day Penny was found.

"Then how can you criticize what parenting is available to the child?"

"There is no parenting. Find one example of an adult helping this child overcome her fears."

"Mrs. Pepas helps me." To everyone's amazement, Penny spoke. "When I am afraid she helps me."

"Go on," said the judge gently.

"Sometimes I am afraid that the things that are outside the bank will get in to get me. Sometimes their shadows come in at night. I can see them."

"And?"

"I told Mrs. Pepas. She said that they were just shadows and that shadows all by themselves couldn't hurt anyone. I didn't have to be afraid. I just had to pretend that they were the shadows of bunnies. That any shadow, if you look at it right, could be the shadow of a bunny. She said I should take my rattle, because I always have my rattle with me, and my ring." She held up her arm to show the teething ring that now sat like a bracelet around her wrist. "She said I should point my rattle at the shadows and say 'You're a bunny,' and then I won't be afraid anymore."

"Did it work?" the judge asked, curious.

"Yes."

The judge looked at CPS and raised his eyebrows. The CPS representative was not pleased. Finally she sniffed and said sharply that it would have been more to the point to teach the child to shake her rattle at the things she thought were outside the bank.

She squatted down in front of Penny. "Darling. These are just silly ideas. We want you to see that. There aren't any monsters. There aren't any bad guys. There isn't anything or anyone outside the bank trying to take you away. It's just nonsense, can you understand that?"

Penny looked at her calmly for a moment. "You are outside the bank," she said. "You are trying to take me away."

Ms. CPS flushed to her hairline and stood up quickly. "Your Honor, the child is sick. She needs help."

"Your help?" the judge asked.

"Our help."

"I disagree." Bang went the gavel and home went Penny to the bank.

CPS tried again and again over the years, but without success, and Penny grew up safe in the bank, but in other ways very much like any girl her age. When she was sixteen and had taken the test to secure a high school equivalency, the Children's Protective Services asked again what future she could have if she never left the Elliotville Bank. Penny explained that she had enrolled in a correspondence course in accounting and she intended to become a teller. The CPS woman, now a little gray but no less forceful, nearly choked. But Treasure was near the age of her majority. Though CPS cajoled and threatened, there was nothing that the department could do.

To celebrate her new legal independence, Penny pierced her ears, straightened her curly hair, and dyed the tips blond. She liked the surprise on people's faces. Customers that she had known her entire life were stunned, but once they looked into her eyes, they knew she was still the same Penny. They broke

into smiles of relief and admired her hair and her dangling earrings and the odd incongruity of her clothing: a camouflage
tank top, a plaid skirt, and over it all a sensible cardigan with
pockets to hold her rattle and teething ring, which she still carried with her wherever she went.

She was working the day before her eighteenth birthday, or
what the authorities thought her eighteenth birthday might be,
when there was an odd disturbance in the doorway. She looked
up from the money she was counting, through the glass window that separated her from the lobby. Standing in the bank
doorway was an extremely tall woman dressed in a crisp black
skirt and suit coat and carrying a shiny black briefcase. For one
moment Penny thought that she was the CPS woman, but this
woman was far more striking. Her hair was silver blond and her
skin was white like cream. Her eyes, even from across the bank
lobby, were a startling blue. She stepped into the lobby like a
queen followed by her minions and her minions were even more
remarkable and less appealing than herself.

There was a troll, a vampire, a few surly-looking dwarves,
three or four pale greenish individuals with sneering faces, and
quite a few animals with unpleasant horns and teeth all in a
crowd that was partially obscured by the mist coming through
the doorway.

"Is it raining?" asked Penny. It had been sunny earlier that
day.

The queenly figure in black must have heard her voice

through the glass. She stepped toward Penny and lifted her briefcase onto the countertop. "I would like to withdraw my niece," she said in a steely voice that hissed on the last sibilant.

Penny swallowed. "Excuse me?" she said.

"My niece," said the woman. "I would like to withdraw my niece." She looked over her shoulder toward the open doorway to the vault and the safety deposit boxes. "She must be around here somewhere. I am sure you see the family resemblance. Her father was mortal and I doubt very much she would take after him."

Penny quickly tilted her head down and pressed a button that rang an alarm in Homer's office. Homer rushed into the lobby and slowed to a stop as he saw the crowd there. More slowly he walked behind the counter and came up behind Penny.

"This lady would like to withdraw her niece," Penny said. She and Homer stared at one another.

"Immediately," prodded the woman on the other side of the counter.

"D—d—d—," said Homer.

"Did you make the deposit?" Penny asked.

"No. I did not. My sister and her husband deposited the baby here, but I am now in charge of their affairs. I would like to withdraw her."

The way she said "in charge of their affairs" made one think it meant no good at all for this unknown mother and father of Penny's.

"And is the original depositor deceased?" Penny asked.

"Deceased?"

"Dead," said Penny.

"No, not yet."

"Well, then, I'm afraid that she will have to make the withdrawal."

"That is impossible."

Penny turned to Homer. "Perhaps a signature on the withdrawal slip would be sufficient?" she asked.

"Uh, huh, yes, I s-suppose so," said Homer.

Penny, very carefully looking down at the paper in front of her, slid a withdrawal slip across the counter. "We'll need to have this filled out and signed," she said in a prim voice.

The elegant creature on the other side of the counter picked up the piece of paper by one corner and looked at it with disgust. "You want this signed?"

"We can't otherwise release your deposit," Penny explained.

"Very well," said the woman. Dangling the paper in front of her, she carried it out of the bank. She was followed by the vampire, the troll, the green people, and assorted unpleasant others.

Homer sighed. Penny rubbed her hands together. "That's once," she said.

The woman was back the next day, bringing rain and mist behind her. The other customers in the bank scattered, leaving an open path to the tellers. The woman headed for a different window, but Penny managed to slide up the counter and displace the teller there before her aunt finished her trip across the lobby.

"My niece," she said, and slid the deposit slip across the counter. Penny studied the slip a moment, turning her head to one side to read the spidery signature.

"You did say that your sister and her husband made the deposit, didn't you?"

"I did," said the woman.

"I am terribly sorry. If it is a joint deposit, we'll need his signature as well to authorize a withdrawal."

"You didn't mention this yesterday," the woman hissed.

No one was better at dealing with unpleasant customers than Penny. "I'm terribly sorry," she said in an officially earnest voice. "But we do need both signatures."

The woman snatched the paper from the desk and swept out the door, sucking the mist away in her wake and disappearing before she'd gone more than a few steps down the street. Penny watched them through the glass doors of the bank. "That's twice," she said.

When the woman returned with the deposit slip, signed, Penny was relieved to see, by two people, she clucked sympathetically and said, "They haven't dated it."

"You are joking."

"No, I am afraid it has . . ."

The woman snapped her fingers and Penny flinched as a pen slid across the counter and jumped obediently into the outstretched hand. The woman looked at the little block calendar next to the teller's window and carefully dated the deposit slip.

". . . to be dated by the signatories," Penny finished as the pen dropped back to the counter.

"I am not pleased, young woman."

"I do apologize," Penny said meekly, her eyes cast down, and when the vampires, the trolls, the nixies, monsters, and minions were gone with the mist, she smiled a different smile and said to Homer, "That's three."

The next day she told the woman that the deposit slip, because it wasn't filled out in the bank, needed to be notarized by a notary public.

"A what?"

"A notary public."

"Do go on," the woman prompted.

Homer spoke up. He had been standing by Penny every day, holding his ground as best he could, ready to offer her any assistance. "A notary public is an 'individual legally empowered to witness and certify the validity of documents and to take affidavits and depositions.'"

"They have a stamp," Penny explained. "They witness the document being signed and then they stamp it and it is a legal document. Until then"—she slid the deposit slip back to the woman—"until then, it's just a slip of paper." She smiled brightly.

The creature on the far side of the counter inhaled in a hiss and held her breath until Penny thought she might lift off the floor like a gas-filled balloon, or go off with a pop like an over-inflated one. The woman looked around the lobby wall as if for a weapon to use, but finding none she turned back with only a glare.

"And where do I find a notary public?" the enchantress asked. "Where? They don't grow on trees where I come from, and while I might be able to arrange one that did, it would take time I don't have to waste."

"Oh," said Penny thoughtfully. "I am a notary public. I could go with you."

She felt Homer's panicked grasp on her wrist, but she turned to reassure him with a look. "Very well, then," said the frightening woman. "Come along, then."

Penny followed her out of the bank. The mist was thinner than it had been before, and rays of sunshine reached through it. Penny, still keeping her eyes cast down, noted that some of the most frightening creatures of the woman's retinue seemed to have shadows shaped like rabbits. She followed the woman into the mist and saw the world around her thin before the mist cleared entirely and she was standing in the middle of a muddy road. On either side were water-soaked fields under low clouds. The fields were deserted and the few trees between them were black and leafless. It was raining and the enchantress was ahead of her, moving down the road. Her short skirt and briefcase were gone. She wore a long black robe with a hood at the back and had a satchel that hung from her shoulder.

"Come," she commanded and Penny followed her. Ahead lay a fairy-tale sort of castle that should have glowed in the sun-

shine with flags flapping in a breeze, but instead it sat gray and
sodden and inert in its blighted surroundings.

It was a twenty-minute walk to the castle and in the first five
minutes, Penny was soaked to the skin. The mud collected on
her boots and they grew heavier and heavier. She noticed that
the rain didn't fall on the enchantress, who was still perfectly
dry, but the vampires looked miserable, and the trolls were no
happier in their bare skin. Only the nixies, being water creatures, were undistressed by the rain. They were, however, un-
used to the mud. They slipped and slid and occasionally
grabbed each other for support. But they weren't pleasant creatures, even to each other, and when one teetered, another was
apt to push her over altogether. Once one fell, she dragged at
the hems of her passing sisters and pulled them down, too, until
they were all a sprawling nest of spiteful hissing and scratching.
Penny watched with interest as a troll stepped on one of the
nixies underfoot and all the others rose up against him. There
was a harpy nearby who took the troll's side and buffeted the
nixies with her wings, calling them rude names and knocking
them back into the mud. The nixies retaliated by grabbing at
her feathers and pulling them out in handfuls. The harpy
squawked with rage and screamed abuse. The vampires stopped
to watch. The various wolflike creatures and the crawling bat-
winged monsters twisted between the bystanders to get a better
look. Penny, who was behind the vampires, had to stop as well.
She ran her fingers through her hair and squeezed the rainwater

out. As she did so she felt something brush her ankles and she jumped in surprise. A black rabbit with malevolent red eyes was fidgeting past a hop at a time, clearly as eager as the others to see the fight, but just as clearly nervous of the teeth and claws around him.

There was a crack of thunder and simultaneous lightning and all looked guiltily at the enchantress, hastily collected themselves, and hurried on. They passed between rows of broken-down houses, which seemed deserted, huddled behind flat expanses of mud that should have been front gardens. Penny thought she saw a face or two watching from behind the broken windows. When they reached the gates of the castle, the wooden doors were blasted and their hinges broken. The stones of the courtyard beyond were heaved and rumpled as if by a sudden frost. The nixies stumbled again and a troll snarled, but they scurried on as best they could into the main hall where the enchantress stood, smiling in satisfaction before two thrones. On one sat a woman in every way but one identical to the enchantress. She had skin like cream and long hair that fell like a waterfall in moonlight to her shoulders. Her eyes were open and empty as she sat on the throne, covered over in a mass of spider webs that bound her to her chair, clinging to her hands and her arms, her eyelids, her lips, the wisping tendrils of her hair. Though she was as still as a statue, Penny could see in a glance that where her sister was all cruelty, this queen was all kindness. Her eyes were as blue, but where her sister's were blue like ice, this queen's were as blue as the sky and as clear. Beside her sat her husband, ensnared the same way, with his eyes open and watching the enchantress. His skin was a warm coffee color, and his black hair was as curly as a lamb's new fur coat. Penny was uncomfortably aware of her own hair, with the heavy water wrung out of it, beginning to regain its natural curl.

The hall was silent except for the dripping of rain and the occasional hiss or snarl of the enchantress's minions. When she held up her hand, the hisses and snarls ceased and there was only the sound of the rain.

"Still here?" she asked the motionless figures. "I am so fortunate to have found you at home. Why yes, there is the teensiest favor you can do for me." She smiled. "Oh it's nothing, less than nothing, but I know you're pleased to help out. You see, we need our form filled out again."

She held out her hand and Penny hurried to her side to offer her the blank deposit slip. The enchantress stepped forward and lifted the limp hand of the queen. She drew a quill pen, black and shiny, from the air and fitted it into the unresponsive fingers. "Sign," she commanded and the fingers moved the pen across the slip of paper while the queen's blue eyes remained empty.

"Date," hissed the enchantress and the pen moved again.

The enchantress moved to the king on his throne and lifted his hand. His head turned ever so slightly and his eyes met Penny's.

The enchantress folded his fingers around the pen. "Oh, don't fuss," she said. "We are so close now, so close. Do this one little thing for me and we are nearly done. I will have you and I will have the princess and I will have the crown and the scepter and there will be none to stand against me, Queen of the Realm." She smiled up at him. "One little thing and the princess is mine."

"Sign," she said. "Date," and the pen moved. "It was your idea, wasn't it? To hide her and the crown and the scepter when you realized I was too strong to be defeated by your paltry virtuous magic, where I wasted eighteen years trying to fetch her out, sending my minions one after another against cold steel and mortal conventions. Did you think I didn't know?" She straightened. "But if I couldn't reach her, neither could you. So she doesn't know the power she has, and I shall see to it that she never will." Pinching the deposit slip between her thumb and long-nailed forefinger she turned to Penny. "Now for our dear friend, the notary public."

Penny stood with her hands tucked into her cardigan pockets and looked back at her. The enchantress stared at Penny, seeing her clearly for the first time in her heavy boots and plaid skirt oddly paired with her sensible cardigan and her black and yellow hair, her earrings, and her clear blue eyes.

Penny pulled her hands free of her pockets. In one hand was her teething ring, in the other, her rattle. She calmly pointed the rattle at the enchantress.

"No—" shrieked the enchantress. "No—"

"You," Penny said firmly, "are a bunny."

Homer came to visit a few weeks later, bringing the rest of the people from the bank, the tellers, the security guard Mr. Pepas, and his wife. They arrived in a patch of mist on the road before the castle. The mud was gone, along with the nixies and the trolls, the vampires and the looming gray clouds. The fields were greening again and filled with farmers repairing the damages of the war and the Dark Queen's brief rule. Penny and her family were there on the road and all walked together to the newly repaired castle. As they passed through the tiny village below its gates, Homer commented on the fenced-in boxes set in every garden.

"Hutches," explained the king, smiling at his daughter. "We have a surplus of rabbits."

The Circuit

by Francisco Jiménez

It was that time of year again. Ito, the strawberry sharecropper, did not smile. It was natural. The peak of the strawberry season was over and the last few days the workers, most of them *braceros,* were not picking as many boxes as they had during the months of June and July.

As the last days of August disappeared, so did the number of *braceros.* Sunday, only one—the best picker—came to work. I liked him. Sometimes we talked during our half-hour lunch break. That is how I found out he was from Jalisco, the same state in Mexico my family was from. That Sunday was the last time I saw him.

When the sun had tired and sunk behind the mountains, Ito signaled us that it was time to go home. *"Ya esora,"* he yelled in his broken Spanish. Those were the words I waited for twelve hours a day, every day, seven days a week, week after week. And the thought of not hearing them again saddened me.

As we drove home Papá did not say a word. With both hands on the wheel, he stared at the dirt road. My older brother, Roberto, was also silent. He leaned his head back and closed his eyes. Once in a while he cleared from his throat the dust that blew in from outside.

Yes, it was that time of year. When I opened the front door to the shack, I stopped. Everything we owned was neatly packed in cardboard boxes. Suddenly I felt even more the weight of hours, days, weeks, and months of work. I sat down on a box. The thought of having to move to Fresno and knowing what was in store for me there brought tears to my eyes.

That night I could not sleep. I lay in bed thinking about how much I hated this move.

A little before five o'clock in the morning, Papá woke everyone up. A few minutes later, the yelling and screaming of my little brothers and sister, for whom the move was a great adventure, broke the silence of dawn. Shortly, the barking of the dogs accompanied them.

While we packed the breakfast dishes, Papá went outside to start the Carcachita. That was the name Papá gave his old black Plymouth. He'd bought it in a used-car lot in Santa Rosa. Papá was very proud of his little jalopy. He had a right to be proud of it. He spent a lot of time looking at other cars before buying this one. When he finally chose the Carcachita, he checked it thoroughly before driving it out of the car lot. He examined every inch of the car. He listened to the motor, tilting his head from side to side like a parrot, trying to detect any noises that spelled car trouble. After being satisfied with the looks and sounds of the car, Papá then insisted on knowing who the original owner was. He never did find out from the car salesman, but he bought the car anyway. Papá figured the original owner must have been an important man because behind the rear seat of the car he found a blue necktie.

Papá parked the car out in front and left the motor running. *"Listo,"* he yelled. Without saying a word Roberto and I began to carry the boxes out to the car. Roberto carried the two big boxes and I carried the two smaller ones. Papá then threw the mattress on top of the car roof and tied it with ropes to the front and rear bumpers.

Everything was packed except Mamá's pot. It was an old, large galvanized pot she had picked up at an army surplus store in Santa Maria. The pot had many dents and nicks, and the more dents and nicks it acquired the more Mamá liked it. *"Mi olla,"* she used to say proudly.

I held the front door open as Mamá carefully carried out her pot by both handles, making sure not to spill the cooked beans. When she got to the car, Papá reached out to help her with it. Roberto opened the rear car door and Papá gently placed it on the floor behind the front seat. All of us then climbed in. Papá sighed, wiped the sweat from his forehead with his sleeve, and said wearily: *"Es todo."*

As we drove away, I felt a lump in my throat. I turned around and looked at our little shack for the last time.

At sunset we drove into a labor camp near Fresno. Since Papá did not speak English, Mamá asked the camp foreman if he needed any more workers. "We don't need no more," said the foreman, scratching his head. "Check with Sullivan down the road. Can't miss him. He lives in a big white house with a fence around it."

When we got there, Mamá walked up to the house. She went through a white gate, past a row of rose bushes, up the stairs to the house. She rang the doorbell. The porch light went on and a tall, husky man came out. They exchanged a few words. After the man went in, Mamá clasped her hands and hurried back to the car. "We have work! Mr. Sullivan said we can stay there the whole season," she said, gasping and pointing to an old garage near the stables.

The garage was worn out by the years. It had no windows. The walls, eaten by termites, strained to support the roof full of holes. The dirt floor, populated by earthworms, looked like a gray road map.

That night, by the light of a kerosene lamp, we unpacked and cleaned our new home. Roberto swept away the loose dirt, leaving the hard ground. Papá plugged the holes in the walls with old newspapers and tin can tops. Mamá fed my little brothers and sister. Papá and Roberto then brought in the mattress and placed it on the far corner of the garage. "Mamá, you and the little ones sleep on the mattress. Roberto, Panchito, and I will sleep outside under the trees," Papá said.

Early the next morning Mr. Sullivan showed us where his crop was, and after breakfast, Papá, Roberto, and I headed for the vineyard to pick.

Around nine o'clock the temperature had risen to almost one hundred degrees. I was completely soaked in sweat and my mouth felt as if I had been chewing on a handkerchief. I walked over to the end of the row, picked up the jug of water we had brought, and began drinking. "Don't drink too much; you'll get sick," Roberto shouted. No sooner had he said that than I felt sick to my stomach. I dropped to my knees and let the jug roll off my hands. I remained motionless with my eyes glued on the hot sandy ground. All I could hear was the drone of insects. Slowly I began to recover. I poured water over my face and neck and watched the dirty water run down my arms to the ground.

I still felt dizzy when we took a break to eat lunch. It was past two o'clock and we sat underneath a large walnut tree that was on the side of the road. While we ate, Papá jotted down the number of boxes we had picked. Roberto drew designs on the ground with a stick. Suddenly I noticed Papá's face turn pale as he looked down the road. "Here comes the school bus," he whispered loudly in alarm. Instinctively, Roberto and I ran and hid in the vineyards. We did not want to get in trouble for not going to school. The neatly dressed boys about my age got off. They carried books under their arms. After they crossed the street, the bus drove away. Roberto and I came out from hiding and joined Papá. *"Tienen que tener cuidado,"* he warned us.

After lunch we went back to work. The sun kept beating down. The buzzing insects, the wet sweat, and the hot dry dust made the afternoon seem to last forever. Finally the mountains around the valley reached out and swallowed the sun. Within an hour it was too dark to continue picking. The vines blanketed the grapes, making it difficult to see the bunches. *"Vámonos,"* said Papá, signaling to us that it was time to quit work. Papá then took out a pencil and began to figure out how much we had earned our first day. He wrote down numbers, crossed some out, wrote down some more. *"Quince,"* he murmured.

When we arrived home, we took a cold shower underneath a water hose. We then sat down to eat dinner around some wooden crates that served as a table. Mamá had cooked a special meal for us. We had rice and tortillas with *carne con chile,* my favorite dish.

The next morning I could hardly move. My body ached all over. I felt little control over my arms and legs. This feeling went on every morning for days until my muscles finally got used to the work.

It was Monday, the first week of November. The grape

season was over and I could now go to school. I woke up early that morning and lay in bed, looking at the stars and savoring the thought of not going to work and of starting sixth grade for the first time that year. Since I could not sleep, I decided to get up and join Papá and Roberto at breakfast. I sat at the table across from Roberto, but I kept my head down. I did not want to look up and face him. I knew he was sad. He was not going to school today. He was not going tomorrow, or next week, or next month. He would not go until the cotton season was over, and that was sometime in February. I rubbed my hands together and watched the dry, acid-stained skin fall to the floor in little rolls.

When Papá and Roberto left for work, I felt relief. I walked to the top of a small grade next to the shack and watched the *Carcachita* disappear in the distance in a cloud of dust.

Two hours later, around eight o'clock, I stood by the side of the road waiting for school bus number twenty. When it arrived I climbed in. Everyone was busy either talking or yelling. I sat in an empty seat in the back.

When the bus stopped in front of the school, I felt very nervous. I looked out the bus window and saw boys and girls carrying books under their arms. I put my hands in my pant pockets and walked to the principal's office. When I entered I heard a woman's voice say: "May I help you?" I was startled. I had not heard English for months. For a few seconds I remained speechless. I looked at the lady who waited for an answer. My first instinct was to answer her in Spanish, but I held back. Finally, after struggling for English words, I managed to tell her that I wanted to enroll in the sixth grade. After answering many questions, I was led to the classroom.

Mr. Lema, the sixth grade teacher, greeted me and assigned me a desk. He then introduced me to the class. I was so nervous and scared at that moment when everyone's eyes were on me that I wished I were with Papá and Roberto picking cotton. After taking roll, Mr. Lema gave the class the assignment for the first hour. "The first thing we have to do this morning is finish reading the story we began yesterday," he said enthusiastically. He walked up to me, handed me an English book, and asked me to read. "We are on page 125," he said politely. When I heard this, I felt my blood rush to my head; I felt dizzy. "Would you like to read?" he asked hesitantly. I opened the book to page 125. My mouth was dry. My eyes began to water. I could not begin. "You can read later," Mr. Lema said understandingly.

During recess I went into the restroom and opened my English book to page 125. I began to read in a low voice, pretending I was in class. There were many words I did not know. I closed the book and headed back to the classroom.

Mr. Lema was sitting at his desk correcting papers. When I entered he looked up at me and smiled. I felt better. I walked up to him and asked if he could help me with the new words. "Gladly," he said.

The rest of the month I spent my lunch hours working on English with Mr. Lema, my best friend at school.

One Friday during lunch hour Mr. Lema asked me to take a walk with him to the music room. "Do you like music?" he asked me as we entered the building. "Yes, I like *corridos,*" I answered. He then picked up a trumpet, blew on it, and handed it to me. The sound gave me goose bumps. I knew that sound. I had heard it in many *corridos.* "How would you like to learn how to play it?" he asked. He must have read my face because before I could answer, he added: "I'll teach you how to play it during our lunch hours."

That day I could hardly wait to tell Papá and Mamá the great news. As I got off the bus, my little brothers and sister ran up to meet me. They were yelling and screaming. I thought they were happy to see me, but when I opened the door to our shack, I saw that everything we owned was neatly packed in cardboard boxes.

The Widow Carey's Chickens

By Gerald Hausman

Thirty miles west of Land's End, England, on the coast of Cornwall, there is a group of islands called the Scilly Isles. Their broken cliffs rise out of the Atlantic, and being in the direct track of vessels bound for the English Channel, they were historically the scene of some disastrous shipwrecks.

Six of the islands are of considerable size, and one of them, lying on the southwestern side of the cluster, is called Bryher. This is a bare but rugged island whose hills are thickly jowled and whose toothy coast meets the sea in spumes of feathered spray.

It was off the loud and violent shore of Bryher one October in 1743 that the *James Moffett* went aground. A hurricane from the southwest drove the ship against the dark reef of rocks. She was loaded to the gunnels with goods, and what passengers there were swiftly drowned.

All, that is, but one.

When the ship foundered, the islanders of Bryher began pouring out of their cottages to lend a hand. They gathered at the pounding shoreline by lantern light. There was nothing to be done except watch the white combers break on the black shelf of rocks. With each heaving billow that blew in, there came ashore pieces of the *Moffet:* washed-up deck chairs, boxes, bales, and endless barrels of assorted cargo.

In the sea wash, too, came the broken bodies of human beings. One after another. The faces of the forlorn, waxen, white, and dead. Some clutched drowned children. Others—open-eyed and openmouthed—seemed about to say something. But their lips were frozen, and their tongues still.

Through the weary night and into the dreary morning the salvagers thronged on the Bryher coast, working in the shadows of their yellow whale-oil lamps. When daylight arrived, they saw a portion of the ship's hull just a few cables' length from where they stood.

There was the *James Moffett,* her spars naked to the winds. Her hull a wreck. Her masts as skeletal as winter trees. By day's end the sea had nattered the *Moffett* all the way to her keel. What remained on the black-rocked reef was the faintest shape of a ship, just a little more than a child's sketch.

How many passengers were on the *Moffett* when she went aground, the islanders couldn't say. The bodies kept showing up on the beach.

And then, miracle of miracles, one proved to be alive.

It was a woman in her midtwenties. She was pretty as a cameo and wet as a rat. The Bryherians carried her to the Inn of the Fishers, which was built in a safe cove close to the shoreline. She was quickly given dry clothes and a warm woolen blanket by some of the fishermen's wives.

For several hours she remained quiet and shaken. Yet after some hot soup and brandy, she decided to tell her tale. Her toneless voice described the deaths of her husband and baby.

"I am the widow Carey," she said. The woman peered at the wondering faces of the people gathered at the inn. "My husband and child were with me on the *James Moffett* bound for Philadelphia from Bristol when we crashed into those awful rocks. That is what has made me a widow, a childless widow."

Her clear oval face was pale and drawn. Her little voice was hard to hear over the roar of the breakers that gnawed at the stormy coastline. "Am I the only one who has survived?"

One of the fishermen spoke up. "How many were on your ship's register, do you know?"

"One hundred or more," she said softly.

The fisherman said, "We found as many bodies as rocks out there, and you're the only one with a living breath."

The widow's eyes were cast toward the sea. Through a window she stared at the reefed sea crags and the outline of a desolated ship.

In the silence of the inn there echoed the grinding sea and crackling fire. No one said a word. Presently the widow Carey was offered a cup of tea. She accepted it absently. Her eyes roved the room but always returned to the window with the view of the *James Moffett*.

The fishermen and their wives shared glances. They sipped their mugs of tea. No one spoke. Speech is a foolish thing when you have lost everything.

Finally the innkeeper's wife came forward. She had a voice that could soothe a lifeless stone. She said, "When, dear lady, your physical strength has in some measure been restored by rest, we shall be glad to take you to St. Mary's, and thence to Bristol, and then—"

The widow Carey looked alarmed.

"Oh, no!" she exclaimed. "I could never—" She broke off and stared out the window at the black rocks. "Here I must stay," she said in a still, small voice.

"But you must go home, dear. I mean, one day you must go back to Bristol, or Philadelphia, or wherever your home might be." These were the gentle words of Georgie Barkham, the innkeeper's wife. "Don't worry," Georgie whispered. "The time will come when you'll want to leave."

"I won't ever leave," the widow Carey said. Her eyes stayed on the line of rocks that had broken the *Moffett* into spars fingered by the crests of foam. She asked in a chilly voice, "Do you think you could tear me from the place where my husband and child perished?"

The women of Bryher exchanged worried glances. The men drank their tea in silence.

The widow asked, "Who among you knows how my husband in his last hour lashed me to the plank of wood that saved my life? Who here can say how he placed me there with our baby, while he waved me away? Who among you knows how my firstborn, my only born, was torn from my hands by the sea before we ever reached this shore?"

The widow's eyes flashed. The wind sang in the flue, and the fire leaped in the hearth, and somewhere in the darkness a dog howled mournfully.

Now the widow's fluid voice had the sound of a chant. "I pray that you may have pity on my little one's soul, and my brave husband's, and those of the others who went down on the *Moffett*. I pray you have pity on me, too, though I have been blessed—or cursed, I know not which—to live. In any case, I will remain here for the rest of my days. I won't eat the bread of idleness. I shall assist you in your needs. I shall nurse you in sickness, and I shall sit with you in suffering, as you stand with me now. But you mustn't ever ask me to leave your island."

There was no answer to this startling speech. The fishermen and their wives patted the woman on the shoulder, and, one by one, they took leave of her.

The people of Bryher had seen victims of tragedy all their lives. They knew that the misfortune of the widow Carey had affected her reason. They were sure that one day she would come to her senses.

After Georgie put the widow to bed, she told her husband, "One day the poor, distracted darling will beg to leave the barren Isles of Scilly. In the meantime we'll see to her welfare. We'll be pleased to have her among us."

So a pact was passed among the villagers. They were to be the widow Carey's guardians. Until such time.

No one could have guessed how long a time that would be.

Where the widow Carey came to live is as much part of her life as anything else. On a little promontory on the southwestern part of Bryher there was an ancient ruin. Built of stone hundreds of years earlier, this place was shaped like a tower over the sea. Some said it had been crafted by Druid priests.

The tower commanded the only perfect view of the sea crags where the *James Moffett* had met her end. Not surprisingly, this was exactly where the widow Carey decided to live.

At first, Georgie and others brought her food. They sought her welfare. But in time she took better care of them than they of her. She tended the sick and was adept at healing them. She was especially good with children, all of whom loved her. As it turned out, she conversed only with the children of the village. To them she sang little songs in a clear soprano voice that delighted all who heard it. Grownups could never get the widow to sing for them; she said she didn't know how. But for the children she was the pied piper of song.

Wherever there was suffering, the widow Carey came and helped. Wherever there was sickness or strife, she appeared. Whenever she departed, those who were in her care had been restored. Yet she rarely if ever spoke to those she cared for. She would not take money for her services, but she gladly accepted food and clothing.

Time washed over the headland hill where the widow Carey lived in her stone tower. Fishermen would often see her standing on the top of the battlement. One morning, as three friends were heading to the sea, the widow stood out like a statue against the rising sun. "She's a faithful landmark atop that pile of rocks," said one of the fishermen.

A second remarked, "You can set your timepiece by that woman."

The third pointed out, "Some say you can see the headland better when she's standing upright on it. Lord knows, she's like a little lighthouse unto herself."

The years passed, and one generation went away and another was born. In time the widow Carey lived beyond the lives of all who had first met her on that tragic day. Before Georgie Barkham died, she was the only one left who had heard the widow Carey begging to stay on Bryher for the rest of her days. Those days, it seemed, were endless for the widow. But not for everyone else.

The widow Carey, in the passage of time, became a kind of living legend. When people were ill, they saw her at a window. Her pale, thin face; her dark black shawl. Phantomlike, she appeared. But she no longer entered homes to perform her miraculous healings. Her presence was merely felt and only fleetingly seen. Sometimes she appeared to sick people in dreams; after seeing her, they got well.

"How is that?" asked a visitor one cold April morning as he sat before the crackling fire at the Inn of the Fishers.

"Well, sir," Georgie's daughter Susan said sweetly, "she came here more than sixty years ago, as my mother told me. It was before I was born. It happened on the night of the *James Moffett*."

"James Moffett . . . who's he?" the stranger asked, taking a gulp of grog.

"She was a four-masted ship," said Susan, wiping the bar clean with a calico cloth. "A ship like all ships, though, that find the reef of a stormy night. Well, she was on that ship, the widow was; she was the lone survivor."

The visitor grumbled. "Is that what the legend's all about?"

"Well, anyone else would've left us by now, but not her. Not our widow Carey. She's as much a part of us as we are of her."

"And as little a part, too," put in a fisherman, who clinked tankards with another.

"Yes. She has her ways," said Susan.

"What do you mean by that?" asked the visitor.

"She doesn't talk anymore. Nor does she show up—unless we're sick. Mostly we see her at the window."

"Doesn't anyone go up to that stone house of hers?"

"No one goes up there, except the children."

"Why are you so curious?" asked one of the fishermen at the bar.

"It's my business to be. I'm a journalist."

The fisherman was puzzled.

"I write newspaper articles," explained the visitor. "Let me introduce myself. My name is Keziah Coffin, and by the way, your saint of the sea cliff will make quite a story."

"I wouldn't write about her if I were you," said Susan.

"We'll see," said Keziah Coffin.

Early the next morning Mr. Coffin hiked out to the headland, notebook in hand. He went toward the south and a little to the west, and he found the widow Carey's tower quite easily. She was there, too. In the light of the new-risen sun she was sitting by herself on a flat gray rock. It was really a bench built by those ancient men the Druids. The writer had never seen a more desolate spot. Or a stranger, lonelier figure than the widow Carey. She looked like the last woman on earth.

Slowly he walked to the top of the hill. The wind was blowing hard. At first he tried to make small talk, but his words were lost in the wind. The widow Carey looked blankly ahead, staring into the foamy fingers that grabbed at the rocks. Her long dark veil blew behind her, and she didn't seem aware that anyone else was there.

Keziah Coffin tried to get the widow to speak with him—but to no avail. At last, after staring out to sea for a long time, she got up abruptly and left him. The door of the tower closed with a bang. The writer shook his head. He had questions but no answers. In the end he stumbled back to the inn, more intrigued than ever. In fact, Mr. Coffin wanted to write this story so badly, he could see the words forming in the air in front of his face. But he wouldn't write a word without more facts.

"You're no different from anyone else, I don't suppose," said Susan, who served him hot tea with a biscuit and salted pilchard. "I don't know how often we've seen her up at that tower. When the fishermen leave at dawn, she's always there. When they come home and the sun's on their shoulder, she's *still* there. Her flag is that dark veil she wears over her face, and it's always blowing in the wind. Did you see it?"

"I stood beside her for the better part of an hour. She was all wrapped up, as you say. Never noticed me. Finally, she got up, went inside her tower."

Keziah Coffin munched down his biscuit. Then, wiping his pink lips, he asked, "Is there anything else about the widow that I might know? I'm itching to write her up. Just itching."

Susan served him a second biscuit. "What do you mean?"

"I need something," he said, "that I could use to build a story on. You know, something that rounds out her character a little. I have to confess, your lady of the tower has me stumped. What's her reason for being so alone up there, all by herself?"

"Maybe that's best left alone, like her."

Keziah Coffin drank his tea and smacked his lips noisily.

"Well," Keziah Coffin prompted, "maybe you know . . . some little piece of information that I could—"

"You could start with this," said a little girl, who seemed to appear out of nowhere.

"Who are you?" said the writer.

"I'm her daughter. My name is Georgie," answered the dark-eyed, dark-haired child. "I know the widow better'n anybody. She's my . . . friend. All the children like her."

"Well, come over here and let me have a better look at you."

Georgie came from around the bar, where she'd been helping her mother.

"Don't you go telling him anything outrageous, my sweet," Susan said. "Stick to the facts, if you tell him anything."

"I don't see the harm in talking about the . . . *chickens*," said the child.

Keziah Coffin grinned. "Now we're getting somewhere. What chickens?"

The little girl's face lit up. "They're the lost souls she watches over."

"Lost souls. I see."

"From people who died on the *James Moffet*."

"I see," said Keziah Coffin. He had his notebook open, and he was writing in it rapidly. "You said they are chickens?"

Georgie's eyes danced. "They're *petrels*. But she's got them so tame everyone on the island calls them chickens."

Keziah Coffin rubbed his brow. It was clear he didn't know what petrels were.

"Sea birds," she told him. "The widow keeps them in her tower at night. She lets them out before sunup. You can see them then."

"And you say they are the souls of the people who died aboard the *James Moffett*?"

Georgie picked up his biscuit plate and empty mug.

"Don't take that away," he said. "I'll have another of . . . everything." He patted his big stomach. The little girl laughed and went to get him some more.

When Georgie returned with a second helping, Keziah Coffin asked, "What other wrecks have been on that reef?"

Susan answered this time. "None. Not since that widow Carey came here."

Keziah Coffin jiggled his teacup and studied the flurry of tea leaves swirling in the white of the bottom. "Now that," he said, "is the work of an angel. If, of course, it's true." He shook his head and smacked his lips. "Trouble is, I have a hard time believing any of this."

Georgie's eyes widened. "I can show you her chickens," she said. She traced her finger across the window that looked out on the reef and made two wings in the breath of moisture on the glass.

"How?"

"You've got to get up before the sun."

"All right."

Georgie skipped off. "See you tomorrow, mister."

Next day, well before first light, Keziah Coffin and Georgie, the innkeeper's daughter, went to see the widow Carey. The heavyset man carried a lantern. The girl scrambled up ahead of him.

They found the widow Carey sitting on the bench, staring at the ocean. The door of the tower was open. As the sun came out of the sea, a storm of dark-winged petrels fluttered out of the doorway. They settled all over the widow, who never stirred. They dropped like leaves all over her head, her shoulders; every part of her was painted in feathers. And the sounds they made: what weird pipings. What strange singings.

Finally, the widow stood up slowly, and the birds departed. They swung out in an arc around the tower, which they circled three times. Then they descended and followed her inside.

That evening at the inn Keziah Coffin sat before the fire, notebook in hand. He wasn't writing. He stared into the flames. But instead of seeing the darting orange light of the fire, he saw wings, ashen wings flickering before his eyes.

The next morning before first light Keziah Coffin awoke with a purpose. Once again he headed southwest along the path that wound up toward the widow Carey's tower. She was there, as usual. Straight and tall, on her bench. He approached as the sun rose. He waited. The petrels didn't come. The door to the tower was closed.

He and the widow looked out at the salmon-colored sky.
Neither of them moved.

Suddenly a gust swept up from the coast, and the widow folded sideways. Keziah Coffin moved quickly and caught her in his arms. At the same time, the petrels made a gentle thunder as they floated out of the open window casements of the tower. But this time they did not settle on the widow; instead they climbed into the sky.

Keziah Coffin noticed that the widow's eyes were shut. A small smile was on her lips. Her body was hard as wood. Around and around the little storm of petrels whirled overhead. They circled the widow Carey three times, and then they flew low over the breakers and lower still to the reeflike rocks. Then they went out to sea, their high, piercing sea cries keening on the wind, until all Keziah Coffin could see of them was a swirl of specks on the white gold of the sky.

There was nothing to do but tell the villagers what had happened. For some reason, he didn't feel it was his right to disturb the widow's final resting place. On the way back down the hill he met Georgie, who looked questioningly into his eyes.

"Is she gone?"

He nodded. "They took her away with them."

For a little while they walked in silence.

Then Georgie said, "The chickens never go out to sea. They never do that; they never fly away."

"Well," he said, "since they did, then I suppose the *James Moffett* is finally put to rest."

"Is she all right?"

"You mean the widow Carey?"

Georgie nodded.

"I don't think she's ever been better."

Walking back to the inn, Georgie said, "I'm going to miss her and her chickens."

"I didn't know her and I'm going to miss her," Keziah Coffin said.

Today the old rough stone battlement still graces the headland hill of Bryher, and some say there is a time of day when the air stirs and is charged with the gentle thunder of wings. Even now, it is considered a mortal sin to harm a petrel, and when the petrels come to Bryher, some people still call them the widow Carey's chickens.

The Special Powers of Blossom Culp

by Richard Peck

My name is Blossom Culp, and I'm ten years old, to the best of my mama's recollection.

I call 1900 the year of my birth, but Mama claims to have no idea of the day. Mama doesn't hold with birthdays. She says they make her feel old. This also saves her giving me a present. You could go through the courthouse down at Sikeston, Missouri, with a fine-tooth comb without turning up my records. But I must have been born because here I am.

Since Mama is hard to overlook, I will just mention her now. She doesn't know her birthday either but claims to be twenty-nine years old. She has only three teeth in her head, but they are up front, so they make a good showing. Her inky hair flows over her bent shoulders and far down her back. Whenever she appeared in daylight down at Sikeston, horses reared. Mama is a sight.

But she's a woman of wisdom and wonderful when it comes to root mixtures, forbidden knowledge, and other people's poultry. We could live off the land, though the trouble is, it's always somebody else's land. Like many of nature's creatures, Mama goes about her work at night. Get your corn in early, or Mama will have our share. Plant your tomatoes up by the house, or Mama will take them off you by the bushel. She likes her eggs fresh, too.

A moonless night suits her best; then off she goes down the hedgerows with a croaker sack flung over her humped shoulder. But nobody's ever caught her. "I can outrun a dawg," says Mama.

It was another of her talents that got us chased out of Sikeston. To hear her tell it, Mama has the Second Sight. For ready money she'll tell your fortune, find lost articles, see through walls, and call up the departed. She can read tea leaves, a pack of cards, your palm, a crystal ball. It doesn't matter to Mama. But because Sikeston was a backward place and narrow in its thinking, her profession was against the law. So her and me had to hotfoot it out of town two jumps ahead of a sheriff's posse.

Mama said that fate was leading her to our next home place. But we'd have hopped a freight in any direction. Aboard a swaying cattle car, Mama grew thoughtful and pulled on her long chin.

"The farther north we get," she said, "the more progressive.

Wherever we light, you'll be goin' to school." She shifted a plug of Bull Durham from one cheek to the other. If Mama had ever been to school herself, she'd have mentioned it. About all she can read is tea leaves.

"I been to school before, Mama," I reminded her. Down at Sikeston, I'd dropped into the grade school occasionally. Though when I dropped out again, I wasn't missed.

"I mean you'll be goin' to school regular," Mama said. "I won't have the law on me—believe it."

So when at last we came to rest at the town of Bluff City, I knew school was in my future without even a glimpse into Mama's crystal ball. I well recall the day I strolled into the Horace Mann School in Bluff City, wearing the same duds from when me and Mama had dropped off a cattle car of the Wabash Railroad.

"Yewww," said many of the girls in the schoolyard, giving me a wide berth. It was no better inside. I was sent to the principal before I had time to break a rule. She was a woman tall as a tree named Miss Mae Spaulding.

"Oh, dear," she said, looking down at me, "we're going to have to find you a comb."

I was small for ten but old for my years. Miss Spaulding grasped this and assigned me to fourth grade. She took me there herself, shooing me on ahead like a chicken. The teacher, name of Miss Cartwright, took a gander at me and said, "Oh, my stars."

"Perhaps you'd have a spare handkerchief to loan Blossom,"

the principal said to Miss Cartwright over my head.

I wiped my nose on my sleeve and noticed all the eyes of the fourth grade were boring holes in me. The boys' eyes were round with amazement. The girls' eyes were mean slits.

"I guess we had better find Blossom a seat," Miss Cartwright said as Miss Spaulding beat a hasty retreat.

A big girl reared up out of her desk. She wore a bow the size of a kite on the back of her head. "She'll not be sitting next to me!" she sang out, and flopped back.

Her name turned out to be Letty Shambaugh, and once again I didn't need Mama's Second Sight to see I had met an enemy for life.

Miss Cartwright cleared her throat and said, "Boys and girls, we have a new class member. I will ask her to introduce herself."

I looked out across the fourth grade, and they seemed capable of anything. Still, I stood my ground. "My name is Blossom Culp, and I hail from down at Sikeston, Missouri."

"Hillbillies," Letty Shambaugh hissed to the girls around her, "or worse."

"Me and Mama have relocated to Bluff City on account of her business."

"And what is your mother's business?" Miss Cartwright inquired.

"Oh, well, shoot," I says, "Mama is well known for her herbal cures and fortunetelling. She can heal warts, too. There's gypsy blood in our family."

Letty Shambaugh smirked. "Ah," says Miss Cartwright. "Are you an only child, Blossom?"

"I am now," I said. "I was born one half of a pair of Siamese twins, but my twin had to be hacked off my side so I alone could live."

"She lies!" Letty Shambaugh called out, though all the boys were interested in my story.

Miss Cartwright had now pulled back to the blackboard and seemed to cling to the chalk tray. "You may take your seat, Blossom." She pointed to the rear of the room.

I didn't mind it on the back row. But as the weeks passed, the novelty of going to school wore thin. My reading wasn't up to fourth-grade standard, either. Still, when we had to rise and read aloud from a library book, I did well. Holding a book up, I'd tell a story I thought of on the spot.

"Lies, lies," Letty would announce, "nothing but lies!" Still, Miss Cartwright was often so fascinated, she didn't stop me.

Then one day she told us that Letty would be having her birthday party on school time. "It is not usual to have a birthday party in class," Miss Cartwright said, "but we are making an exception of Letty."

People were always making an exception of Letty. Her paw was the president of the Board of Education. "Mrs. Shambaugh has very kindly offered to provide a cake," Miss Cartwright said, "and ice cream punch."

At recess I was in the girls' restroom, which has partitions for modesty. From my stall I eavesdropped on Letty talking to the bunch of girls she rules: Tess and Bess, the Beasley twins; Nola Nirider; and Maisie Markham.

"Now shut up and listen," Letty told them. "I am looking for some first-rate presents from you-all for my birthday. Don't get me any of that five-and-dime stuff."

I was so interested in Letty's commandments that I leaned on the door of my stall and staggered out into full view.

"Oh, there you are, Blossom," Letty sniffed. "Since you do nothing but tell lies and snoop, I'll thank you not to give me a present at all. You are a poor girl and can't afford it. Besides, I want nothing from the likes of you."

The bell rang, and they all flounced off like a gaggle of geese. But Letty turned back to fire a final warning at me. "And don't let me catch you spying on us again, Blossom!"

You won't, I said, but only to myself.

I sat up that night, waiting for Mama to come home. We'd taken up residence in an abandoned structure over past the streetcar tracks. It must have been midnight before Mama came in and eased her croaker sack down.

Then she busied herself shaking out everything she'd harvested from nearby gardens. From the look of some of it, she'd detoured past the dump. It was late in the season, so all there was to eat was a handful of pale parsnips.

"Well, Mama, I've got me a problem," I told her. "A stuck-up girl at school is having a birthday party, and I mean to give her a present like anybody else."

Mama surveyed her night's haul. "See anything here you can use?"

She held up a lady's whalebone corset straight off the trash heap and busted beyond repair. Besides, it wouldn't go halfway around Letty. The rest of the stuff was worse, except for a nice hatbox only a little dented with the tissue paper still inside. When I reached for it, Mama only shrugged, and picked between two of her three teeth.

The school days droned on, but I kept my wits about me. In one of my read-alouds, I went too far. Holding up a library copy of *Rebecca of Sunnybrook Farm,* I told the class about the time Mama came across the severed head of a woman and how Mama could identify the murderer with her Second Sight.

"A pack of lies!" Letty bawled out. "And disgusting!"

"That will do, Blossom," Miss Cartwright said in a weary voice. So after that, I had little to occupy myself with but to lie low and snoop on other people's business.

On the afternoon of Letty's party, a cake was wheeled in as large and pink as Letty herself. The classroom was stacked with tastefully wrapped presents, and no learning was done that afternoon. Miss Cartwright hung at the edge while Letty was the center of attention, where she likes to be.

We played some games too childish to interest me, but I

managed three slabs of cake and copped an extra slice for Mama. Then it was time for the presents.

"Oh heavens, you shouldn't have!" says Letty, her pudgy fingers fluttering over the vast heap. "Land sakes, I don't know which one to open first!"

"Start with this one." I nudged the hatbox toward her with the toe of my shoe. I'd dressed it up with a bow I found in the schoolyard and some gold star stickers I'd come across in a teacher's desk.

Miss Cartwright was standing by. Though strict, she sometimes eyed me sympathetically, though it might only have been pity. "Yes, Letty," she said. "Start with Blossom's present."

So Letty had to. She shook the box but heard nothing. She lifted the lid and ran a hand through the issue paper. "But there's nothing in it," she gasped, shooting me a dangerous look.

Some of the boys snickered, but the girls just pursed up their lips. "Oh, dear," Miss Cartwright remarked. Now Letty had turned the hatbox upside down. The tissue paper dropped out and with it a small note I'd hand-lettered. She read it aloud:

> *To Letty,*
>
> *Since I am too poor to buy you a present, I will share with you my own personal Gift.*
> *Believe it.*
>
> *Blossom Culp*

Letty glanced longingly at her other presents. "What is this so-called personal Gift of yours, Blossom?"

"Just a little demonstration of the Special Powers I inherited from my mama," I replied.

Letty shook a fist at me. "Blossom, you aren't going to ruin my party by showing off and telling lies!"

"For example," I said, cool as a cucumber, "before you even open up your other presents, I can tell what's in them with my Inner Eye. It's a Gift, and I have it down pat."

The girls were fixing to turn on me, but a boy said, "Then do it."

I could read the card on Nola Nirider's. "Now, you take Nola's present." I pointed it out. "No, I don't want to touch it. Just give me a minute." I let my head loll. Then I let my eyes roll back in my head. It was a ghastly sight, and the class gasped. In a voice faint and far off I said, "Within the wrappings, I see . . . a woman! She is a dainty creature cut in two at the waist!" I let my eyes roll back in place and looked around. "What did I say?"

Letty was already tearing open Nola's present. She pulled out a dainty china powder box in the shape of a lady. It was in two parts. The lid was the upper half. The boys blinked, and the girls looked worried.

Reading the card on Maisie's present from afar, I said, "Now, you take that one from Maisie Markham." And back flipped my eyes, and my head bobbed around till it like to fall off. "Deep within that fancy package," I moaned weirdly, "is a sealed bottle of apple-blossom toilet water—retailing at seventy-nine cents. I sense it with my Inner Nose."

Letty ripped open the box, coming up with that selfsame bottle of toilet water. "How am I doin'?" I asked the class.

It was like that with Tess's brush-and-comb set and Bess's four hair ribbons in rainbow hues. My eyes rolled back so often, showing my whites, that I thought I'd never get them straight in their sockets.

By now Letty sat sprawled in a heap of wrapping paper. The tears streamed down her red face. She was clouding up and ready to squall and had to stand to stamp her foot. "You have ruined my party with your showing off, Blossom. I knew you would, and you have!" She pounded out of the room before she even got to any presents from the boys, which was just as well. The other girls followed her as usual.

Now I was left with the boys, who showed me new respect, unsure of my Special Powers. But then the bell rang and they trooped out, taking final swipes at the remains of the cake.

"One moment, Blossom," Miss Cartwright said before I could make it to the door. "Could it be as you say—that you have . . . unearthly powers? Or could it merely be that you eavesdropped in the restroom often enough to hear those girls telling each other what they were giving Letty—and then you added that business with your eyes?"

Her chalky hand rested on my shoulder. "No, don't tell me," she said. "I don't want to know."

I was ready to cut out, but Miss Cartwright continued. "It has not taken you long to make a name for yourself at Horace Mann School. You will never be popular. But I have hopes for your future, Blossom. You will go far in your own peculiar way."

And I only nodded, as it's never wise to disagree with a teacher. Then she turned me loose, and I went on my way.

A White Heron

By Sarah Orne Jewett

The woods were already filled with shadows one June evening, just before eight o'clock, though a bright sunset still glimmered faintly among the trunks of the trees. A little girl was driving home her cow, a plodding, dilatory, provoking creature in her behavior, but a valued companion for all that. They were going away from whatever light there was, and striking deep into the woods, but their feet were familiar with the path, and it was no matter whether their eyes could see it or not.

There was hardly a night the summer through when the old cow could be found waiting at the pasture bars; on the contrary, it was her greatest pleasure to hide herself away among the high huckleberry bushes, and though she wore a loud bell she had made the discovery that if one stood perfectly still it would not ring. So Sylvia had to hunt for her until she found her, and call "Co'! Co'!" with never an answering moo, until her childish patience was quite spent.

If the creature had not given good milk and plenty of it, the case would have seemed very different to her owners. Besides, Sylvia had all the time there was, and very little use to make of it. Sometimes in pleasant weather it was a consolation to look upon the cow's pranks as an intelligent attempt to play hide-and-seek, and as the child had no playmates she lent herself to this amusement with a good deal of zest.

Though this chase had been so long that the wary animal herself had given an unusual signal of her whereabouts, Sylvia had only laughed when she came upon Mistress Moolly at the swampside, and urged her affectionately homeward with a twig of birch leaves. The old cow was not inclined to wander farther; she even turned in the right direction for once as they left the pasture, and stepped along the road at a good pace. She was quite ready to be milked now, and seldom stopped to browse.

Sylvia wondered what her grandmother would say because they were so late. It was a great while since she had left home at half past five o'clock, but everybody knew the difficulty of making this errand a short one.

Mrs. Tilley had chased the horned torment too many summer evenings herself to blame anyone else for lingering, and was only thankful as she waited that she had Sylvia, nowadays, to give such valuable assistance. The good woman suspected that Sylvia loitered occasionally on her own account; there never was such a child for straying about out-of-doors since the world was made!

Everybody said that it was a good change for a little maid who had tried to grow for eight years in a crowded manufacturing town, but as for Sylvia herself, it seemed as if she never had been alive at all before she came to live at the farm. She thought often with wistful compassion of a wretched geranium that belonged to a town neighbor.

"'Afraid of folks,'" old Mrs. Tilley said to herself with a smile, after she had made the unlikely choice of Sylvia from her daughter's houseful of children and was returning to the farm. "'Afraid of folks,' they said! I guess she won't be troubled no great with 'em up to the old place!" When they reached the door of the lonely house and stopped to unlock it, and the cat came to purr loudly, and rub against them, a deserted pussy, indeed, but fat with young robins, Sylvia whispered that this was a beautiful place to live in, and she never should wish to go home.

The companions followed the shady wood road, the cow taking slow steps and the child very fast ones. The cow stopped long at the brook to drink, as if the pasture were not half a swamp, and Sylvia stood still and waited, letting her bare feet cool themselves in the shoal water, while the great twilight moths struck softly against her. She waded on through the brook as the cow moved away, and listened to the thrushes with a heart that beat fast with pleasure. There was a stirring in the great boughs overhead. They were full of little birds and beasts that seemed to be wide awake, and going about their world, or else saying good night to each other in sleepy twitters. Sylvia herself felt sleepy as she walked along. However, it was not much farther to the house, and the air was soft and sweet. She was not often in the woods so late as this, and it made her feel as if she were a part of the gray shadows and the moving leaves.

She was just thinking how long it seemed since she first came to the farm a year ago, and wondering if everything went on in the noisy town just the same as when she was there; the thought of the great red-faced boy who used to chase and frighten her made her hurry along the path to escape from the shadow of the trees.

Suddenly the little woods-girl was horror-stricken to hear a clear whistle not very far away. Not a bird's whistle, which would have a sort of friendliness, but a boy's whistle, determined, and somewhat aggressive. Sylvia left the cow to whatever sad fate might await her, and stepped discreetly aside into the bushes, but she was just too late. The enemy had discovered her, and called out in a very cheerful and persuasive tone, "Halloa, little girl, how far is it to the road?" and trembling Sylvia answered almost inaudibly, "A good ways."

She did not dare to look boldly at the tall young man, who carried a gun over his shoulder, but she came out of her bush and again followed the cow, while he walked alongside.

"I have been hunting for some birds," the stranger said kindly, "and I have lost my way, and need a friend very much. Don't be afraid," he added gallantly. "Speak up and tell me what your name is, and whether you think I can spend the night at your house, and go out gunning early in the morning."

Sylvia was more alarmed than before. Would not her grandmother consider her much to blame? But who could have foreseen such an accident as this? It did not seem to be her fault, and she hung her head as if the stem of it were broken, but managed to answer "Sylvy" with much effort when her companion again asked her name.

Mrs. Tilley was standing in the doorway when the trio came into view. The cow gave a loud moo by way of explanation.

"Yes, you'd better speak up for yourself, you old trial! Where'd she tucked herself away this time, Sylvy?" But Sylvia kept an awed silence; she knew by instinct that her grandmother did not comprehend the gravity of the situation. She must be mistaking the stranger for one of the farmer lads of the region.

The young man stood his gun beside the door, and dropped a lumpy game bag beside it; then he bade Mr. Tilley good evening, and repeated his wayfarer's story, and asked if he could have a night's lodging.

"Put me anywhere you like," he said. "I must be off early in the morning, before day; but I am very hungry indeed. You can give me some milk at any rate, that's plain."

"Dear sakes, yes," responded the hostess, whose long-slumbering hospitality seemed to be easily awakened. "You might fare better if you went out to the main road a mile or so, but you're welcome to what we've got. I'll milk right off, and you make yourself at home. You can sleep on husks or feathers," she proffered graciously. "I raised them all myself. There's good pasturing for geese just below here toward the ma'sh. Now step round and set a plate for the gentleman, Sylvy!" And Sylvia promptly stepped. She was glad to have something to do, and she was hungry herself.

It was a surprise to find so clean and comfortable a little dwelling in this New England wilderness. The young man had known the horrors of its most primitive housekeeping, and the dreary squalor of that level of society which does not rebel at the companionship of hens. This was the best thrift of an old-fashioned farmstead, though on such a small scale that it seemed like a hermitage.

He listened eagerly to the old woman's quaint talk, he watched Sylvia's pale face and shining gray eyes with ever-growing enthusiasm, and insisted that this was the best supper he had eaten for a month, and afterward, the new-made friends sat down in the doorway together while the moon came up.

Soon it would be berry time, and Sylvia was a great help at

picking. The cow was a good milker, though a plaguy thing to keep track of, the hostess gossiped frankly, adding presently that she had buried four children, so Sylvia's mother, and a son (who might be dead) in California were all the children she had left.

"Dan, my boy, was a great hand to go gunning," she explained sadly. "I never wanted for pa'tridges or gray squer'ls while he was to home. He's been a great wand'rer, I expect, and he's no hand to write letters. There, I don't blame him, I'd ha' seen the world myself if it had been so I could."

"Sylvia takes after him," the grandmother continued affectionately, after a minute's pause. "There ain't a foot o' ground she don't know her way over, and the wild creatur's counts her one o' themselves.

"Squer'ls she'll tame to come an' feed right out o' her hands, and all sorts o' birds. Last winter she got the jay-birds to bangeing here, and I believe she'd 'a' scanted herself of her own meals to have plenty to throw out amongst 'em, if I hadn't kep' watch.

"Anything but crows, I tell her, I'm willin' to help support— though Dan he had a tamed one o' them that did seem to have reason same as folks. It was round here a good spell after he went away. Dan an' his father they didn't hitch—but he never held up his head ag'in after Dan had dared him an' gone off."

The guest did not notice this hint of family sorrows in his eager interest in something else.

"So Sylvy knows all about birds, does she?" he exclaimed, as he looked round at the little girl who sat, very demure but increasingly sleepy, in the moonlight. "I am making a collection of birds myself. I have been at it since I was a boy." (Mrs. Tilley smiled.) "There are two or three very rare ones I have been hunting for these five years. I mean to get them on my own ground if they can be found."

"Do you cage 'em up?" asked Mrs. Tilley doubtfully, in response to this enthusiastic announcement.

"Oh no, they're stuffed and preserved, dozens and dozens of them," said the ornithologist, "and I have shot or snared every one myself. I caught a glimpse of a white heron a few miles from here on Saturday, and I have followed it in this direction. They have never been found in this district at all. The little white heron, it is," and he turned again to look at Sylvia with the hope of discovering that the rare bird was one of her acquaintances. But Sylvia was watching a hop-toad in the narrow footpath.

"You would know the heron if you saw it," the stranger continued eagerly. "A queer tall white bird with soft feathers and long thin legs. And it would have a nest perhaps in the top of a high tree, made of sticks, something like a hawk's nest."

Sylvia's heart gave a wild beat; she knew that strange white bird, and had once stolen softly near where it stood in some bright green swamp grass, away over at the other side of the woods.

There was an open place where the sunshine always seemed strangely yellow and hot, where tall, nodding rushes grew, and her grandmother had warned her that she might sink in the soft black mud underneath and never be heard of more. Not far beyond were the salt marshes and just this side the sea itself, which Sylvia wondered and dreamed much about, but never had seen, whose great voices could sometimes be heard above the noise of the woods on stormy nights.

"I can't think of anything I should like so much as to find that heron's nest," the handsome stranger was saying. "I would give ten dollars to anybody who could show it to me," he added desperately, "and I mean to spend my whole vacation hunting for it if need be. Perhaps it was only migrating, or had been chased out of its own region by some bird of prey."

Mrs. Tilley gave amazed attention to all this, but Sylvia still watched the toad, not divining, as she might have done at some calmer time, that the creature wished to get to its hole under the doorstep and was much hindered by the unusual spectators at that hour of the evening. No amount of thought, that night, could decide how many wished-for treasures the ten dollars, so lightly spoken of, would buy.

The next day the young sportsman hovered about the woods, and Sylvia kept him company, having lost her first fear of the friendly lad, who proved to be most kind and sympathetic. He told her many things about the birds and what they knew and where they lived and what they did with themselves. And he gave her a jackknife, which she thought as great a treasure as if she were a desert islander.

All day long he did not once make her troubled or afraid except when he brought down some unsuspecting singing creature from its bough. Sylvia would have liked him vastly better without his gun; she could not understand why he killed the very birds he seemed to like so much.

But as the day waned, Sylvia still watched the young man with loving admiration. She had never seen anybody so charming and delightful; the woman's heart, asleep in the child, was vaguely thrilled by a dream of love. Some premonition of that great power stirred and swayed these young creatures who traversed the solemn woodlands with soft-footed silent care.

They stopped to listen to a bird's song; they pressed forward again eagerly, parting the branches—speaking to each other rarely and in whispers; the young man going first and Sylvia following, fascinated, a few steps behind, with her gray eyes dark with excitement.

She grieved because the longed-for white heron was elusive, but she did not lead the guest, she only followed, and there was no such thing as speaking first. The sound of her own unquestioned voice would have terrified her—it was hard enough to answer yes or no when there was need of that.

At last evening began to fall, and they drove the cow home together, and Sylvia smiled with pleasure when they came to the place where she had heard the whistle and was afraid only the night before.

* * * *

Half a mile from home, at the farther edge of the woods, where
the land was highest, a great pine tree stood, the last of its generation. Whether it was left for a boundary mark, or for what
reason, no one could say; the wood choppers who had felled its
mates were dead and gone long ago, and a whole forest of sturdy
trees, pines and oaks and maples, had grown again. But the
stately head of this old pine towered above them all and made a
landmark for sea and shore miles and miles away.

Sylvia knew it well. She had always believed that whoever
climbed to the top of it could see the ocean; and the little girl
had often laid her hand on the great rough trunk and looked up
wistfully at those dark boughs that the wind always stirred, no
matter how hot and still the air might be below.

Now she thought of the tree with a new excitement, for
why, if one climbed it at break of day could not one see all the
world, and easily discover from whence the white heron flew,
and mark the place, and find the hidden nest?

What a spirit of adventure, what wild ambition! What fan-
cied triumph and delight and glory for the later morning when
she could make known the secret! It was almost too real and too
great for her childish heart to bear.

All night the door of the little house stood open and the
whippoorwills came and sang upon the very step. The young
sportsman and his old hostess were sound asleep, but Sylvia's
great design kept her broad awake and watching.

She forgot to think of sleep. The short summer night seemed

as long as the winter darkness, and then at last when the whip-poorwills ceased, and she was afraid the morning would after all come too soon, she stole out of the house and followed the pasture path through the woods, hastening toward the open ground beyond, listening with a sense of comfort and companionship to the drowsy twitter of a half-awakened bird, whose perch she had jarred slightly in passing.

Alas, if the great wave of human interest which flooded for the first time this dull little life should sweep away the satisfactions of an existence heart to heart with nature and the dumb life of the forest!

There was the huge tree asleep yet in the paling moonlight, and small and silly Sylvia began with utmost bravery to mount to the top of it, with tingling, eager blood coursing the channels of her whole frame, with her bare feet and fingers, that pinched and held like birds' claws to the monstrous ladder reaching up, up, almost to the sky itself.

First she must mount the white oak tree that grew alongside, where she was almost lost among the dark branches and the green leaves heavy and wet with dew; a bird fluttered off its nest, and a red squirrel ran to and fro and scolded pettishly at the harmless housebreaker. Sylvia felt her way easily. She had often climbed there, and knew that higher still one of the oak's upper branches chafed against the pine trunk, just where its lower boughs were set close together. There, when she made the dangerous pass from one tree to the other, the great enterprise would really begin.

She crept out along the swaying oak limb at last, and took the daring step across into the old pine tree. The way was harder than she thought; she must reach far and hold fast, the sharp dry twigs caught and held her and scratched her like angry talons, the pitch made her thin little fingers clumsy and stiff as she went round and round the tree's great stem, higher and higher upward. The sparrows and robins in the woods below were beginning to wake and twitter to the dawn, yet it seemed much lighter there aloft in the pine tree, and the child knew she must hurry if her project was to be of any use.

The tree seemed to lengthen itself out as she went up, and to reach farther and farther upward. It was like a great mainmast to the voyaging earth; it must truly have been amazed that morning through all its ponderous frame as it felt this determined spark of human spirit wending its way from higher branch to branch.

Who knows how steadily the least twigs held themselves to advantage this light, weak creature on her way! The old pine must have loved his new dependent. More than all the hawks, and bats, and moths, and even the sweet-voiced thrushes, was the brave, beating heart of the solitary gray-eyed child. And the tree stood still and frowned away the winds that June morning while the dawn grew bright in the east.

Sylvia's face was like a pale star, if one had seen it from the ground, when the last thorny bough was past, and she stood trembling and tired but wholly triumphant, high in the treetop. Yes, there was the sea with the dawning sun making a golden dazzle over it, and toward that glorious east flew two hawks with slow-moving pinions.

How low they looked in the air from that height when one had only seen them before far up, and dark against the blue sky. Their gray feathers were as soft as moths; they seemed only a little way from the tree, and Sylvia felt as if she too could go fly-ing away among the clouds. Westward, the woodlands and farms reached miles and miles into the distance; here and there were church steeples, and white villages; truly it was a vast and awesome world!

The birds sang louder and louder. At last the sun came up bewilderingly bright. Sylvia could see the white sails of ships out at sea, and the clouds that were purple and rose-colored and yellow at first began to fade away. Where was the white heron's nest in the sea of green branches, and was this wonderful sight and pageant of the world the only reward for having climbed to such a giddy height?

Now look down again, Sylvia, where the green marsh is set among the shining birches and dark hemlocks; there where you saw the white heron once you will see him again; look, look! A white spot of him like a single floating feather comes up from the dead hemlock and grows larger, and rises, and comes close at last, and goes by the landmark pine with steady sweep of wing and outstretched slender neck and crested head.

And wait! Wait! Do not move a foot or a finger, little girl, do not send an arrow of light and consciousness from your two eager eyes, for the heron has perched on a pine bough not far beyond yours, and cries back to his mate on the nest and plumes his feathers for the new day!

The child gives a long sigh a minute later when a company of shouting catbirds comes also to the tree, and vexed by their fluttering and lawlessness the solemn heron goes away. She knows his secret now, the wild, light, slender bird that floats and wavers, and goes back like an arrow presently to his home in the green world beneath.

Then Sylvia, well satisfied, makes her perilous way down again, not daring to look far below the branch she stands on, ready to cry sometimes because her fingers ache and her lamed feet slip. Wondering over and over again what the stranger would say to her, and what he would think when she told him how to find his way straight to the heron's nest.

"Sylvy, Sylvy!" called the busy old grandmother again and again, but nobody answered, and the small husk bed was empty and Sylvia had disappeared.

The guest waked from a dream, and remembering his day's pleasure hurried to dress himself that might it sooner begin. He was sure from the way the shy little girl looked once or twice yesterday that she had at least seen the white heron, and now she must really be made to tell.

Here she comes now, paler than ever, and her worn old frock is torn and tattered, and smeared with pine pitch.

The grandmother and the sportsman stand in the door together and question her, and the splendid moment has come to speak of the dead hemlock tree by the green marsh.

But Sylvia does not speak after all, though the old grandmother fretfully rebukes her, and the young man's kind, appealing eyes are looking straight in her own. He can make them rich with money; he has promised it, and they are poor now. He is so well worth making happy, and he waits to hear the story she can tell.

No, she must keep silence! What is it that suddenly forbids her and makes her dumb? Has she been nine years growing and now, when the great world for the first time puts out a hand to her, must she thrust it aside for a bird's sake? The murmur of the pine's green branches is in her ears, she remembers how the white heron came flying through the golden air and how they watched the sea and the morning together, and Sylvia cannot speak; she cannot tell the heron's secret and give its life away.

Dear loyalty, that suffered a sharp pang as the guest went away disappointed later in the day, that could have served and followed him and loved him as a dog loves! Many a night Sylvia heard the echo of his whistle haunting the pasture path as she came home with the loitering cow. She forgot even her sorrow at the sharp report of his gun and the sight of thrushes and sparrows dropping silent to the ground, their songs hushed and their pretty feathers stained and wet with blood.

Were the birds better friends than their hunter might have been—who can tell? Whatever treasures were lost to her, woodlands and summertime, remember! Bring your gifts and graces and tell your secrets to this lonely country child!

Jimmy Takes Vanishing Lessons

by Walter R. Brooks

The school bus picked up Jimmy Crandall every morning at the side road that led up to his aunt's house, and every afternoon it dropped him there again. And so twice a day, on the bus, he passed the entrance to the mysterious road.

It wasn't much of a road anymore. It was choked with weeds and blackberry bushes, and the woods on both sides pressed in so closely that the branches met overhead, and it was dark and gloomy even on bright days. The bus driver once pointed it out.

"Folks that go in there after dark," he said, "well, they usually don't ever come out again. There's a haunted house about a quarter of a mile down the road." He paused. "But you ought to know about that, Jimmy. It was your grandfather's house."

Jimmy knew about it, and he knew that it now belonged to

his aunt Mary. But Jimmy's aunt would never talk to him about the house. She said the stories about it were silly nonsense and there were no such things as ghosts. If all the villagers weren't a lot of superstitious idiots, she would be able to rent the house, and then she would have enough money to buy Jimmy some decent clothes and take him to the movies.

Jimmy thought it was all very well to say that there were no such things as ghosts, but how about the people who had tried to live there? Aunt Mary had rented the house three times, but every family had moved out within a week. They said the things that went on there were just too queer. So nobody would live in it anymore.

Jimmy thought about the house a lot. If he could only prove that there wasn't a ghost . . . And one Saturday when his aunt was in the village, Jimmy took the key to the haunted house from its hook on the kitchen door, and started out.

It had seemed like a fine idea when he had first thought of it—to find out for himself. Even in the silence and damp gloom of the old road it still seemed pretty good. Nothing to be scared of, he told himself. Ghosts aren't around in the daytime. But when he came out in the clearing and looked at those blank, dusty windows, he wasn't so sure.

Oh, come on! he told himself. And he squared his shoulders and waded through the long grass to the porch.

Then he stopped again. His feet did not seem to want to go up the steps. It took him nearly five minutes to persuade them to move. But when at last they did, they marched right up and across the porch to the front door, and Jimmy set his teeth hard and put the key in the keyhole. It turned with a squeak. He pushed the door open and went in.

That was probably the bravest thing that Jimmy had ever done. He was in a long dark hall with closed doors on both sides, and on the right the stairs went up. He had left the door open behind him, and the light from it showed him that, except for the hat rack and table and chairs, the hall was empty. And then as he stood there, listening to the bumping of his heart, gradually the light faded, the hall grew darker and darker—as if something huge had come up on the porch behind him and stood there, blocking the doorway. He swung round quickly, but there was nothing there.

He drew a deep breath. It must have been just a cloud passing across the sun. But then the door, all of itself, began to swing shut. And before he could stop it, it closed with a bang. And it was then, as he was pulling frantically at the handle to get out, that Jimmy saw the ghost.

It behaved just as you would expect a ghost to behave. It was a tall, dim white figure, and it came gliding slowly down the stairs toward him. Jimmy gave a yell, yanked the door open, and tore down the steps.

He didn't stop until he was well down the road. Then he had to get his breath. He sat down on a log. "Boy!" he said. "I've seen a ghost! Golly, was that awful!" Then after a minute, he thought,

What was so awful about it? He was trying to scare me, like that smart Alec who was always jumping out from behind things. Pretty silly business for a grown-up ghost to be doing.

It always makes you mad when someone deliberately tries to scare you. And as Jimmy got over his fright, he began to get angry. And pretty soon he got up and started back. I must get that key, anyway, he thought, for he had left it in the door.

This time he approached very quietly. He thought he'd just lock the door and go home. But as he tiptoed up the steps he saw it was still open; and as he reached out cautiously for the key, he heard a faint sound. He drew back and peeked around the door jamb, and there was the ghost.

The ghost was going back upstairs, but he wasn't gliding now; he was doing a sort of dance, and every other step he would bend double and shake with laughter. His thin cackle was the sound Jimmy had heard. Evidently he was enjoying the joke he had played. That made Jimmy madder than ever. He stuck his head farther around the door jamb and yelled "Boo!" at the top of his lungs. The ghost gave a thin shriek and leaped two feet in the air, then collapsed on the stairs.

As soon as Jimmy saw he could scare the ghost even worse than the ghost could scare him, he wasn't afraid anymore, and he came right into the hall. The ghost was hanging on to the banisters and panting. "Oh, my goodness!" he gasped. "Oh, my gracious! Boy, you can't *do* that to me!"

"I did it, didn't I?" said Jimmy. "Now we're even."

"Nothing of the kind," said the ghost crossly. "You seem pretty stupid, even for a boy. Ghosts are supposed to scare people. People aren't supposed to scare ghosts." He got up slowly and glided down and sat on the bottom step. "But look here, boy; this could be pretty serious for me if people got to know about it."

"You mean you don't want me to tell anybody about it?" Jimmy asked.

"Suppose we make a deal," the ghost said. "You keep still about this, and in return I'll—well, let's see; how would you like to know how to vanish?"

"Oh, that would be swell!" Jimmy exclaimed. "But—can you vanish?"

"Sure," said the ghost, and he did. All at once he just wasn't there. Jimmy was alone in the hall.

But his voice went right on. "It would be pretty handy, wouldn't it?" he said persuasively. "You could get into the movies free whenever you wanted to, and if your aunt called you to do something—when you were in the yard, say—well, she wouldn't be able to find you."

"I don't mind helping Aunt Mary," Jimmy said.

"Hmm. High-minded, eh?" said the ghost. "Well, then—"

"I wish you'd please reappear," Jimmy interrupted. "It makes me feel funny to talk to somebody who isn't there."

"Sorry, I forgot," said the ghost, and there he was again, sitting on the bottom step. Jimmy could see the step, dimly, right through him. "Good trick, eh? Well, if you don't like vanishing, maybe I could teach you to seep through keyholes. Like this." He floated over to the door and went right through the keyhole, the way water goes down the drain. Then he came back the same way.

"That's useful, too," he said. "Getting into locked rooms and so on. You can go anywhere the wind can."

"No," said Jimmy. "There's only one thing you can do to get me to promise not to tell about scaring you. Go live somewhere else. There's Miller's, up the road. Nobody lives there anymore."

"That old shack!" said the ghost, with a nasty laugh. "Doors and windows half off, roof leaky—no thanks! What do you think it's like in a storm, windows banging, rain dripping on you—I guess not! Peace and quiet, that's really what a ghost wants out of life."

"Well, I don't think it's very fair," Jimmy said, "for you to live in a house that doesn't belong to you and keep my aunt from renting it."

"Pooh!" said the ghost. "I'm not stopping her from renting it. I don't take up any room, and it's not my fault if people get scared and leave."

"It certainly is!" Jimmy said angrily. "You don't play fair and I'm not going to make any bargain with you. I'm going to tell everybody how I scared you."

"Oh, you mustn't do that!" The ghost seemed quite disturbed and he vanished and reappeared rapidly several times. "If that got out, every ghost in the country would be in terrible trouble."

So they argued about it. The ghost said if Jimmy wanted money he could learn to vanish; then he could join a circus and get a big salary. Jimmy said he didn't want to be in a circus; he wanted to go to college and learn to be a doctor. He was very firm. And the ghost began to cry. "But this is my *home,* boy," he said. "Thirty years I've lived here and no trouble to anybody, and now you want to throw me out into the cold world! And for what? A little money! That's pretty heartless." And he sobbed, trying to make Jimmy feel cruel.

Jimmy didn't feel cruel at all, for the ghost had certainly driven plenty of other people out into the cold world. But he didn't really think it would do much good for him to tell anybody that he had scared the ghost. Nobody would believe him, and how could he prove it? So after a minute he said, "Well, all right. You teach me to vanish and I won't tell." They settled it that way.

Jimmy didn't say anything to his aunt about what he'd done. But every Saturday he went to the haunted house for his vanishing lesson. It is really quite easy when you know how, and in a couple of weeks he could flicker, and in six weeks the ghost gave him an examination and he got a B plus, which is very good for a human. So he thanked the ghost and shook hands with him and said, "Well, goodbye now. You'll hear from me."

"What do you mean by that?" said the ghost suspiciously. But Jimmy laughed and ran off home.

That night at supper Jimmy's aunt said, "Well, what have you been doing today?"

"I've been learning to vanish."

His aunt smiled and said, "That must be fun."

"Honestly," said Jimmy. "The ghost up at grandfather's taught me."

"I don't think that's very funny," said his aunt. "And will you please not—why, where are you?" she demanded, for he had vanished.

"Here, Aunt Mary," he said, as he reappeared.

"Merciful heavens!" she exclaimed, and she pushed back her chair and rubbed her eyes hard. Then she looked at him again.

Well, it took a lot of explaining and he had to do it twice more before he could persuade her that he really could vanish. She was pretty upset. But at last she calmed down and they had a long talk. Jimmy kept his word and didn't tell her that he had scared the ghost, but he said he had a plan, and at last, though very reluctantly, she agreed to help him.

So the next day she went up to the old house and started to work. She opened the windows and swept and dusted and aired the bedding, and made as much noise as possible. This disturbed the ghost, and pretty soon he came floating into the room where she was sweeping. She was scared all right. She gave a yell and threw the broom at him. As the broom went right through him and he came nearer, waving his arms and groaning, she shrank back.

And Jimmy, who had been standing there invisible all the time, suddenly appeared and jumped at the ghost with a "Boo!" And the ghost fell over in a dead faint.

As soon as Jimmy's aunt saw that, she wasn't frightened anymore. She found some smelling salts and held them under the ghost's nose, and when he came to she tried to help him into a chair. Of course she couldn't help him much because her hands went right through him. But at last he sat up and said reproachfully to Jimmy, "You broke your word!"

"I promised not to tell about scaring you," said the boy, "but I didn't promise not to scare you again."

And his aunt said, "You really are a ghost, aren't you? I thought you were just stories people made up. Well, excuse me, but I must get on with my work." And she began sweeping and banging around with her broom harder than ever.

The ghost put his hands to his head. "All this noise," he said. "Couldn't you work more quietly, ma'am?"

"Whose house is this, anyway?" she demanded. "If you don't like it, why don't you move out?"

The ghost sneezed violently several times. "Excuse me," he said. "You're raising so much dust. Where's that boy?" he asked suddenly. For Jimmy had vanished again.

"I'm sure I don't know," she replied. "Probably getting ready to scare you again."

"You ought to have better control of him," said the ghost severely. "If he was my boy, I'd take a hairbrush to him."

"You have my permission," she said, and she reached right through the ghost and pulled the chair cushion out from under him and began banging the dust out of it. "What's more," she went on, as he got up and glided wearily to another chair, "Jimmy and I are going to sleep here nights from now on, and I don't think it would be very smart of you to try any tricks."

"Ha, ha," said the ghost nastily. "He who laughs last—"

"Ha, ha, yourself," said Jimmy's voice from close behind him. "And that's me, laughing last."

The ghost muttered and vanished.

Jimmy's aunt put cotton in her ears and slept that night in the best bedroom with the light lit. The ghost screamed for a while down in the cellar, but nothing happened, so he came upstairs. He thought he would appear to her as two glaring, fiery eyes, which was one of his best tricks, but first he wanted to be sure where Jimmy was. But he couldn't find him. He hunted all over the house, and though he was invisible himself, he got more and more nervous. He kept imagining that at any moment Jimmy might jump out at him from some dark corner and scare him into fits. Finally he got so jittery that he went back to the cellar and hid in the coal bin all night.

The following days were just as bad for the ghost. Several times he tried to scare Jimmy's aunt while she was working, but she didn't scare worth a cent, and twice Jimmy managed to sneak up on him and appear suddenly with a loud yell, frightening him dreadfully. He was, I suppose, rather timid even for a ghost. He began to look quite haggard. He had several long arguments with Jimmy's aunt, in which he wept and appealed to her sympathy, but she was firm. If he wanted to live there he would have to pay rent, just like anybody else. There was the abandoned Miller farm two miles up the road. Why didn't he move there?

When the house was all in apple-pie order, Jimmy's aunt went down to the village to see a Mr. and Mrs. Whistler, who were living at the hotel because they couldn't find a house to move into. She told them about the old house, but they said, "No, thank you. We've heard about that house. It's haunted. I'll bet," they said, "*you* wouldn't dare spend a night there."

She told them that she had spent the last week there, but they evidently didn't believe her. So she said, "You know my nephew, Jimmy. He's twelve years old. I am so sure that the house is not haunted that, if you want to rent it, I will let Jimmy stay there with you every night until you are sure everything is all right."

"Ha!" said Mr. Whistler. "The boy won't do it. He's got more sense."

So they sent for Jimmy. "Why, I've spent the last week there," he said. "Sure. I'd just as soon."

But the Whistlers still refused.

So Jimmy's aunt went around and told a lot of the village people about their talk, and everybody made so much fun of the

Whistlers for being afraid, when a twelve-year-old boy wasn't, that they were ashamed, and said they would rent it. So they moved in. Jimmy stayed there for a week, but he saw nothing of the ghost. And then one day one of the boys in his grade told him that somebody had seen a ghost up at the Miller farm. So Jimmy knew the ghost had taken his aunt's advice.

A day or two later he walked up to the Miller farm. There was no front door and he walked right in. There was some groaning and thumping upstairs, and then after a minute the ghost came floating down.

"Oh, it's you!" he said. "Goodness sakes, boy, can't you leave me in peace?"

Jimmy said he'd just come up to see how he was getting along.

"Getting along fine," said the ghost. "From my point of view it's a very desirable property. Peaceful. Quiet. Nobody playing silly tricks."

"Well," said Jimmy, "I won't bother you if you don't bother the Whistlers. But if you come back there . . ."

"Don't worry," said the ghost.

So with the rent money, Jimmy and his aunt had a much easier life. They went to the movies sometimes twice a week, and Jimmy had all new clothes, and on Thanksgiving, for the first time in his life, Jimmy had a turkey. Once a week he would go up to the Miller farm to see the ghost and they got to be very good friends. The ghost even came down to the Thanksgiving dinner, though of course he couldn't eat much. He seemed to enjoy the warmth of the house and he was in very good humor. He taught Jimmy several more tricks. The best one was how to glare with fiery eyes, which was useful later on when Jimmy became a doctor and had to look down people's throats to see if their tonsils ought to come out. He was really a pretty good fellow as ghosts go, and Jimmy's aunt got quite fond of him herself. When the real winter weather began, she even used to worry about him a lot, because of course there was no heat in the Miller place and the doors and windows didn't amount to much and there was hardly any roof. The ghost tried to explain to her that heat and cold didn't bother ghosts at all.

"Maybe not," she said, "but just the same, it can't be very pleasant." And when he accepted their invitation for Christmas dinner she knitted some red woolen slippers, and he was so pleased that he broke down and cried. And that made Jimmy's aunt so happy, *she* broke down and cried.

Jimmy didn't cry, but he said, "Aunt Mary, don't you think it would be nice if the ghost came down and lived with us this winter?"

"I would feel very much better about him if he did," she said.

So he stayed with them that winter, and then he just stayed on, and it must have been a peaceful place, for the last I heard he was still there.

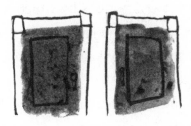

The Lady or the Tiger?

by Frank Stockton

In the very olden time there lived a semi-barbaric king, whose ideas, though somewhat polished and sharpened by the progressiveness of distant Latin neighbors, were still large, florid, and untrammeled, as became the half of him which was barbaric. He was a man of exuberant fancy, and, withal, of an authority so irresistible that, at his will, he turned his varied fancies into facts. He was greatly given to self-communing, and, when he and himself agreed upon anything, the thing was done. When every member of his domestic and political systems moved smoothly in its appointed course, his nature was bland and genial; but, whenever there was a little hitch, and some of his orbs got out of their orbits, he was blander and more genial still, for nothing pleased him so much as to make the crooked straight and crush down uneven places.

Among the borrowed notions by which his barbarism had become semified was that of the public arena, in which, by exhibitions of manly and beastly valor, the minds of his subjects were refined and cultured.

But even here the exuberant and barbaric fancy asserted itself. The arena of the king was built, not to give the people an opportunity of hearing the rhapsodies of dying gladiators, nor to enable them to view the inevitable conclusion of a conflict between religious opinions and hungry jaws, but for purposes far better adapted to widen and develop the mental energies of the people. This vast amphitheater, with its encircling galleries, its mysterious vaults, and its unseen passages, was an agent of poetic justice, in which crime was punished, or virtue rewarded, by the decrees of an impartial and incorruptible chance.

When a subject was accused of a crime of sufficient importance to interest the king, public notice was given that on an appointed day the fate of the accused person would be decided in the king's arena, a structure which well deserved its name, for, although its form and plan were borrowed from afar, its purpose emanated solely from the brain of this man, who, every barleycorn a king, knew no tradition to which he owed more allegiance than pleased his fancy, and who ingrafted on every adopted form of human thought and action the rich growth of his barbaric idealism.

When all the people had assembled in the galleries, and the king, surrounded by his court, sat high up on his throne of royal state on one side of the arena, he gave a signal, a door beneath him opened, and the accused subject stepped out into the amphitheater. Directly opposite him, on the other side of the enclosed space, were two doors, exactly alike and side by side. It was the duty and the privilege of the person on trial to walk directly to these doors and open one of them. He could open either door he pleased; he was subject to no guidance or influence but that of the aforementioned impartial and incorruptible chance. If he opened the one, there came out of it a hungry tiger, the fiercest and most cruel that could be procured, which immediately sprang upon him and tore him to pieces as a punishment for his guilt. The moment that the case of the criminal was thus decided, doleful iron bells were clanged, great wails went up from the hired mourners posted on the outer rim of the arena, and the vast audience, with bowed heads and downcast hearts, wended slowly their homeward way, mourning greatly that one so young and fair, or so old and respected, should have merited so dire a fate.

But, if the accused person opened the other door, there came forth from it a lady, the most suitable to his years and station that his majesty could select among his fair subjects, and to this lady he was immediately married, as a reward of his innocence. It mattered not that he might already possess a wife and family, or that his affections might be engaged upon an object of his own selection; the king allowed no such subordinate arrangements to interfere with his great scheme of retribution and reward. The exercises, as in the other instance, took place immediately, and in the arena. Another door opened beneath the king, and a priest, followed by a band of choristers, and dancing maidens blowing joyous airs on golden horns and treading an epithalamic measure, advanced to where the pair stood, side by side, and the wedding was promptly and cheerily solemnized. Then the gay brass bells rang forth their merry peals, the people shouted glad hurrahs, and the innocent man, preceded by children strewing flowers on his path, led his bride to his home.

This was the king's semi-barbaric method of administering justice. Its perfect fairness is obvious. The criminal could not know out of which door would come the lady; he opened either he pleased, without having the slightest idea whether, in the next instant, he was to be devoured or married. On some occasions the tiger came out of one door, and on some out of the other. The decisions of this tribunal were not only fair, they were positively determinate: the accused person was instantly punished if he found himself guilty, and, if innocent, he was rewarded on the spot, whether he liked it or not. There was no escape from the judgments of the king's arena.

The institution was a very popular one. When the people gathered together on one of the great trial days, they never knew whether they were to witness a bloody slaughter or a hilarious wedding. This element of uncertainty lent an interest to the occasion which it could not otherwise have attained. Thus, the masses were entertained and pleased, and the thinking part of the community could bring no charge of unfairness against this plan, for did not the accused person have the whole matter in his own hands?

This semi-barbaric king had a daughter as blooming as his most florid fancies, and with a soul as fervent and imperious as his own. As is usual in such cases, she was the apple of his eye, and was loved by him above all humanity. Among his courtiers was a young man of that fineness of blood and lowness of station common to the conventional heroes of romance who love royal maidens. This royal maiden was well satisfied with her lover, for he was handsome and brave to a degree unsurpassed in all this kingdom, and she loved him with an ardor that had enough of barbarism in it to make it exceedingly warm and strong. This love affair moved on happily for many months, until one day the king happened to discover its existence. He did not hesitate nor waver in regard to his duty in the premises. The youth was immediately cast into prison, and a day was appointed for his trial in the king's arena. This, of course, was an especially important occasion, and his majesty, as well as all the people, was greatly interested in the workings and development of this trial. Never before had such a case occurred; never before had a subject dared to love the daughter of the king. In after years such things became commonplace enough, but then they were in no slight degree novel and startling.

The tiger cages of the kingdom were searched for the most savage and relentless beasts, from which the fiercest monster might be selected for the arena; and the ranks of maiden youth and beauty throughout the land were carefully surveyed by competent judges in order that the young man might have a fitting bride in case fate did not determine for him a different destiny. Of course, everybody knew that the deed with which the accused was charged had been done. He had loved the princess, and neither he, she, nor anyone else thought of denying the fact; but the king would not think of allowing any fact of this kind to interfere with the workings of the tribunal, in which he took such great delight and satisfaction. No matter how the affair turned out, the youth would be disposed of, and the king would take an aesthetic pleasure in watching the course of events, which would determine whether or not the young man had done wrong in allowing himself to love the princess.

The appointed day arrived. From far and near the people gathered, and thronged the great galleries of the arena, and crowds, unable to gain admittance, massed themselves against its outside walls. The king and his court were in their places, opposite the twin doors, those fateful portals, so terrible in their similarity.

All was ready. The signal was given. A door beneath the

royal party opened, and the lover of the princess walked into the arena. Tall, beautiful, fair, his appearance was greeted with a low hum of admiration and anxiety. Half the audience had not known so grand a youth had lived among them. No wonder the princess loved him! What a terrible thing for him to be there!

As the youth advanced into the arena he turned, as the custom was, to bow to the king, but he did not think at all of that royal personage. His eyes were fixed upon the princess, who sat to the right of her father. Had it not been for the moiety of barbarism in her nature it is probable that lady would not have been there, but her intense and fervid soul would not allow her to be absent on an occasion in which she was so terribly interested. From the moment that the decree had gone forth that her lover should decide his fate in the king's arena, she had thought of nothing, night or day, but this great event and the various subjects connected with it. Possessed of more power, influence, and force of character than anyone who had ever before been interested in such a case, she had done what no other person had done—she had possessed herself of the secret of the doors. She knew in which of the two rooms, that lay behind those doors, stood the cage of the tiger, with its open front, and in which waited the lady. Through these thick doors, heavily curtained with skins on the inside, it was impossible that any noise or suggestion should come from within to the person who should approach to raise the latch of one of them. But gold, and the power of a woman's will, had brought the secret to the princess.

And not only did she know in which room stood the lady ready to emerge, all blushing and radiant, should her door be opened, but she knew who the lady was. It was one of the fairest and loveliest of the damsels of the court who had been selected as the reward of the accused youth, should he be proved innocent of the crime of aspiring to one so far above him; and the princess hated her. Often had she seen, or imagined that she had seen, this fair creature throwing glances of admiration upon the person of her lover, and sometimes she thought these glances were perceived, and even returned. Now and then she had seen them talking together; it was but for a moment or two, but much can be said in a brief space; it may have been on most unimportant topics, but how could she know that? The girl was lovely, but she had dared to raise her eyes to the loved one of the princess; and, with all the intensity of the savage blood transmitted to her through long lines of wholly barbaric ancestors, she hated the woman who blushed and trembled behind that silent door.

When her lover turned and looked at her, and his eye met hers as she sat there, paler and whiter than anyone in the vast ocean of anxious faces about her, he saw, by that power of quick perception which is given to those whose souls are one, that she knew behind which door crouched the tiger, and behind which stood the lady. He had expected her to know it. He understood her nature, and his soul was assured that she would never rest until she had made plain to herself this thing, hidden to all other lookers-on, even to the king. The only hope for the youth in which there was any element of certainty was based upon the success of the princess in discovering this mystery; and the moment he looked upon her, he saw she had succeeded, as in his soul he knew she would succeed.

Then it was that his quick and anxious glance asked the question: "Which?" It was as plain to her as if he shouted it from where he stood. There was not an instant to be lost. The question was asked in a flash; it must be answered in another.

Her right arm lay on the cushioned parapet before her. She raised her hand, and made a slight, quick movement toward the right. No one but her lover saw her. Every eye but his was fixed on the man in the arena.

He turned, and with a firm and rapid step he walked across the empty space. Every heart stopped beating, every breath was held, every eye was fixed immovably upon that man. Without the slightest hesitation, he went to the door on the right, and opened it.

Now, the point of the story is this: Did the tiger come out of that door, or did the lady?

The more we reflect upon this question, the harder it is to answer. It involves a study of the human heart which leads us through devious mazes of passion, out of which it is difficult to find our way. Think of it, fair reader, not as if the decision of the question depended upon yourself, but upon that hot-blooded, semi-barbaric princess, her soul at a white heat beneath the combined fires of despair and jealousy. She had lost him, but who should have him?

How often, in her waking hours and in her dreams, had she started in wild horror, and covered her face with her hands as she thought of her lover opening the door on the other side of which waited the cruel fangs of the tiger!

But how much oftener had she seen him at the other door! How in her grievous reveries had she gnashed her teeth, and torn her hair, when she saw his start of rapturous delight as he opened the door of the lady! How her soul had burned in agony when she had seen him rush to meet that woman, with her flushing cheek and sparkling eye of triumph; when she had seen him lead her forth, his whole frame kindled with the joy of recovered life; when she had heard the glad shouts from the multitude, and the wild ringing of the happy bells; when she had seen the priest, with his joyous followers, advance to the couple, and make them man and wife before her very eyes; and when she had seen them walk away together upon their path of flowers, followed by the tremendous shouts of the hilarious multitude, in which her one despairing shriek was lost and drowned!

Would it not be better for him to die at once, and go to wait for her in the blessed regions of semi-barbaric futurity?

And yet, that awful tiger, those shrieks, that blood!

Her decision had been indicated in an instant, but it had

been made after days and nights of anguished deliberation. She had known she would be asked, she had decided what she would answer, and, without the slightest hesitation, she had moved her hand to the right.

The question of her decision is one not to be lightly considered, and it is not for me to presume to set myself up as the one person able to answer it. And so I leave it with all of you: Which came out of the opened door—the lady, or the tiger?

Afterword

Perhaps you're like me—one of those readers who love a novel, one so compelling that it keeps you wide awake nights turning its 200, 300, even 400-plus pages. There are times, however, when I just don't have time to wallow in a big fat book. I need something to grab and read on the run. Then I'll reach for a magazine or a collection of short stories, hoping for the best, because, sad to say, choices for short fiction are not as satisfying as they once were.

Now, I know when I say that I sound exactly like the grandmother I've become, but it's true. When I was growing up, there were lots of magazines that carried stories by America's best-known writers. Today, there are only a handful. Happily, a new day is dawning. Publishers are beginning to realize that the short story, long an important literary form, could again become a popular form if readers were offered a smorgasbord of stories that appealed to a wide variety of tastes.

In *Best Shorts: Favorite Short Stories for Sharing,* you are being offered just such a feast. At the same time, those of us involved in this book are hoping that its publication will encourage magazines and other book publishers to seek out and print many more stories that will make us, the readers, laugh, shiver, think, and feel deeply and that, in rare instances, will move us to tears.

Although you may read these stories alone, in your room or under the covers with a flashlight—we hope that you will also find that they can be shared aloud and talked about in families or in classrooms. We all know that a feast eaten with others is much more delicious than one eaten alone. This is often the case in reading.

Do read these stories with your family, your friends, or your classmates. Try reading one aloud. Sometimes when you hear a story read aloud, your ears catch details that your eyes skipped over. Talk about what you didn't understand or what particularly spoke to you as you read. I belong to a book club, and I always find that the discussion of what the group has read makes my experience of the work much richer. I think I can promise that your enjoyment will deepen as you discover what meanings a story has had for someone else. Perhaps he or she got something from the story that had never occurred to you. In the same way, your understanding of the story will enrich someone else's experience.

Don't be afraid to disagree. If you've read or listened carefully, you'll have great fun backing up your argument with evidence you've gathered from the story and challenging your friends and family to do the same. Still, remember that a good story has more than one level. There is never only one "right" meaning, so everyone will gain from listening to other views.

So here it is—this smorgasbord of stories all laid out for you. We hope you enjoy the spread. And we hope that, because of you, others will, too.

Katherine Paterson
2006

Contributors

Avi is the author of more than sixty books for children, including the 2003 Newbery Medal winner *Crispin: The Cross of Lead* and two Newbery Honors, *Nothing but the Truth* and *The True Confessions of Charlotte Doyle*. His most recent book is the short story collection *Strange Happenings*. He lives with his family in Denver, where he continues to write.

Lloyd Alexander decided to be an author when he was fifteen, but seventeen more years went by before he published his first children's book. Since then, he has written more than forty books, including *The Town Cats and Other Tales. The High King,* the last novel in his acclaimed fantasy series The Chronicles of Prydain, was awarded the Newbery Medal. He lives in Philadelphia.

The author of the contemporary classic *Tuck Everlasting,* **Natalie Babbitt** ranks as one of today's most gifted children's book writers. Her novel *Kneeknock Rise* received a Newbery Honor. *The Devil's Storybook* and *The Devil's Other Storybook* feature short stories about a devil constantly bested by mortals. She lives in Rhode Island.

Andrew Benedict is just one of more than fifteen pen names used by Robert Arthur, who died in 1969. He was a film writer, magazine editor, anthologist, and the author of many books. He thrice received the Edgar Allen Poe Award for his mystery writing.

Marian Flandrick Bray wrote her first short story about a race-horse when she was in ninth grade. Since then, she's written many books and short stories, most of which feature animals. The story "The Pale Horse" is included in the anthology *Stay True: Short Stories for Strong Girls.*

Walter R. Brooks was a writer best known for his short stories and a talking pig named Freddy, the star of twenty-six books. His short story "Ed Takes the Pledge" was the basis for the popular 1960s TV series *Mister Ed.* Born in 1886, he died in 1958.

The versatile poet and author **Paul Fleischman** grew up in a house imbued with stories and music. He received a 1982 Newbery Honor for *Graven Images,* a trio of short stories, and the 1989 Newbery Medal for *Joyful Noise: Poems for Two Voices.* He lives in California.

Born in 1820 to a Boston literary family, **Lucretia P. Hale** wrote books for both children and adults. Many of her stories for young people were first published in magazines and later collected in *The Peterkin Papers* and *The Last of the Peterkins.* She died in 1900.

The award-winning author and storyteller **Gerald Hausman** was born in Maryland and grew up in New Jersey and Massachusetts. His interest in animals, folklore, and the natural world has led him to create books like *Dogs of Myth: Tales from Around the World* and *Castaways: Stories of Survival.* Gerald Hausman lives in Florida with his wife, two dogs, two cats, and a parrot from the Amazon.

Considered America's first master of the short story, **Washington Irving** also wrote essays, poems, biographies, and travel pieces. Today he's best known for the enduring popularity of the stories "Rip Van Winkle" and "The Legend of Sleepy Hollow." Born in New York City in 1783, he died in 1859.

Sarah Orne Jewett, a short story writer and novelist born in 1849, lived her entire life in the coastal village of South Berwick, Maine. As a girl she accompanied her father, a country doctor, on his horse-and-buggy rounds, and the people she met during those trips often appear in her work. She died in 1909.

As a child, the award-winning author **Francisco Jiménez** immigrated from Mexico to California. His books *The Circuit: Stories from the Life of a Migrant Child,* a Boston Globe–Horn Book Award recipient, and its sequel, *Breaking Through,* are based on his experiences growing up. He lives in California.

The acclaimed author **Margaret Mahy** has written everything from picture books to novels for young adults. Her novels *The Haunting, The Changeover,* and *Memory* have each won the Carnegie Medal. She writes full-time at her home near Christchurch, New Zealand.

Internationally known storyteller and author **Rafe Martin** grew up in a family that loved to tell stories. His work includes the picture books *The Rough-Face Girl* and *The Boy Who Lived with Seals,* as well as the story collection *Mysterious Tales of Japan.* The novel *Birdwing* is his most recent book. He lives in New York.

Patricia McKissack traces her love of books and language to the oral storytellers in her family. Her books have received legions of awards, including a Coretta Scott King Award and a Newbery Honor for *The Dark Thirty: Southern Tales of the Supernatural* and a Caldecott Honor for *Mirandy and Brother Wind.* She lives in Missouri, where she is a frequent collaborator with her husband, Frederick.

Lensey Namioka wrote her first book on scraps of paper sewn together with thread when she was eight. Today her most popular books, including *Yang the Youngest and His Terrible Ear* and *Yang the Third and Her Impossible Family,* feature a Chinese American family. Like her fictional Yangs, Lensey Namioka lives in Seattle, Washington.

Katherine Paterson is a renowned and much loved author of international acclaim. Her books *Bridge to Terabithia* and *Jacob Have I Loved* are both Newbery Medal winners. She has twice received the National Book Award for Children's Literature, and has received both the Hans Christian Andersen Award and the Astrid Lindgren Memorial Award for her body of work.

Richard Peck, the author of more than thirty books, is the recipient of the Margaret A. Edwards Award for lifetime achievement in young adult literature. His novel *A Year Down Under* won the Newbery Medal in 2001, and his book *Past Perfect, Present Tense* is a collection of short stories he's written over the course of many years.

Chris Raschka is the well-loved, award-winning author and illustrator of many books for young children, including *Yo! Yes?* (A Caldecott Honor book), *Can't Sleep, Charlie Parker Played Be Bop,* and *Mysterious Thelonius.* His book, *The Hello, Goodbye Window,* written by Norton Juster, was awarded the 2006 Caldecott Medal.

Robert D. San Souci is highly regarded for his retellings of folktales, found in collections such as *Cut from the Same Cloth: American Women of Myth, Legend, and Tall Tale.* His most recent short story collections include *Dare to Be Scared* and *Double Dare to Be Scared*. He lives in California.

Carolyn Shute is an editor and free-lance writer who has worked in educational publishing and in the children's book field for fifteen years.

Isaac Bashevis Singer won the Nobel Prize for Literature in 1978. Most of Singer's writing for young readers consists of collections of short stories, including *Zlateh the Goat and Other Stories* and *The Fools of Chelm and Their History*. He died in 1991.

Frank Stockton was once one of America's most popular storytellers and humorists. Born in 1834, he began writing stories in high school and published his first book, *Ting-A-Ling*, in 1870. Two of his best-known short stories, *The Griffin and the Minor Canon* and *The Bee-Man of Orn*, have been memorably illustrated by Maurice Sendak. He died in 1902.

Theodore Taylor began writing at thirteen as a cub reporter covering high school sports for his local newspaper. His popular novel *The Cay* received the Lewis Carroll Shelf Award and was made into a movie. He lives in California.

Fantasy and everyday life often meet in the work of **Megan Whalen Turner**. Her first book, a collection of short stories, is called *Instead of Three Wishes*. Her second book, *The Thief*, was awarded a Newbery Honor. Her most recent book is *The King of Attolia*, a sequel to *The Thief*. She lives in Ohio.

Born in 1885, **Louis Untermeyer** was an author, poet, editor, and anthologist. During his lifetime, he published more than one hundred books for readers of all ages, including the anthologies *The Golden Treasury of Poetry* and *Old Friends and Lasting Favorites*. He died in 1977.

As a boy, the Canadian **Tim Wynne-Jones** dreamed of becoming an architect, but he grew up to be a writer instead. His short story collections include *Some of the Kinder Planets,* recipient of the Governor General's Award for Children's Literature, *The Book of Changes,* and *Lord of the Fries.* His most recent book is the novel *A Thief in the House of Memory.* He lives in Ottowa.

Credits